Anonymous

A Letter to the West Country Farmers,

concerning the difficulties and management of a bad harvest. Written in the end of

the year 1772

Anonymous

A Letter to the West Country Farmers,
concerning the difficulties and management of a bad harvest. Written in the end of the year
1772

ISBN/EAN: 9783337411442

Printed in Europe, USA, Canada, Australia, Japan

Cover: Foto ©Andreas Hilbeck / pixelio.de

More available books at **www.hansebooks.com**

A

LETTER

TO THE

WEST COUNTRY FARMERS,

CONCERNING THE

DIFFICULTIES and MANAGEMENT

OF A

BAD HARVEST.

Written in the end of the Year 1772.

PAISLEY:

Printed by A. WEIR and A. M'LEAN.

Sold by A. WEIR bookfeller there; J. DUNCAN bookfeller, Trongate, Glafgow; A. LOW, bookfeller, Ayr;
J. MEUROS, bookfeller, Kilmarnock; N. STUART,
bookfeller, Irvine; W. WHYTE, bookfeller, Beith;
and J. FORSYTH, bookfeller, Greenock. 1773.

[Price Eightpence.]

A D V E R T I S E M E N T.

SHOULD any profit arife from the fale of this letter, the author having devoted it to a beneficent purpofe, hopes that no perfon will reprint it without his leave. By this, however, he means not to preclude the periodical writers from publifhing extracts from it; if they fhall think proper.

TO THE

PRESES AND MANAGERS

OF THE

KILBARCHEN FARMER-SOCIETY.

Good Friends,

OF all laborious employments yours is the *Husbandry* most useful, and perhaps, upon the whole, *a pleasant* it is the most pleasant and healthful. There are, *and health-* however, inconveniencies, toils, and hazards at- *ful employ-* tending it, which greatly diminish both its com- *ment.* forts and its profits. These chiefly arise from your climate and seasons, which in the west country, are not often very favourable to your operations and hopes. But of all the calamities attending husbandry, none gives the farmer so much trouble as bad harvest seasons. These produce at times the most painful anxiety: they increase the labours and expences of the husband- man. And the more he has improved his fields, *Bad harvest* and has seen upon them the fruits of his skill and *weather the* industry, the greater often is his loss, and the *greatest af-* more grievous his disappointment. Nor does it *fliction to the* add a small matter to his grief, that his misfor- *farmer.* tune happens at the very time when he thought of enjoying the returns of all his labours. The happiness, the joy of harvest, which is so much celebrated in ancient writings, and has afforded their finest allusions ; that joy which, in happier climates, is still the cause of mirth and song,

you,

you, my friends, feldom tafte, in full fecurity
and eafe. And mixed as it often is, with toil-
fome days and reftlefs nights, with many cares
and fears, with much lofs and vexation, you can
hope for no compenfation for your loffes, but in
your own ingenuity and induftry; no compaffion for your fufferings, but in the mercy of heaven.

Neither. are you, my friends, the only fuffer-
ers, by bad harvefts; the tradefman, the mecha-
nic, and the common labourer, are all concern-
ed in the quantity and the quality of the grain
which you bring to market. Nay, the public
may be fometimes faid to fuffer more from the
injuries of a bad harveft, than even fome of yourfelves do. For on fuch occafions, the advanced
price makes up in part the lofs, at leaft to thofe
of you who hold the largeft farms. At the fame
time, in the fmaller farms of the weft, your own
families often add to the demands upon the public markets, and help to increafe the price of all
the victual brought to them. In a word, I imagine, it will be found on trial, and may be con-
fiftent with the remembrance of the oldeft and
moft experienced farmers, that victual never rofe
much above its ordinary price, but from the lofs
which the crop fuftained in harveft. Nor was it
ever difgufting to the tafte, or hurtful to the
health of man or beaft, but from the injuries it
received in that feafon.

For thefe reafons, amidft all the valuable inftructions upon improvements, which are given
by the writers on hufbandry, a few hints on harveft-work may not be unprofitable. And that
farmers may enjoy the benefit of them, as of all
other inftructions, I would defire that they would
give them a patient hearing and trial.

The writer of this letter does not claim the
public attention, from his long experience in
farming, nor from the number of obfervations
which

which he may have made upon that bufinefs. *claim to the* His manner of life did not afford him fufficient *public atten-* leifure, nor his farm fufficient opportunities for *tion.* thefe purpofes. What, however, he enjoyed of either he did not overlook; nor was he inatten- tive to things of common benefit, which he could learn from books, or from the obfervations and practice of others. Befides, as he did not whol- ly depend upon his farm, nor was altogether in- different to its advantages, he confidered himfelf as in a middle ftate; neither able to throw out expence upon extravagant projects, nor yet un- willing to run the rifk of a promifing experi- ment; by which he himfelf, or any of his neighbours, could be inftructed and convinced of its ufefulnefs. Upon thefe and the like grounds only, he claims at prefent a little of your time and attention.

It has long been a queftion with me, Whe- ther, in refpect to the difficulties and dangers *Whether an* in harveft, it be better upon the whole, for the *early or late* farmer to have his crops early or late in that *harveft be* feafon? I have indeed no doubt of the advan- *moft eligible.* tage of early plowing, nor even of early fowing fuch grain as takes a long time to ripen. No- thing, I imagine, can be more abfurd, than for our farmers to have their plowing to begin in the month of March, and their fowing in the month of April; while they fuffer fome of the fineft weather in January, or February, to pafs without any field-employment. This neglect often o- bliges them to plow in all weathers, and either to fow in a very indifferent feafon, or to delay it till it is fo late, that the produce is both thin in the grain, and comes by far too late in harveft. But the earlinefs, or latenefs of our harvefts does not altogether depend on our fowing early or late in the fpring, unlefs the difference be very great between the two. The odds at harveft is oft as great between a warm and cold foil, and between early and late feed.

But

But unto whatever caufes we afcribe our earlinefs, or latenefs in harveft, the queftion ftill returns upon us, Which of the two is fafeft in general for the farmer ? And having long confidered it, and made feveral trials of both ways, I am
ftill unable to refolve it to my own fatisfaction.
Having an early foil myfelf, I got the earlieft feed,
and both plowed and fowed among the firft; and
for two or three years I triumphed in the earlinefs of my crop; my fields being fometimes almoft cleared before my neighbours had begun to
reap. And as we are fond of having our good fortune appear to be the effect of reafon and judgment, I ufed to fay, that in our northern climate
and fhort fummers, the very term *late*, whatever it was applied to, had fomething in it difa-
greeable and inconfiftent, that could never be my
choice—That my corns enjoyed a longer day, a
much higher and warmer fun, which contributed
to perfect them more effectually, both before
and after they were reaped; of all which the
later corns were deprived. But I did not always
rejoice in my own earlinefs. In fome of the
worft harvefts my lateft neighbours triumphed in
their turn. Nor was there wanting on their fide
a fhew of reafon, that feemed to vindicate their
negligence. Our Lambafs floods, faid they,
often vie with our equinoctial, or as they call
them, our Bulloch ftorms. Befides, early feed
corn is more apt to grow than late feed, for in
this very readinefs to germinate confifts much of
its earlinefs : add to all, if the weather is moift and
rainy, corn of every kind grows ftill more readily, on account of its being cut early in the feafon,
for then it has more of the fummer's heat to make
it fpring. Thefe arguments feem to balance
one another pretty nearly, and the latter end of
harveft being as often good weather as the beginning of it, it is impoffible to fay, whether an early
or late harveft can be moft depended on. For my
own

own part, I have been convinced of late, that a greater proportion of late feed is preferable upon light foils. I have not however given up the practice of sowing it as early as possible, and I would recommend the same practice to those especially who have heavy foils; at the same time that they keep some of the earliest feed for their latest sowings. Beans, for example, may be sown with advantage, in February or earlier. And if our pease are not sown then, they may be sown with near as much advantage in the end of April. The same treatment may be given to late and early oats. And if the farmer has a proper assortment of feed, he can both catch the different seasons of sowing in spring time, and have his whole fields more under his command in the time of reaping them: which last must be of particular advantage in regard to harvest-work; because if one does not live in the neighbourhood of some town or village, from which he can be supplied with reapers at pleasure, it must be peculiarly inconvenient for him to have all his fields upon him at once.

The result uncertainty.

I recollect no other management previous to the harvest labour itself, that tends to facilitate the affairs of that season, but one; it is this, That we take care to have our crops as clean as possible; for no corns suffer more from a bad harvest, than those which are full of grass and other weeds; none succeed better than those which are perfectly free of all mixture. This, amongst many more important considerations, should recommend to us, the practices in use with our English neighbours; I mean those of hand-weeding and hand-hoeing, or rather those of horse-hoeing and summer-fallowing. Some of those practices are used for the benefit of the present crop, and all of them are profitable for the succeeding crops. But though the safety of their corns in harvest may be scarce considered in such operations, yet do

The cleanliness of corns an advantage in bad harvests.

Weeding, hoeing, and summer-fallowing recommended.

they

they alfo enjoy this benefit of them, in an important degree, if I am not much miftaken. One can
fcarce indeed account for their getting in their
whole corns, fo foon after reaping them, merely
from climate, even though theirs fhould be better
than ours. Such a remarkable difference in this
(for they will carry in their wheat on the day after it is reaped, and other corns in proportion)
cannot be accounted for, but from a combination
of different caufes ; of which their better climate
may be one ; better methods of preferving corns
after they are got in, may be another ; and a
third may be that which we have here touched at,
the cleannefs of their crops.

The dangers in harveft arife from high winds and heavy rains. But paffing thefe previous operations, we proceed to the more immediate defign of this letter ;
which is to treat of the dangers, and remedies of
bad harveft feafons. I therefore obferve, that the
dangers in harveft time arife from high winds,
and great rains.

Of HIGH WINDS.

Of high winds. There feems to be no effectual precaution a-
gainft fhaking, from violent winds ; except a fpecial attention to thofe fields, which by their elevated fituation, or north weft pofition, ly more expofed to danger. One fingle obfervation may
however be ufeful, to fuch as can attend to circumftances, and govern themfelves accordingly.

Their dan- ger about the full and change. It is, That high winds commonly happen during
the fpring tides, as they are called, that is, about
three days before, and as many after the full and
change. If a field therefore much expofed, happens to be ripe at the approach of thefe periods,
it fhould, if poffible, be cut down before they
come on. Befides, as fuch winds commonly
bring rain at laft, in order to fave the trouble of
again introducing this circumftance, I here alfo
obferve, That if we have a field ready for ingathering

thering on thefe occafions, it ought not to be deferred beyond thefe times. Though fuch obfervations may feem but trifling, to fuch as never
thought of their importance, yet I muft confefs,
I have paid a fcrupulous regard to them thefe
twenty years paft; and have often cut down a
field a day or two before the time, in hopes of efcap-
ing the winds expected at fuch periods; and even
fometimes have done it at the diftance, which I
thought fufficient, in favourable weather, to win
the corn before the next period of danger fhould
overtake me: and I have frequently fucceeded in
both. If what I apprehended at the full, or more
commonly at the change of the moon, did not
happen, I did not repent my attention to it; becaufe it might have happened, and have caught
me unprepared.

After the hufbandman has fuffered by a
fhaking wind, his lofs admits of no remedy, nor
aleviation from the common practice in Scotland. *The only re-*
In England, indeed, their cuftom is to mow their *medy, a fuf-*
oats and barley, and to prepare them for the rick *ficient num-*
or barn, as they do hay; fo that by raking them *ber of poul-*
backwards and forwards upon the ftubble, a good *try.*
deal of the grain and ears are left upon the ground;
a quantity equal perhaps to the lofs fuftained by a
fhakewind. But while the love of a frefh meat
meal may have at firft quickened invention,
their perpetual wafte by this method of reaping
fecures to them a cuftomary remedy. They rear
a good number of poultry, particularly geefe,
if they have wafte grounds for that purpofe; or
they buy in a fufficient number from the wilds
and moorifh grounds, where they are commonly
reared for fale. Thefe they lay upon their cleared grounds, to gather up what is left upon them.
In a few weeks after, they can bring them to market at a good advanced price; or in very good
order to their own tables. By this management
next to nothing is loft. The grain left upon the

B

ground

ground brings the farmer as much perhaps, as it could have done, had it been carried into the barn upon the ftraw. Befides, fuch is the tafte of our neighbours fouthward, that had all of it been faved and gathered in, it would have probably gone to the fame ufe in the court-yard, that it goes to in their cloffes and open fields.

I have heard of expedients to prevent corns *Another hint,* from being fhaken, fuch as laying them down *of fome un-* flat upon the ground, with crofs ropes drawn over *certainty.* them, from end to end of the ridges. I never faw this practifed, and imagine the effect muft at beft be but trifling; and even fometimes dangerous, fo far as it could be made effectual. For as great rains commonly fucceed high winds, I fhould think a field quite broken down and lying flat, in a very bad ftate for fuch an event, and which I would by no means hazard, could I help it. I do indeed *A narrative* remember a ftorm, about fixteen or feventeen *of a ftorm* years ago, that came on with wetnefs, and ended *without bad* without damage to the ftanding corn, though al-*effects on the* moft the whole high grounds were unreaped. It *growing* begun an hour or two before midnight, out of the *corn.* fouth, attended with a dreadful rain, which laid every ftalk flat upon the ground. Betwixt one and two of the morning it turned directly north, as in January 13,—39, and it blew fo hard and dry till morning, that in gathering a peafe ftack, which it had blown down, and fcattered into the ditches and hollows, we found not a drop of water in them. Many trees were broke over, and tore up by the roots; many ftacks and barns were blown down; yet in travelling four or five miles, I could not fee one loofe corn pickle lying on the ground. Every ear and ftalk adhered to the earth indeed, being laid fo flat by the rain, that it did not rife till gathered up by the reapers. The only lofs here lay in the difficulty of reaping it, and in the dirtinefs both of the ftraw and corn. Nothing amazed me fo much as to fee no corn fhaken,

till

till I reflected on the circumstances in the beginning of the storm. For had the hard wind blown *The reason of this.* first, I was of opinion, that the fifth, or sixth part, could not have been preserved. The saving seemed to be providential, which we cannot always expect, nor can we imitate the means of it. I observe therefore, that our best security against high winds, is to gather a sufficient number of hands, to cut down the field quickly, by day or by night. Our best remedy, after the damage is done, is a sufficient number of poultry to gather up the grain ; unless we generously leave it to the fowls of the air, who have a right to their share, and notwithstanding our most invidious oeconomy,—*Will*, as the poet says, *vindicate their grain.* So much for high winds.

Of RAINY WEATHER.

With us, however, the most common harvest calamities arise from the wetness of our seasons. *Wetness dangerous.* This makes our corns grow and rot in the fields ; and is oft the occasion of their being hurried into the barn or yard, where they suffer as much as they could have done without. Sometimes our wet weather is extreme, both in its degree and continuance. It seems to combat, and often conquers every ordinary measure of foresight or precaution, and even disappoints the utmost efforts of ingenuity and activity. Nevertheless as, in most cases, it allows some scope for prudence and diligence, if the farmer thinks in time ; it is highly requisite that we bestow a particular attention to this capital branch of our subject.

There are three periods of harvest-work, in all of which a close attention, and strict caution may *Three periods of harvest-work require attention.* be useful to the farmer. I shall speak particularly to them all.

The first is the period of cutting down ;

The second is the period of drying and wining ;

The

The third is the period of ingathering, and securing the crop.

In all thefe different periods directions and hints may be given, upon the proper management, and requifite care, keeping conftantly in our eye the dangers of a weft country climate: for there the harveft weather is frequently alarming; and if we had been all along fufficiently aware of its dangers, one would imagine they might have produced the moft ingenious contrivances, and fecured to us the beft cuftoms of any corner in Scotland. But though we are far from being perfect in our methods of hufbandry, there may be ftill fomething found among us, in relation to harveft-work, that is worth imitating. The more favourable weather, upon the eaftern coafts, feldom calls for extraordinary efforts of ingenuity; nor does it oblige the farmer to fo ftrict an adherence to good rules and cuftoms. Hence, I have heard a very intelligent eaft country farmer fay, after he had for fometime refided in the weft, That if he were to educate his fon to be a compleat farmer, he would firft teach him the Eaft Lothian methods of culture, and then fend him to the weft, to learn harveft-work. For he had obferved, that when a bad harveft happened in the eaft, the farmers there were in hazard of being ruined by it; and that from a too general neglect of thofe common precautions, which the frequency of danger obliged others to obferve conftantly. How far the cafe may be altered of late, I cannot well judge. Farming, for fome time paft, is become more an object of thought and ftudy; and as we in the weft have adopted fome of the eaft country methods of improvement, 'tis likely that they may be paying more attention to the precautions abfolutely neceffary in the weft.

But to come more directly to the fubject, you'll remember,

remember, that the firſt period of harveſt-work *Of reaping.*
relates to reaping, and what belongs to that o-
peration.

Now, the firſt and moſt obvious rule here is, *The firſt rule,*
Never to cut down corns under rain, nor imme- *not to reap*
diately after it, that they may always have time *in rain.*
to dry before the reapers are ſet to work. Wet
ſhearing is commonly the beginning of moſt of
the evils which accompany a bad harveſt. And *Extended.*
therefore this rule may be extended ſo far, as to
caution farmers againſt ſetting out too early in a
miſty morning. The avarice of ſome maſters
ſometimes becomes a ſnare to them. When many
ſhearers are beſpoke at a fixed wage for the day,
ſuch maſters are deſirous of having a great day's
labour out of them. But it would be better for
themſelves, to truſt an hour in the morning, till
they ſaw how the evening might make it up ; or
to loſe the time altogether, than to riſk any thing
doubtful in the event. If indeed a dewy morning
ſeems to uſher in a fine day, one may venture
in ſuch hopes, to uſe the morning with freedom,
and be ſufficiently ſafe. The ſame caution may
be extended to corns that have been much lodged, *Farther ex-*
under a continued dropping weather. They ought *tended.*
not to be touched upon their firſt dry appearance ;
becauſe their under parts, which ly cloſs to the
ground, will be found to be very wet, and perhaps growing ; for it requires more than one,
or even two days drought, after wetneſs, to make
a lodged field fit for reaping. If, however, the
field is begun, for want of ſufficient attention to
its real ſtate, or perhaps for want of other work,
then the wet handfuls, if worth preſerving,
ſhould be clapped upon an outſide, inſtead of
being thrown careleſly into the very heart of the
ſheaf. But if they feel ſoapie, and have begun
to grow in the head, it would be better to leave
them uncut, or to throw them down in parcels
ſeparate from the ſheaf. They can be gathered
afterwards

afterwards by themselves, if they are found of any value. But it is scarce to be conceived, of how little value they often are; and yet that very little shall be gathered up with great care, and put into the heart of a sheaf, where it never can dry; the farmer will encumber himself with it; and it may be, for the sake of it, or the dampness which it occasions, the ingathering of the whole field shall be delayed, and hazarded in the highest degree. Is it not better, to lose at first frankly, what must be lost at last, notwithstanding all the labour that can be used, and all the risk that must be run, in order to save it?

The second rule.

Though all good farmers have acknowledged the danger of this practice, and declared openly against it, yet corns of all kinds will be cut wet at times. In this case, the next rule is, Never to bind them up wet if it can be helped :—I say, if it can be helped. So precarious is the state of every thing depending upon the weather, that no rule can be made about it, wholly absolute, or unconditional. Besides, the commission of one error generally leads to another. The farmer who has cut his corns wet, lies at the mercy of the weather, and is obliged sometimes also to bind them wet; for by long lying on the ground, the side next it begins to grow, and the sheaves must be set on end, to drain off the wetness and give them air. After this happens, they should always be set up single, as shall be directed afterwards, till they dry. If in their wet condition they are put up in stook or hut, they must certainly suffer by this management.

Argument.

From what has been said above, you will easily perceive, that when victual has been cut and bound up in a wet condition, the farmer has put it wholly out of his own power and skill to preserve or amend it. He must entirely depend upon the goodness of the weather; and which is more, none but the very best will serve his turn. But this,

this, however neceffary and defireable, he neither can command, nor has he right to expect. On the other hand, if the farmer cuts and binds up dry, he hath his corns fo much in his own power and management, that he alone is to blame if they fhould be afterwards loft : for he can cover them up fo effectualiy, that nothing but the worft of weather, and of the longeft continuance, can in any meafure hurt them. If therefore the want of all other labour fhould force him into any fuch bad meafures, it would be fafer for him to cut or bind his beans, or peafe, in a wet condition, than his wheat, oats, or barley. And if ever he tranf-greffeth farther, it fhould be with thofe only of a clean, large, and firm ftraw. Upon the whole, however, it would be more eligible to avoid, if poffible, fuch dangerous practices, with regard to all forts of ftuff, rather than to venture them with any. A wife man will rather run the hazard of fome expence, and lofs of time, than venture a danger which neither fkill nor pains afterwards may enable him to remedy. In one word, in the worft harvefts I ever faw, the lofs was chiefly in thofe fields that were cut, bound up, and ftooked wet. In the beft harvefts I ever faw, the fields which had received that bad treatment at the beginning, have always fuffered more or lefs in the end, whilft every thing elfe hath efcaped fafe and well.

If then the farmer is confcious to himfelf, that *Rule third.* this error has been committed in any part of a field, though never fo fmall a part, inftead of ftooking it with the reft, and fuffering it to take its common hazard, becaufe the weather comes in fine and promifing, my advice is to keep his eye upon it, and to take the firft good day to un-bind and expofe the corn of it to the air, before it hath time to grow, and be irrecoverably loft. Every labourer knows the difficulty of drying corn in that grown ftate, and the lofs it muft fuftain by

being

being torn afunder for that purpofe. Every one knows how eafily it may be recovered, when taken early, if the weather be favourable. I once loft almoft the whole of a fet of land, by not knowing till the laft, that it had been cut and bound wet. The oats were clean and good, as any ever I had. The weather was perfectly fine from the day it was cut, and the ftooks ftood all firm and well covered. On the day when it fhould have been got in, my fervants examined the field, and pronounced it ready, without exception of any part. They returned too foon with their verdict, and I fufpected the examination had been but fuperficial. I went myfelf, while the horfes were getting ready. I found the fheaves on that particular fet of land, to be double the ordinary fize, for even this advantage had been taken of my abfence; and to crown all, every fheaf was growing within. To be fhort, the horfes were countermanded, and the fheaves were all fpread out. Two days were fpent in drying that piece, and after all, the half of the corn was loft; all of which might have been faved, in much lefs time at firft. What a leffon was here, to fuch as could learn from it!

Rule fourth. I add but one caution more upon this period of harveft-work. It is, that the fheaves be made rather fmall than large; and at any rate, as near an equal fize as can be obtained. The farmer fhould confider here, for he knows it well, that the fmalleft fheaf is fooneft ready: and if there is a great inequality among them, the one half of the field muft wait for the other, in the beft weather; and in the worft weather, runs an unneceffary hazard, by the delay. I know the difficulty of managing a great number of reapers: but I know alfo what a prudent and peremptory mafter can do, if he ftands to his point. If he indolently gives it up, he deferves the lofs. It is better to give fervants a fmart word at firft, than a galling reproach at laft.

The

The second period of harvest-work comprehends *The second pe-* the time wherein corns stand out in the field for *riod of har-* drying and wining. *vest-work.*

The management consists in using the best and most approved methods of setting them up, and *General ma-* covering them, so as both to dry them, and to *nagement.* preserve them most effectually, from the rains and storms, till they are ready for the barn or yard.

Before we speak of setting corns out to the *Two things* drought, we should first think of removing them *premised.* from an inconvenient or dangerous situation, to one more convenient and safe. 1st, All corns *To remove* upon the level banks of rivers, or on any hollow *corns from* grounds that are naturally wet, or occasionally *the hazard* subject to land-floods and inundations, should be *of overflood-* removed as soon as they are bound. How absurd *ing.* is it to delay this, till the stooks are standing in water, or going off with the current? How foolish is it on these occasions, to see men scratching their heads, and bemoaning their loss, when they should be blaming their own stupidity? 2dly, Where there is no such danger from floods, it may *From calm si-* be very inconvenient to leave corns for drying *tuations.* under the cover of rising grounds, woods, or high hedges, where there is no free circulation of air to be of service to them. They should be immediately carried to the opener fields, and higher, grounds, where they have every advantage of situation. To delay this is at best but loss of time; in a bad harvest corns must suffer from their very situation, and by a late removal they must suffer by their carriage. Besides, the straw itself turns soft and brittle by long standing; so that it cannot again be set up aright, nor endure the least wind, without being demolished and blown about by it.

Observe, after corns are carried from these incon- *Kittling of* venient and dangerous situations, above-mention- *corn bad.* ed, into a more open exposure, the huts, or stooks

C   should

should never be set up too near one another; least by preventing the free paffage of air among them, we should even hurt the very intention of removing them.

Having premifed thefe particulars, we return to the bufinefs of our fecond period of harveft-work, which is the management of corn, in order to fit it for ingathering. This to us is a moft important, and fometimes a very tedious work: for while other parts of the kingdom get in moft of their corns in three, four, or five days ftanding, when the weather favours, ours take commonly twelve or fourteen days, with all advantages; and in bad feafons half as many weeks, if not more. The queftion then is, in what manner they fhould be fet out, for the beft advantage, both of wining and protecting them? Now, we have three different methods of fetting out wheat, barley, and oats.

Viz. { Gayting,
Stooking, and
Hutting.

And though thefe different operations may be generally known, and practifed through Scotland; yet there are better and worfe methods of performing each of them. I fhall therefore give a fhort account of each, for the fake of a few rules and cautions that may be annexed.

I. Of GAYTING CORNS.

Of gayting.

The manner of doing it.

This is performed by fetting up a fingle fheaf feparately. If the fheaf is bound too near the bottom for the purpofe, the farmer firft of all draws up the ftrap a little towards the crop end; then fetting the whole down upon the ground, with fome force, in order to beat in the inequalities of its bottom, he fpreads this out with one hand in a circular form: and, as he leaves a little vacancy in the middle of the circle, he admits
the

the air into it by a fmall opening towards the wind fide. Laft of all, collecting together the loofe heads, and twifting them about the top, he leaves it to its chance.

The ufe of gayting is chiefly for preferving wet and green corns, that need immediate drying; and in their wet condition, cannot fo properly be put together in ftooks or huts. The coarfer the ftraw and larger the fheaf, the more is it fit for ftanding fingle, and the more does it require gayting. The operation feems to be fimple; yet errors are often committed in performing it. The firft that occurs, is an attempt to widen too much the circle of the bottom on which it ftands; and thereby breaking too much of the ftraw below the ftrap. The intention here indeed is, to make the fheaf ftand better upon an enlarged bafe; and for this purpofe it is thruft down ftrongly. But the effect is the very contrary of that intention; for after the ftraw is entirely broke, it cannot ftand at all, in any weather. The fecond error lies, in breaking down the ftraw all round above the ftrap, in order to let in to the heart of the fheaf, the fun and air from above; but unlefs the field can be carried in immediately, this too defeats its own intention. For a fpread head prefents to the rain a kind of cup or filler, to take into the heart of the fheaf all that falls within half a yard, or three quarters diameter. Befides, whatever is below the cup above formed, hangs over the ftrap, like the hair of a new combed head, and effectually prevents both fun and wind from reaching the wetteft part of all the fheaf. Every farmer knows this lies in the ftrap itfelf, and in that part of the fheaf which is immediately within it, and ftraitened by its binding. How have I been galled oftimes to fee thefe errors going on and perfifted in, from abfolute thoughtleffnefs? In fhort, a fervant fhall fcarce pafs through a gayted field, where he has no work at the time,

The ufe of it.

Errors committed.

Breaking the ftraw below the ftrap.

Breaking it above the ftrap.

but

but he will, after repeated admonitions, spoil every *The figure of* gayted sheaf within the reach of his arm. The *a gayt sheaf.* true figure of a right gayted sheaf is that of a circular cone, which, while widened at the bottom, should be drawn, as near as possible, to a point at the top, to prevent the rains from ever entering it. And the only management of them when fallen down, is to set them up again with all the care possible. If the wind blows hard, so that they cannot stand single, then one of them should be set to the leeward of another, leaning on it; and if one will not do to support the other, a third, in the same position, may secure the whole, till the storm blows over. The straw never should be broken, either above or below the strap, but when one thinks of getting in the field, and that there shall be no further occasion for setting up the sheaves any more. Gayting, if the work is wise-

The input- ly managed, is indeed the speediest, and most ef- *ting or co-* fectual way to dry wet, or to deaden green corns. *vering of* It would however be convenient to put in such as *gayted corn* soon as they are ready. If this cannot be done, *not to be de-* they should be hutted up, and covered from dan- *layed.* ger in the field itself. It is true, that large sheaves are not so fit for huts; and broken straw, according to the common state of gayted corn, will not stand in stooks. The corns should, however, be some way protected, when ready; otherwise one shower in this condition, will undo a week's attention, and put them in a worse state than ever. And if the farmer recollects, that rain is much more hurtful to old shorn corn, than at any former period, he will scarce hesitate, in securing what is now ready, but still in great danger.

OF STOOKING CORNS.

The second method of setting out corns, in common use, is stooking. When corns are cut
and

and bound up dry, ſtooking, though not the quickeſt way of wining is yet the beſt way to preſerve them in dangerous weather, till they are quite ready for ingathering. Good methods muſt however be uſed in putting up the ſtooks, and great care uſed in keeping them up; otherwiſe every puff of wind overturns them, and diſappoints the intended ſecurity: whereas, if rules are ſtrictly obſerved at firſt, and proper care taken afterwards, it is hardly poſſible for the farmer to ſuffer any material loſs, even in a long courſe of bad weather.

A ſtook, in the weſt country faſhion, conſiſteth either of ten ſheaves, eight of which are ſet upon the ground, and may be called ſtandards, two are reſerved for their covering, and are called hoodings; or it may conſiſt of thirteen ſheaves, ten of which are ſet upon the ground, and three are reſerved for hoodings. The deſign of the odd ſheaf here, is, that when ſet in the middle, as a rider, it may ſupport the heads of the end hoodings; which in ſo long a ſtook would, without it, fall down too much towards the level, before they reached one another, ſo as to give and to receive mutual ſupport from each other. Thus the hoodings might be in danger of growing, like any other ſheaf that lies long on the level ground : for all ſheaves ſuffer in wet weather, from their level poſition, or their approaching too near it ; whereas the wetneſs drains off the more quickly, the more they are raiſed in their tops. In the ten ſheaves-ſtooks the middle rider is ſcarce neceſſary ; becauſe the end hoodings, if choſen large enough, meet more readily for the ſupport of each other, before they incline too much to the level. After all, when a ten ſheaves-ſtook hath long ſtood under a weight of rain, the hoodings begin to ſink their heads, and grow faſt. This invites the crows and pigeons, to ſit down in great numbers upon them, which preſs them down ſtill lower;

A ſtook conſiſts of ten or of thirteen ſheaves.

The rider, and its uſe.

Not neceſſary in a ten ſheaves-ſtook.

and

and while they confume the grain, they alfo promote the growth of what they leave. In thefe

Though fome-times conve-nient.

events I have often wifhed for, and have fometimes put in a middle rider between the hoodings; that by raifing their heads a little, the rain might drain better downward, and the fowls might not have fuch fure footing, nor fo much room to ftand on. I likewife thought,

To prevent wetnefs and growing, & confequently the crows from fitting down on the hoodings.

that if my rider had been put in foon enough, the growing of the hooding, and the temptation to appetite, arifing from a tendency towards it, might have both been prevented: for crows &c. are fond of corn when fwelled, and ready to burft its cheft; and perhaps more fo from the fweet tafte it may acquire by growing. And on the other hand, they fcarce touch it, either in fpring or autumn, till it begins to approach towards that ftate. What I have faid above chiefly refpects Polifh oats; which (whether from the fhortnefs of their ftraw or the weight of their head) I have always found moft ready to fink down to a level as hoodings; and which alfo (whether from their natural tafte, or aptnefs to grow) I have found moft inviting to the birds.

Of the ftandard fheaves.

As I prefer the ten fheaves-ftooks, becaufe the eafieft dryed and win, I fhall here give my thoughts, upon the beft and fureft method of putting them up.

How fet up.

Suppofe then two men employed, becaufe they are fometimes neceffary in windy weather, each of them takes a fheaf in every hand, and if the ground is level, he choofes them as near of a fize as poffible, without lofing time; if the ground declines to any fide, the talleft and heavieft goes to the loweft fide. Then the labourers turning their faces to each other, every man fets down his pair together. This is done, by giving their bottoms a fufficient knock upon the ground, in order to beat in their inequalities, that they may ftand folid. At the fame time, inclining their heads towards each

each other, care is taken, that they be placed exactly opposite to, and bear equally upon, one another. This being done by both labourers, each of them again 'takes up another pair, which he chooses and sets by his first pair, with the same care and exactness. The reasons for this accuracy are obvious, for if all the several pairs are not equally balanced, the heaviest must in time push over the lightest. If they are not set exactly opposite to each other, they soon lose their hold of one another; and sliding down they lie across the stook, and so set out their heads on both sides of it, like the points of a St Andrew's cross. Lastly, If they are not set firm upon their bottoms, by a knock upon the ground, they stand only upon a few pens of their straw that jut out beyond the rest, and by their slight hold of the earth, they lose their balance, and are either blown down, or twisted out of their place, by every puff of wind. One may think lightly of these hints, as niceties of no consequence; but if he were passing through a field negligently stooked, but ten days after it was set up, he would soon perceive the effects of carelessness, in the distorted appearance of every stook. And if he had any concern in the field, he would soon feel the effects of such general dislocation: for every shower that fell, and every wind that blew, would hurt him greatly. Whereas, on the other hand, a field well put up at first, if it is not afterwards disordered by storm, will, at some weeks distance, stand firm and upright to the eye; and be able both to resist a hard gale, and to defend an ordinary rain, incomparably beyond the other.

The reasons for adhering strictly to method.

When the eight standard sheaves of a stook are set properly, an open passage is left between the two sides, so wide that a little dog could easily pass through, from end to end of the whole. Further, though every sheaf of the pair leans upon its fellow on the opposite side, yet ought not the

An air passage from end to end.

Air passages across.

end

end pair to lean upon the pair next them, so as to have their tops too close upon one another; that even here sufficient room may be left about the straps, for the wind to pass freely between pair and pair, when it blows across the stook. Lastly,

The corn knot to be under cover. When the standard sheaves are set up, care should be taken to turn the corn knot of them all inwards, that it may be sheltered from the weather. For it shall be shewn afterwards, that this is the first part of the sheaf which begins to grow, when it is exposed to wet weather.

These are the rules and cautions that should be observed in setting up the standard sheaves of a corn stook. After a little attention to the practice, it is performed with perfect ease and readiness, by any labourer of common sense. When this part of the work is done, the labourers

Of hooding stooks. proceed next to the hooding of the stook. For this purpose each man takes hold of the largest, greenest, or wettest sheaf at hand, and prepares it for laying on, as a covering to the whole. But

A few cautions necessary. this being one of the most important operations for the harvest security, a few rules and cautions become necessary here also.

The first caution is, to hood always with the

The first. To keep up the crops of the hoodings. crop end of the hooding uppermost. By this position, the rain that falls drains from the corn head downwards to the bottom of the hood sheaf. Likewise, the corn being elevated above the whole stook, is exposed to the free passage of the air, and to the full influence of the sun for drying it. I have been told, that it is common in the east, either not to hood at all, which in very bad seasons is dangerous to the whole, or to hood with the bottoms uppermost: by this means the corn hanging down claps close round the lower parts of the standard sheaves. But this also is greatly hurtful. For by such a position, the corn of the hooding, instead of having the wetness drained from it, as above-mentioned, has

it

it all drained to it; fo that, by a conftant feeping from above, it is kept long wet, even after the rain is over. Nay, there the wetnefs muft abide; for the corn being wrapt about the bottom of the ftook, lies fo clofs to it, that it can leave no paffage through itfelf for the tranfmiffion of the fun beams, nor the free circulation of the air or wind. Still more, though the outfide of the corn fhould be hazzarcd by the fun or wind, the infide muft ever be damp, from its nearnefs to the ground, and clofenefs to the damp bottoms of the ftandards.

I did not here depend wholly upon reafoning; it might be fallacious. For my own fatisfaction, I have made repeated trials, year after year, and *Experience* according to cuftom in the neighbouring rows of *the beft in-* the fame field. I can therefore affure the farmer, *ftructor.* from undoubted experience, that the eaft country practice of putting up the bottoms, and keeping down the corn of their hoodings, is moft perni- cious. For, in thefe rows, I have feldom loft in wet feafons, lefs than triple the quantity of what I loft by our own method. All my reafonings therefore, in pages 21ft and 22d, proceeded upon the fuppofition that the weft country practice was ufed. An exception fhould be made of wheat, which prefents a cup to the rain.

Our fecond caution in putting on our hoodings *The fecond* is, to open the fheaf under the corn knot, in *caution.* order to lay it on with that fide lowermoft. The *To cover the* defign of this is to preferve the corn knot from *corn knot* rain, under the cover and protection of the whole *from the* fheaf. For, as was already obferved, that knot, *weather.* retaining the rain, begins firft to grow. It is no doubt eafier to open the hood fheaf under the binder's knot, becaufe at that place it was juft now put together. Here therefore lies the temptation to lazinefs. But befides the lazinefs often im- puted to fervants, the ignorance and inattention of the farmer himfelf may be juftly blamed; if he

D   either

either does this himfelf, or fuffers it to be done by any fervant. I remember that, twenty years ago, after long wet and hazy weather, I croffed a field both put up and hooded in this erroneous way; and perceiving its bad effects, I called out the farmer who was otherwife an active and ingenious man. I took notice to him, that all his hoodings were green at the corn knot, and beginning to chip throughout the whole. I here reafoned with him, for he could hearken to it——That a hard knot did not part with rain, like the ftraight corn fet up on one end. On this account, if the corn knot gets rain it begins firft of all to grow. After which it almoft never parteth with the wetnefs, till it be torn afunder, and every ftraw and pickle of it expofed to the drought. I obferved further, that when the corn knot is in this wet and growing ftate, the moifture of it will naturally communicate with, and infect the neighbouring parts of the fheaf; efpecially about the binding, where he could not but obferve, that the grain was already begun to fwell and chip; and had even ftraitened the fheaf to that degree, that no moifture could pafs fo as to drain downwards, which in a little would entirely deftroy it. I likewife defired him to examine the ftandard fheaves fo fet, and compare them with their neighbours, that had the corn knot concealed from the weather. He faw, and was fully convinced of his error, and never, I dare fay, needed another leffon on the point. In the mean time he loft for that year near a third part of a ten acres field: by far too great a price for any piece of inftruction, which he might have purchafed much cheaper, with a little obfervation of his own, or a little attention to the conduct of his more experienced neighbours. That which aggravated his affliction was, that he was clever, and even knew himfelf to be fo. What then can be expected of many, who may be faid, like the

idols

idols of the nations, to have eyes but fee not, ears bu thear not, neither will they underftand.

The prudent farmer, having ftooked his field with all the care and exactnefs above recommended, looks back upon it with fatisfaction and fecurity; for it ftands fair and upright to his eye : and confcious of his care and pains about it, he perhaps thinks his labour over with regard to it, for that year. Indeed fo it is, if the weather continues mild; yet, after his ftooks have ftood ten or twelve days in good weather, the fheaves begin to dry, and turn lighter; and tho', if the weather continues, he hopes in a day or two to gather it in fafely; yet let him not be too fecure : the wind perhaps rifes from the fouth, or fouth weft, and begins to blow off his hoodings; then gradually increafing, it tumbles down and fcatters all his ftooks over the field. He ftands aghaft and terrified. But, while he is a dreaming what he fhould do, a flood of rain comes on, and continues, till there is fcarce a fheaf in the field which is not thoroughly drenched. Here his whole labour is undone in an hour; hope deferred makes his heart fick; danger increafed leads him to defpondence. This furely is a miferable ftate to the poor farmer. Let us fee however, if there is no provifion for, no precaution againft, fo defolating a ftroke. I imagine there is, and fhall mention two fecurities, which long ufe has recommended to myfelf.

Stooks in danger of being blown down.

The firft lies in a certain method of putting on the hood fheaves. And this may be confidered as a third caution in hooding. It is performed thus, After the hood fheaf, fplit as above directed, is laid on, and in the common fafhion fpread about the end of the ftook, the workman ftanding at that end, grafps in each hand a parcel of the lappets of the hooding, which hang down on each fide, and thrufts both his hands, thus filled, round the firft pair of ftandards next himfelf; this pair and hooding he draws gently towards his bofom, till he

Third caution.

To faften on the hood fheaves.

gets

gets room, between it and the fecond pair, to crofs the handfuls over each other. This done, he lets go his hold of them, and with both his hands preffes the whole (pair and hooding) gently back to their former pofition, till they take hold of the croffed handfuls, that are now held between the firft and fecond pair of ftandards. The whole of this operation is done in an inftant, as foon as the hoodings are put on; and by the fame hand that put them on, and alfo before he moves from his place. —But leaft the croffed handfuls fhould lead in the wetnefs, which falls upon the hood fheaf, towards the heart of the ftook, where they themfelves terminate, a few loofe ftraws, from the fame lappets, may be fpread over their place of entering, in order to carry the droppings down the outfide of the ftook. So that, after the whole is finifhed, the entry of the crofs handfuls is both covered from the weather, and even from the eye itfelf, as one paffes along.

This operation I furely learnt of fome body, and I foon convinced myfelf of its effects by a fair trial. I have had however difficulties in perfuading my fervants to comply with it. And as I am fond *Proof by trial.* of governing dependents, rather by their own underftanding and conviction, than by the mere authority of a mafter, I have had many occafions of repeating the fame trials, to fatisfy their minds. And as a hint to other mafters, my method was this, I allowed my fervants to put up one row of ftooks in any field, after their fafhion; I took the next row upon myfelf, which I executed with the precaution above defcribed; and having made fmall wagers between us, upon the event, both of us exerted ourfelves to the utmoft. I need not tell the iffue of the trials. The wager indeed never was exacted, it being chiefly defigned as a fpur and memorial, and was commonly paid by the winner. In the laft inftance, I remember particularly the trial came out like ten to one, there

being

being fifty hoodings down on their row, when mine had loft but five. The reafon is indeed obvious. When the ftook has had time to fit together, which it muft have had, before the hoodings became fo light, as to be eafily blown off, the hold taken of them is fo good, that they can only be raifed from their feats by a wind that will tear up the whole end of the ftook in which they are faftened. And if after they were faftened below, their crops alfo were fomewhat united, and mingled with each other above, they would there likewife take fuch hold through time, that they could only be torn from their feats, by fuch a tempeft as was able to overturn at once the whole ftook from the bottom. And give me leave to obferve, that this fcarce ever happens, for the fheaves are commonly blown off, one by one, or pair by pair. If it happens otherwife, it can only be in fuch ftooks as are leaning half over already; or fuch as are much diftorted from thofe erroneous methods of ftooking, which have been already mentioned (page 23.)

In cafe the foregoing fecurity fhould have been neglected, or fhould actually fail from the abfolute violence of the wind, there is yet another method of preventing the effects of fuch ftorms, as are defcribed above, (page 27) if one could catch the time rightly. This too I have practifed fuccefsfully, and can give the hiftory of one inftance from my laft year's operations. I take the fact from thence, becaufe it is recent, and becaufe it may be remembered by a hundred people, that were occafionally witneffes of the whole tranfaction.

In harveft 1771, I had a fmall field of between two and three acres, cut and bound dry; fo that it came to be ftooked in good order; but on account of my abfence, the precaution of faftening the hoodings as above, had been neglected. About a fortnight after, upon a Saturday morning,

when

when the field was near ready for the ſtack, it blew a hard gale from the ſouth. My harveſt people were of opinion, that if the wind continued without rain, in a little time it could be taken in, in good order. However fond I was of catching the occaſion, yet the ſouth wind being doubtful, and a blackneſs beginning to appear, I ordered them to the barn, which was in ſight of the field, that they might not be engaged in any work, which they could not leave at a minute's warning; and I bade them look out, now and then, to the field and weather. At ten o'clock the wind and blackneſs were increaſed, and danger was to be feared about noon. Then I told the ſervants, that I had given up thoughts of getting in the corn on that day; but was reſolved if poſſible to keep on the hoodings, and to ſecure every thing againſt Monday, if the weather then ſhould favour us. I aſſured them, that the rain *Of the au* would be on before one of the clock, againſt *thor's atten* which time I was afraid the field would be in *tion to its* bad order to receive it, unleſs they exerted them *approaches.* ſelves ſtrenuouſly. They either not foreſeeing the danger, or unwilling to leave the cover of the barn, in the approach of a viſible tempeſt, did not ſeem to enter frankly into my views; rather attempting to frame difficulties. After ſome reaſoning, I was obliged to tell them, in a ſtronger ſtile, (I remember the words) That the devil, the prince of the power of the air, was juſt going to throw down the whole field; and then, like a dog as he was, to lift his leg and piſs upon it; but I was reſolved to diſappoint him, through the help of heaven, and their aſſiſtance. This language ſtruck; and Will ſmiled at the thoughts of a battle, and promiſed to give me notice of the firſt hooding that fell. I retired a little. At eleven the wind preſſing moſt vehemently, I run out again; and finding one of the lads at the corner of the barn, looking at the field; we both

together

together saw the first hooding fall. In five minutes we reached the field; but by that time, fifty
or sixty stooks were uncovered, and some down
altogether. We began however resolutely, three
hands to the row of stooks, because four sheaves
were to be set up together, and in some violent
blasts they were to be held up, till four more were
added. Then, and not till then, I found that
the above-mentioned precaution, of fixing the
hoodings properly, had been neglected. I now
saw the reason of the total overthrow of the corn,
and expresly ordered every hooding to be fixed
on with care. I followed after the servants my
self, picking up, and replacing firmly every sheaf
that fell behind them. By the time we were
half, or little more than half through the field,
the servants despaired of the work, and would
have given it up. Many hoodings had fallen
behind them, all was flat before them, and the
rain began to spit through the wind, now become
a tempest. Secure myself of the effect, so far as
we could go, and not yet without hopes of finish-
ing the whole, I urged their perseverance with
good humour, upon the old topic, of resisting
the devil. They smiled, and went on vigorous-
ly; I still brought up the rear. In a word, the
whole was finished about five or six minutes after
the rain came on. We then left the field under
a heavy rain, but perfectly well covered and secured: for though we often turned to look at it,
we had no occasion to return to it; not a sheaf
being down when we entered the barn, nor at
any time after when we surveyed it, till it was
taken down for carriage. Which is still more,
not a sheaf was hurt by what fell upon it, either
before, or after it was put up. The clear proof
of our success was, that we had the whole field in
a stack upon Monday, whilst scarce a carr or waggon in the parish, was yoked for several days
thereafter; nor could have been in a fortnight,

*His diligence
in keeping up
the corn, and
on the hood-
ings.*

His success.

unlefs the weather had been very good that week.

The ufe of the above hiflo- rical narra- tive. I have narrated this hiftory minutely, for the fake of the many things that may be learned from it. For 1*ft*, It fhews the good effects of faftening on the hoodings rightly, and the bad effects of careleffnefs in this point. 2*dly*, It fhews the importance of a ftrict attention to the weather, and a forefight of the dangers arifing from the fudden changes of it. 3*dly*, It fhews how much a fudden ftorm, and the appearances of danger and difficulty from it, will rather ftartle and confound the farmer, than roufe him to proper thought, and a vigorous exertion. And what is ftill of more importance, 4*thly*, This hiftory fhews what a bold atteempt, and refolute perfeverance will fometimes do, beyond all firft conception or belief. The fervants who on Saturday would not enter into the hurry going then on, againft Monday's evening boafted their fuccefs; and upon Tuefday were triumphing over their neighbours, who had fcarce as yet been able to touch a fheaf. The people on the high way, and the villagers, who, overlooking the field, thought us mad, and came out of their back doors to fee our diftraction, as they called it, were equally amazed to fee the waggon on the field upon Monday morning; and till the corn was almoft wholly carried off it, could fcarce comprehend the meaning of our Saturday's hurry.

I doubt not, but there may be many farmers through the country, who can tell fimilar inftances of their vigilance, equally furprizing in their fuccefs and efficacy, with what is narrated above. Were fuch tranfactions faithfully recorded, and minutely attended to, they could not fail of making impreffions, where dry precept and argument might be forgotten. For which reafon, I have often wifhed, that fome of your occafional meetings were employed in hearing any well attefted

tefted accounts of fuch tranfactions; and that
fome fmall part of your charity funds were allotted, as encouragements, to fuch as had exerted their ingenuity, prudence, and activity
fuccefsfully, in their affairs of hufbandry. This
might have a tendency to ftir up others, to employ their thought and reflection upon their bufinefs; in the courfe of which, the difficulties and
dangers of their way of life might occur to them,
and the proper remedies be fought out, and at
hand as it were. Thus difficulties might be en-
countered with firmnefs and fuccefs: And is not
this better, than for a man to be ftanding with
folded arms, and a vacant face, gazing at them,
and dreaming about them, till he is overwhelmed
with them?

Of HUTTING CORNS.

The third method of fetting up corns in order
to preferve them, is hutting. Though a wife
man will prefer a well made ftook, to every other
way of preferving or wining corn in the fields,
yet hutting is fometimes neceffary, before particular kinds can be fitted for the barn, or yard. It
is therefore ufed in light grounds, hot gravels,
or thin foils near the rock; where the ftraw is
fmall, and the bottoms of the fheaves are full of
weeds, or natural grafs.

A hut of corn is a fmall clump or ftack, refem-
bling a hay quoil or rick; and confifts of about *A hut*
forty, fifty, or more fheaves, according to the *fcribed.*
nature and ftate of the victual at the time. The
defign of it is to preferve the corn upon the top of
the fheaf from future damage, after it is pretty well
dried in the ftook, or gayt fheaf; and to expofe
to the air the wet and graffy bottoms, that cannot
be fo well cured and win, while they ftand upon the damp earth. It is therefore peculiarly neceffary, to certain corns and foils; efpecially in

E   calm

calm and dropping feafons. From this general intention of hutting, it is eafy to fee, that the operation cannot be fo well performed immediately after the corn is reaped, or when the crops of the fheaves are wet. If this was done, unlefs the quantity put together was very fmall, it would probably heat too much in the hut, and fpoil both the colour and quality of the grain.

Further, from the fize and figure of a hut, as well as the intention of it, it muft alfo be obvious to a man of fenfe, in what manner it ought to be built ; and equally eafy to him to detect any errors in the common practice, that may be committed through ignorance or inattention. But paffing all obfervations upon an erroneous practice, we fhall 1ft, in as few words as poffible, give the moft approved practice in common ufe. Then 2dly, we fhall give a fmall improvement on it, which may be of advantage, in cafe a bad feafon fhould force the farmer to hut his corns before they are fufficiently dried, or deadened for that operation.

The common way of hutting corn. And firft, of the moft approved method of hutting, in common ufe. You will obferve, that as huts are generally made of the ftooks, or gayt fheaves, which have ftood fome time, the farmer chufes, from thofe around him, a fufficient number of dry fheaves, of the cleaneft and ftrongeft ftraw, for the foundation of his hut. Thefe he fets up like the ftale of a ftack, in a circular form, but not preffing it too clofs together ; and about it he fclates on fome of a leffer fize, that do not reach the ground. His care is, by this fecond courfe, to cover all round the open fpaces in the ftale below it. This brings the top of the work to its full breadth, and nearly to a level. Upon this again he begins another courfe, firft by filling the heart well with his dry hoodings, and other fheaves, chofen from the windy and drieft end of his ftooks ; and then he takes the wetter and more graffy bottomed fheaves, to be fclated upon the

out-

outfide as before. After thefe are put on properly, that is, by fpreading their bottoms a little, and thereby covering, as directed above, all the open fpaces between fheaf and fheaf in the courfe below them, he again fets up a few hoodings, or fuch like in the center, as many as he thinks neceffary to contract the circle towards the top; and having chofen fome of his greeneft and wetteft fheaves, he again fclates them on, both around and above the other, till he brings the whole to a proper point, or top. Here he does not care how wet or green his fheaves be, becaufe he trufts to their height, and outfide fituation, for their drying: and is not even difpleafed, that they have fome more than ordinary weight in them, to refift the wind, that they may not fo readily be blown off till the whole fits together a little, or can be fufficiently faftened together. For this laft purpofe, and as a further covering to the whole, the farmer looks about him for one of the largeft and greeneft fheaves in the field, for a top fheaf; and if he is not properly fitted with one, he tyes two fheaves together in one ftrap, pretty near the crop. This he fits on above all, fpreading its bottom round the whole, and as far downward as it will reach. If the weather is windy, two thumb ropes of ftraw are put on acrofs each other, round the neck of the top fheaf, and faftened below at each end. This finifhes the hut, and will fecure it againft all weather for a confiderable time. For by fclating on all the outfide fheaves, with their heads fufficiently raifed, the rain that falls drains off, as from a thatched roof; and by fpreading their bottoms rightly, fo as to cover all vacant fpaces between fheaf and fheaf, none of it gets admittance to the body of the hut.

In very bad weather, when the farmer cannot find a fufficient number of dry and deadened fheaves, for the ftale of his huts, an ingenious neighbour begins his operations in the following

manner.

manner. He choofes fheaves of the cleaneft and
ftrongeft ftraw; and with thefe he fets up two
ftooks, croffing each other in the middle, and
extending fo far on all fides, as he defigns the
widenefs of his hut fhould be. And having put
them up in the beft manner directed on the article
of ftooking, they give him four logies or funnels,
pointed to four quarters of the heavens; fo that
blow the wind how it will, it paffeth freely from
fide to fide of the hut ftale, and communicates its
influence to the infides of all the fheaves in the
crofs ftooks. The quarters between their ends
he fills up but flightly, by a fingle large fheaf or
fo; that the air having fufficient room here alfo,
may communicate its influence to the outfides of
the crofs ftook fheaves. This is excellent. But
it is eafy to fee, that fuch a foundation will not
bear a great quantity of ftuff above it; neither
does the condition in which we fuppofed it to
be, admit of one's putting too much of it together.
The farmer therefore obferving the rules of hutting, above prefcribed, by fetting his beft dried
hoodings and other fheaves in the middle, and
by fclating on his wet and graffy bottomed on the
outfide of them, he quickly brings it to a top;
which he finifhes off as neat and clofs as he can,
to prevent the entry of rain into the heart of the
hut. A hut put up in this fafhion, by an exact
hand, while it preferves the ftuff from danger,
will alfo win it, in half the time that would be
required for a large quantity, put up in the common fafhion; and it will give it out in better
condition, to the carrs and waggons, when it is
to be carried off the field.

But if corns are put up in tolerable good cafe
either of the ways, they will ftand a long time in
fafety, and with the common intervals of fair
weather, or of windy weather though fcarcely
fair, they will improve confiderably, and be got
in at laft in very good condition. The farmer
therefore

An improve-
ment upon
the common
method.

The fecurity
acquired by
hutting corn.

therefore acquires a kind of temporary eafe, and fecurity of mind, when his fields that require hutting are put up in good condition, and with a proper care and accuracy in the workmanfhip.

Upon the whole of what hath been faid, on this fecond period of harveft-work, it may be obferved, that whether corns are gayted, ftooked, or hutted, the farmer's fecurity in all feafons, depends 1ft, upon his having fome knowledge of the beft methods of performing his work, and his thinking a little of what he is about. 2dly, Upon a fufficient pains and accuracy in the execution of it. And if he begins with right methods, he fhall foon acquire a facility and exactnefs in every manual operation. It will at laft become a habit, or fecond nature to him. To encourage him therefore, to take the neceffary care and pains, I could affure him of his faving more than half of what is commonly loft, or fpoiled by a bad harveft. For, in following the very cuftoms that are in common ufe, even that is the difference, I may fay, between a prudent and a thoughtlefs, an active and a flothful management. If the farmer thinks otherwife, and indulges himfelf in careleffnefs, or diffipation, he muft content himfelf with being bankrupt, before half his tack is run; or if, by a fortunate fituation, he fees it out, he muft refolve to fatisfy himfelf with being a great deal poorer at the end of it, than otherwife he might have been. I know what is commonly thought and faid by many of you, when your neighbour grows rich and you poor, or when he fucceeds in any operation which mifgave in your hands. You never imagine him more fkilful and careful than you; you don't blame yourfelves for ignorance or negligence: No. Thefe things feldom enter into your thoughts; you fay, he is always lucky; every thing goes well with him: I am for ever unfortunate; nothing fucceeds with me, defign what I will. Both in your religious

and

and worldly concerns, many of you think, or
feem to think, that heaven has taken the whole of
them upon itfelf; and appear as afraid of inter-
fering with it. So much do you depend, or feem
to depend on its grace, that you fcarce attempt to
do what it expects and requires of you. Thefe
are often the pretences and excufes of floth. For,
though the race is not always to the fwift, nor the
battle to the ftrong; neither bread always to the
wife, nor favour to men of underftanding: yet in
the general courfe of things, a good fortune, or
rather, the grace and providence of heaven, commonly attend the footfteps of wifdom and induftry.

With refpect to the *peafe* and *bean* crops, they
are feldom covered; nor can they be well employed, in ftook or hut, as coverings to themfelves.
And therefore, if coverings are to be put upon
them, it would be beft to protect them with oat
fheaves, or thatch ftraw. The common practice
however is, after they are bound, to fet them up
in the way of ftook, fix or eight fheaves together,
without any covering at all. If this naked method is approved, it would appear to me better to
put only four fheaves together; then, all of them
would be alike expofed to the air and drought;
and all alike ready, when they were to be carried
off the field. If one would wifh to have them
covered when they are near dry, then ten or
twelve fheaves may be fet together in the way of
ftook, and covered with four or five riders and
hoodings of green corn if at hand. But, unlefs
the peafe or beans be full of grafs and weeds, I
fhould not be fond of moving them from their
feats, nor even of laying them down, till the day,
or the day before, I hoped to take them home.
The reafon is, that, after they have ftood long under alternate rain and drought, the leaft motion
makes them open their pods, and fhakes out their
grain. The practice however, of laying down
corns

corns of all kinds, to air their bottoms before they are carried in, is generally useful, and sometimes necessary; especially when they have stood long upon a wettish soil, and under wet weather. But our rules and observations upon the management of this part of the harvest-work, we refer to the next period of it.

The third period of harvest-work comprehends *The third* every operation that may be necessary, from the *period of* time that the corns appear to be ready for inga- *harvest-* thering, till the whole is finished, and the victual, *work.* put into the barn or barn-yard, is brought into a state of perfect soundness for use, and of perfect safety for preservation.

· Here then let me observe, that notwithstanding the best intentions of the farmer, to have his corns in good condition for being carried off the field, —to put them into stack or barn in good keeping order,—and to secure them effectually against all future dangers; notwithstanding he has used his utmost care and diligence, to answer his good intentions in all these particulars; yet by some change of weather, some hurry in his operations, some inattention or neglect, soon or late, errors are committed, and necessaries unprovided, so that the honest man suffers in one or other particular, and meets an unexpected disappointment. Therefore, that we may overlook nothing material to his security, which he himself may forget, we shall divide the business of ingathering, and securing his crops, into the following heads.

1*st*, Of the operations immediately preparatory *The division* for leading corns. *of the subject*

2*dly*, Of the operations preparatory for stack- *belonging to* ing and mowing corns. *it.*

3*dly*, Of the methods of building, covering, and roping stacks; and the provisions necessary for these operations.

4*thly*, Of the means used for recovering heated

corns,

corns, either in mow or ſtack ; and the proviſion that may be made for rendering this an eaſy work.

In all theſe we proceed upon the ſuppoſition of unfavourable weather ; and at the ſame time, that ſome room is left for human prudence and activity. And we ſhall be as particular on the whole, as is neceſſary to be underſtood and believed by any farmer of common thought and reflection.

1ſt, Of the operations immediately preparatory for leading corns.

In entering upon this point, it is neceſſary to obſerve, that the farmer ought never to begin his leading upon mere conjecture that his corn is ready. He himſelf ſhould examine it, in all its different parts and poſitions. It was not perhaps all cut in one day, nor in the ſame condition of dryneſs or ripeneſs ; nor laſtly, was it all alike expoſed to the influence of the drought. He ſhould therefore examine it ſtrictly with his own hands and eyes, left after he has diſengaged his ſervants from other occupations, and yoked his cattle, he be diſconcerted, and obliged either to proceed with danger, or to leave off with ſhame and loſs of time. It were better this trial were made the day before, than on the day of ingathering ; that he may have time to be well concerted, or even to remedy what he may find amiſs. On this occaſion, a few of the worſt ſheaves may be marked where they ſtand, and a few others laid out to dry ; that by inſpecting ſuch at ſome hours diſtance, he may be able to judge of the whole field at preſent ; and even to underſtand what time it might require, to mend the worſt of it. And if he viſited the field in the ſame evening, or in the morning of the next day, with the ſame care, he could not fail of being concerted and prepared for the beſt.

If, upon his firſt trial, the farmer finds his corns in good order, and the ground itſelf perfectly dry beneath his ſtooks ; he has no more to do, but

order

order his men and horfes to be got ready, at an appointed time, that his work may go on brifkly.

If he finds no faults, but a little dampnefs in the bottoms, arifing from their long ftanding upon a wettifh foil; and that the whole might be better of an hour's drought, all hands may be called together, in order to lay it out, that no time may be loft. In this operation, the hoodings are firft pulled off, and fet at the end of the ftook, not directly in the wind; then the operator takes hold, with both his hands, of the crops of the eight ftanding fheaves, and pulling them towards himfelf, he wheels them about to the fun or wind in one piece, as he lays the whole down upon its fide. If the two fides of the ftook are unequally dried—For example, if the winds have blown for two or three days from one quarter, or the fouth fide has enjoyed a warm fun, or the dew is yet hanging on the north fide; in that cafe, it is beft to turn the damp fide uppermoft: for which purpofe nothing more is requifite, but that the operator ftand upon the drieft fide, while he pulls the ftook towards him, and wheels its bottoms to the fun or wind: for in laying the whole down, the drieft fide will be always lowermoft, the wetteft fide always uppermoft. And it might not be amifs, before he parts with it, if he drew his hand acrofs the bottoms, to open the pens of the ftraw a little; or if he turned a parcel of every wet fheaf inward, in order to the admiffion of the air or fun beams. If this be all that is requifite, and the operation be performed in a good morning, then, by the time breakfaft is over, and the cattle yoked, the work may begin, upon that fide of the field which was firft laid down. The judgment of the farmer however muft be confulted upon every point; for no language can make rules fo accurate and precife, as to hit the various degrees of wet or dry, green or win, that may be in a field.

Of laying down ftooks to air their bottoms.

Which fide to lay uppermoft.

F

If,

If laft of all, the ftate of the corn, is fo bad as to require more handling, and a longer time before it is carried off, then the moft clear and certain me-

Of waling and forting corn in bad order.
thod is, to wale and fort the whole field, fheaf by fheaf. This, if done with diftinctnefs and care, leaves nothing afterwards under any degree of doubtfulnefs, to caufe delay, or a repetition of labour. In this operation, the dry hood fheaves, and all others in good condition, fhould be laid on that fide of the ridge along which the waggon comes, turning any part of the fheaf to the wind, that requires a little drought. All the fheaves in bad condition, fhould be laid or fet out upon the oppofite fide; but with much more care and attention. This diftinct fituation of good and bad fheaves, fhould be invariably obferved over the whole field, by all the labourers employed in forting it. A few experienced hands fhould be fet to this work: they will be able to know a good fheaf by its comparative lightnefs, and loofenefs in the ftrap: and a bad fheaf by its weight, and the tightnefs of its binding. A doubtful one muft be tried, by thrufting one's hand into the middle of it, or his finger beneath the binder's knot. What is found in very bad condition, fhould have its worft fide laid carefully out to the drought; its bottom fhould be tiezed up, or if need be, the band fhould be loofed, and the fheaf fpread out at full breadth, or in any other way expofed, that will beft amend its faults. All the while, particular care fhould be taken of both knots of the ftrap, that they be opened and effectually dried; otherwife it would be more profitable to throw it afide, and to make a new one.

The waling repeated.
It is eafy to fee that, after the above forting, the waggons may go over the whole field, and carry off but half of its contents. There is however no time loft by that circumftance; for, before the whole of the dry corn is taken away, that which was laid out to dry on the other fide of the ridge,

may

may be either wholly ready for carrying, or so great a part of it may be ready, that it can be again separated from the bad, by the same hands employed in the first sorting; and the bad itself may be so managed, as to have those parts, which had hitherto escaped the drought, anew exposed to it. In this second sorting it would be wise, in my opinion, and I have already hinted it, rather to throw aside a growing strap or handful, and to bind up the sound by itself for carriage, than, for the sake of what would not amount to a dozen sheaves, to expose some hundreds of a field to unnecessary danger or delay. Nay, 'tis better for the whole, the earlier this separation can be made; for it prevents all future trouble, or delay in securing the best; and the worst itself, laid out in small percels, would soon dry; and might, as was formerly hinted, be gathered at leisure. Thus, with the addition of a few hands, the same field can be finished in the same time it would have required, had the weather been all along good, and the corns in the best possible condition for carrying in.

The same pains may be used, when necessary, to separate the good and bad of gayted corn, or of corn in huts. Indeed it is convenient to load a waggon from the huts themselves, and if the corn is generally in good condition, as one might expect it would be, after it had been already sorted, in the building of the huts, perhaps the waggoner and forker together may be trusted, without more ado about the matter. For it is perfectly easy to them, with the least attention, to throw aside a bad sheaf that comes through both their hands. This then should be enjoined them, and even to the stack builder, since all labourers need from time to time, to have their attention roused to any thing expected from them, which is not their immediate work. Indeed, if much of this by-work is to be done, better a separate hand were

employed,

employed, than to run the rifk of their neglecting either of their proper employments, in minding other matters.

A caution not to lay down much in doubtful weather.

Having now difcuffed the feveral points, relating to the work in the field, I cannot, at prefent, recollect any thing material omitted, but one advice, which is never to fpread out much corn at once, unlefs pretty fure of the weather. To be overtaken with rain, in this ftate of the field when every part is almoft ready, muft be highly diftreffing to the careful farmer. I fhould therefore take occafion here, from thefe and the like accidents, to recommend to him a careful ftudy, and obfervation of the weather; treafuring up every judicious hint upon this fubject that he hears from others, as well as what may have occured to himfelf. The fhepherd of Banbury's obfervations have been printed, and are much talked of. To me indeed they appear to have been made upon a plain, or nearly fo; for he takes no notice of the figns upon high hills, commonly marked by all who have them within view. Befides fome of his obfervations do not ftrike. Perhaps indeed I have not been fufficiently attentive to thefe matters; perhaps too, the obfervations being made in an inland or plain country, his figns may not exactly correfpond with thofe obferved on a fea coaft, or among a clufter of hills. Some of his obfervations are however ftriking; and if any one is curious to compare them with his own experience and obfervation, he may find an abftract of them printted (before the calendar) in the Edinburgh almanack, for the year 1773. If farmers are acquainted with the ordinary figns of good or bad weather, in the places where they live, a weatherglafs might be ufeful to them; but not without a ftrict attention to it; daily marking its rifings and fallings, obferving their progrefs, and even their indications of continuing, upon the top of the mercury, according to the directions given along

The ftudy of the weather recommended.

along with it. Be wary however of trufting to the barometer alone. But if the figns of the weather without, correfpond with the indications of it upon the weatherglafs, one may more fe-curely truft to it.

I now leave the fields, and muft lead you from thence to the barn and barn-yard. There we fhall employ a little more of your time and leifure, if you can beftow it this way.

The fecond point.

This was our fecond point, upon the third pe-riod of harveft-work. And here, keeping a wef-tern climate, or a bad feafon, ftill in our eye, we cannot but commend the ufages of the weft, par-ticularly, in building large barns and fmall ftacks.

Of the ope-rations pre-paratory for ftacking, corns.

A large barn is of great advantage in variable weather. One, for example, may throw into his barn two or three waggon loads, when he dares not fet the ftale of a ftack, however fmall. Little ftacks are equally convenient, for one of ten bolls may be begun and finifhed, when one of thirty or for-ty muft not be undertaken. Befides, the advan-tage of a fmall fize is vifible, when one cannot truft to the good condition of his corn. In fuch ftacks, the external air penetrates to their very centers, or very near them. The heat of them therefore can never be very great, nor widely ex-tended. If it fhews itfelf at all, it can only be when the ftack through time fubfides, and fhuts its pores, fo to fpeak. This commonly happen-ing very late, may furprife the farmer, perhaps, after he thought all danger was over ; but it is its only inconvenience : for a fheaf or two pulled out to the leeward, in order to let out the fteam, will cure it as foon as it is perceived. And if he pleafes, one or two pulled out to the windward will affift its flight, and fupply its room with cool air. If the farmer finds it needful, he can multi-ply fuch air paffages, at different heights, and in different directions, at pleafure ; and that with-out any inconvenience, if he only takes care, that the

Large barns and fmall ftacks conve-nient.

The advan-tage of fmall ftacks.

Eafily cured of heating.

the balance of the ſtack be not deſtroyed, by pulling out too much on one ſide, in the very great hurry of mending it. If the weight above tends to fill up the air holes, a few branches thruſt into them will keep them open, till all danger is over.

If the ſmallneſs of the barn-yard obliges the farmer, or his own conceit inclines him, to have large ſtacks, writers on huſbandry recommend a *Of funnels in* funnel, drawn up in the center of the ſtack, from *large ſtacks.* the bottom to whatever height is moſt convenient. This is made in England, by ſetting a ſack full of chaff in the middle of the ſtale, and building round it; as the ſtack advances, the ſack is drawn upwards, from time to time, till the funnel is high enough; and then the ſack may be pulled out, and the hole above drawn to a point, or covered. The heated air, ſay they, finds its way upward by this *An improve-* conveyance, and ſo flies out at the top. It would *ment on them.* however be an improvement of this convenience, were the air from without admitted into it, from time to time. This might eaſily be done by a level pipe, reaching from the outſide of the ſtack upon the windward ſide, to the center funnel, or near to the ſame. And the pipe may be laid upon the ground, or even two or three foot above the ground, if that height is neceſſary to catch the wind.

Others recommend well hewed ſtone pillars and *Of ſtone pil-* covers, clad above with ſmall timber and bruſh-*lars and co-* wood, on which the corn is laid. Theſe founda-*vers.* tions have ſeveral advantages; the corns are lifted up into the air, out of the reach of dampneſs from the earth; the wind blows through beneath them, as well as round them, with good effect: *Their advan-* and laſtly, if they are rightly made, and the pil-*tages.* lars three feet above the ground, no rats nor mice can get into the ſtack. This laſt advantage is the chief deſign of ſuch pillars; and indeed it is a great ſaving, in ſome years, and in ſome particular ſituations. In the mean time, care muſt be taken,

to

to leave no ſtraw beneath the ſtacks that are built upon them, no poles nor ladders leaning to them; by which ſuch vermine may get up or down, other-wiſe all the expence and labour, ſo far as regards them, is wholly loſt. The expence of them is in-deed great for a poor farmer, who hath not much to ſpare, after his rent is payed. A circular one, that could hold from forty to ſixty bolls, coſts in ſtone, hewing, &c. about ſix pounds. One I have, that holds from ſixteen to twentyfour bolls, coſt me in ſtone work above three pounds, beſides half a guinea for the ſmall timber and bruſh-wood. Yet I would not have wanted its convenience, not to ſay its beauty, theſe few years paſt, for more than the money. But however elegant and uſeful they may be, let us rather conſider them here as a kind of ornament to the barn-yard of a gentleman farmer, than as conveniences for his poor tenants, that cannot ſpare the expence. And let us recomend to them a cheaper, and at the *A cheaper* ſame time an equally uſeful plan. A plan which, *plan equally* while it anſwers every purpoſe of the other, ſhall *uſeful.* ſcarce coſt ſo many ſhillings as it does pounds. It was contrived and executed by a farmer, Thomas Orr in Ernock, who has experienced its advan-tages for ſome years paſt.

This farmer has his ſtack-yard upon a little riſing ground, in reſpect of the neighbouring fields. He began by cutting a ſmall trench from *A deſcripti-* the outſide of his yard dyke, to the place where *on of it.* the center of his ſtack was deſigned to be. This trench, ſtraight in the bottom, and as near the level as the riſe allowed him, was about eighteen inches or two feet wide. He lined it on both ſides with common field ſtones; over which he laid a covering of flagg ſtones, leaving a vent hole open under the center of his ſtack, to let up the wind into it. This vent-hole, like the reſt of his pipe, might be about nine inches wide. And having dreſſed down the earth, that was thrown out of

his

his trench, over the flagg coverings, and into any hollow places around him, his work was done for the time. Againft the harveft feafon 'Thomas gathered a good bundle of fmall fticks, or rods, which he laid up to dry, and be ready for ufe. When he begins to build his ftack, he fets up his bundle of rods over the center vent-hole, fpreading them a little below, that they may ftand firm ; and tying them loofely above, by a withy, or thumb rope of ftraw. Around this bundle, he builds his ftack to what circumference he pleafes ; and at laft above it, to what height he pleafes. And when it is finifhed, he is at eafe with refpect to fo much.

By this trifling expence, fcarce above two days labour of his own hands, does this ingenious man fecure his corns in the yard againft all poffible *Its advanta-* danger. For his logie from the outfide draws the *ges.* air fo ftrongly, if the wind is near that quarter, that he fears no danger from heating in the ftacks. Nor 2*dly*, does he run half the hazard in the fields, that his neighbours do, by keeping out their corns a long time to win them ; for he dares to put in his, if cut dry, much fooner than they can with fafety venture theirs. And laftly, which is ftill more notable, he makes ufe of his logie and funnel pipe, for the capital purpofe of the pillared fteddings above defcribed. For if he fufpects that any of his ftacks are infefted with mice, he diflodges and deftroys them in an hour, or fo, at almoft no expence at all. Whenever he finds that the wind anfwers him, he carries out a fhovel full of hot cinders, and having placed them in the logie, or mouth of his funnel, he only ftrows upon them a little bruifed brimftone. This in a little time, begins to fhew its effects throughout the whole ftack ; fo that, by applying his ear to any fide of it, he can hear within a ruftling noife, attended with a cheeping cry, which fhew the whole mice to be in motion, and, at the fame
time,

time, in diſtreſs from the very air they breathe. After this they begin to ſet out their heads for a gulp of freſh air ; and may now be ſeen by an attentive eye. Thomas goes round with the grey plaid about him, and contemplates the effects of his own ingenuity, with peculiar pleaſure ; for he expects them, and looks for them. At laſt the mice being no longer able to endure the ſtench within purſuing them, are forced to deſert their winter habitations ; and ſo drop down in their preſent ſickly and feeble ſtate, an eaſy prey to the dog and cat, who are both of them taught to watch and deſtroy them, on ſuch occaſions.

All this is moſt natural, and when told with ſimplicity by the man himſelf, can ſcarce admit a doubt. Thomas adds further, that this ſcheme is *Moſt uſeful* much more effectual to all his purpoſes, in a pretty *in large and* large and cloſs built ſtack, than in a very ſmall and *cloſs built* looſe built one : becauſe, when the ſtack is of little *ſtacks.* compaſs, and not preſſed ſufficiently together by its weight, the air finds more eaſily and readily, ſome vent for itſelf near the bottom, through which it eſcapes, without paſſing thro' the whole ſtuff, and ſo producing all its deſigned effects. Whereas, in a greater and more compact body of corn, the air is obliged to find its way through every ſmall ſpace between the ſtraws, before it can get out. This too is abundantly natural and obvious. Inſtead then of doubting the facts, as ſome at a diſtance may incline to do, or of deſpiſing the efforts of genius, as ſome neighbours may do, who cannot doubt the facts, we ought all to be ready to make a fair trial, before we decide againſt the meaſure : and the rather that, while our own intereſt is at ſtake, the experiment can coſt us nothing.

Some will perhaps object, that their barn-yards *Objections* are not convenient for ſuch experiments. For ex- *from ſituati-* ample, they may think them not ſufficiently raiſ- *on anſwer-* ed, not expoſed to the weſt wind, which is the *ed.*

G   trade

trade wind of this country; or that they are too clofs on all hands, to receive any benefit from fuch trials. But none of thefe difficulties appear to me infurmountable. Suppofe the barn-yard were not above the level of the neighbouring grounds, the air pipe might be built, if of ftone, above the furface itfelf; or a rhone of wood could be made for the purpofe, communicating with the center; and it might be either laid on the ground, or two feet above it among the ftuff, in order to catch the wind the better. If the ftack-yard declines to the north, or eaft, a trench caft in any of thefe directions, would certainly anfwer the purpofe, nearly as well as one to the weft or fouth. For if the wind is not fo violent in fuch directions, it is generally harder, and more drying in its nature. Laft of all, if the barn-yard is too clofs fenced, it muft, at any rate, be very bad for the purpofe of keeping victual; therefore it fhould be laid more open: and the fituation muft indeed have been at firft ill chofen, if it does not afford a proper opening on fome fide. But not to ftay on fuch particulars, a willing mind will conquer the difficulties of any fituation whatever.

The fame principles and works will apply to a barn-mow, as to a ftack in the yard; and will doubtlefs have the fame effect. A little paffage might eafily be made through the foundation for the back mow, at the time of building; the fore mow may be fupplied with air from the open fpace between the doors, by a fmall wooden rhone placed on the floor, or at what heighth above it may feem neceffary: or, laft of all, either of thefe may be fupplied, by placing a triangular rhone in the three cornered windows, commonly made in country barns. If the air is conveyed by thefe, three or four feet within the body of the mow, it will anfwer the purpofe, when the mow is rightly built, or has any opening for the air to afcend by. A friend of mine has contrived fomewhat

what of this kind ; but he carries his rhone, or
conveyance, acrofs the barn, from window to window, with openings to let out the air in its paffage. My opinion was, that he would be better
to have no communication from air hole to air
hole, for thus the wind was apt to pafs through
too rapidly for any great effect; but if he meant
to force it up through the whole mafs of ftuff, it
would be better for him to cut out five or fix
feet from the middle of his rhone, that the piece
at each fide might terminate in the folid mow, or
near any fmall vent upwards. Then, on whatever fide the wind blew, it would be forced to afcend, and to find its way through fome part of
the mafs. The piece cut out might be better employed elfewhere.

Air holes in barn walls are certainly ufeful in
fome meafure, without any additional improvement. But as they ftand at prefent, their ufe is
very fmall ; for when the mow begins to fubfide,
as all mows do through time, it naturally clofes
up its own pores and interftices, fo that little air
can be admitted to the center, where it begins to
heat, and needs it moft. Add to this, the more
damp the corn is, and the greater its danger of
heating, the weightier is it, and the readier to fink
and clap together, which muft in courfe haften
and increafe its difeafe. Laft of all, the very finking and contraction of the mow loofens it in
fome meafure from the walls, leaving a fmall fpace
between them and the corn, into which the air,
admitted by the barn windows, enters ; and round
which it circulates, without penetrating the corn
itfelf. From all which views of the cafe, air holes,
as they ftand at prefent, are not fo ufeful as they
might be made. But if the air admitted by them
was conveyed, by means of a wooden rhone, or a
little brufh-wood, two, three, or four feet, within
the body of the mow, where the real danger is,

Air. holes i
barn wal
examined.

Not fo ufefi
as might l
thought.

Improved .
real ufe.

G 2   it

it might do the moſt effectual ſervice to heating, or already heated corn.

There is nothing to hinder theſe four or five feet rhones, to be laid in ſtacks of any ſize, at the building of them, on different ſides, and at different heights, and to what number, and indeed of what greater lengths the farmer ſees needful. If ſuch implements of huſbandry were in common uſe, and prepared for the purpoſe, I ſhould not be ſurprized to hear the ſtack-builder calling for them, when he was laying on a waggon-load of his greeneſt or dampeſt corn. Their obvious advantages would ſoon recommend them to every body.

The expence little or no-thing. Obſerve, that one homeward grown fir-tree, from a ſhilling to eighteen pence price, ſawed into boards an inch thick, and cut into proper lengths and breadths, would ſerve all the purpoſes of an ordinary barn and yard. They might be three cornered in their form, and ſcarce above three or four inches in their ſides. And what is the expence in compariſon with the riſk yearly run, and the damage often ſuſtained, in both barn and yard? Nay, what is it in compariſon of the toil and anxiety, occaſioned by ſuch accidents?

The way of managing rhones and air pipes to the beſt advantage. Further, my opinion concerning the management of theſe rhones, and of all other air pipes or funnel, is this, that they ſhould be ſhut up for eight or ten days, and perhaps more, after the ſtack or mow is built, till the heat begins to ſhew itſelf on the end of the hand-ſtaves, for heat itſelf, when kept in due bounds, is an excellent drier. When the heat begins to be felt by drawing out one of the hand-ſtaves, and we may judge from thence, that the air within is beginning to

Heat rarifies the air. rarify and expand itſelf; then is the critical time of opening the holes, and admitting the cold air into the mow or ſtack: for at that time the vacuum, ſo to ſpeak, occaſioned by rariſaction and ſudden condenſation, will attract and draw the

freſh

freſh air, like a well going chimney, over a well kindled fire. This freſh recruit of air again, mixing with the moiſt and warm vapour within, will in time alſo be expanded and rarified; and ſo carrying the vapour along with it, will eſcape through every pore and interſtice of the ſtuff, into the open air, till nothing is left behind but cool air. And if the ſtack, or mow, was in very bad condition, by being ſuffered to heat too much, the ſteam, as is common in ſuch caſes, will be even viſible to the eye as it flies off. This is the philoſophical account, which I gave to Thomas Orr and others, of the effect. The language may be ſtrange to common farmers; but the reaſoning is juſt, and experience will incline ſuch reaſonable minds as have attended to the effect, to believe it will hold, though the language in which it is expreſſed, may not be ſo familiar to them, or the properties of air be not underſtood. If the farmer makes the trial, I could wiſh he would ſuffer the heat to be ſenſibly felt before his trial, that he may be convinced of the change that muſt happen. On the other hand, I hope he will not ſuffer the heat to increaſe too much, or to continue too long, before he opens his vent-holes, and gives his corns the neceſſary refreſhment. And this is all the caution needed upon the point.

Condenſed by the admiſſion of cold air produces a vacuum into which the air ruſhes violently.

If any of thoſe methods for preſerving victual were tried, and the farmer were well provided with every thing neceſſary before-hand, that the trial might be thoroughly made; I am convinced, that much of the corns, which in bad harveſts are loſt, or ſpoiled, might be preſerved perfectly found, for the uſe of man or beaſt. If this were the caſe, the farmer could never be in hazard of loſing his next years crop, by ſowing feed too much browned at the ends by mow-hurning. A calamity that is but too often, and ſeverely felt by the careleſs ſluggard; while, from the ſame circumſtance, the prudent farmer is ſometimes obliged to renew his

Mow-burnt corn a bad feed.

his feed, when there is otherwife no immediate call for that expence or trouble.

I have faid nothing here, as yet, of building ftacks or mows, for their prefervation from heating. If no air funnel is carried up the middle of either, it would be certainly neceffary to fet a great deal of the corn upon one end, in the place of fuch funnels ; that is, fetting the ftale a new, above the ground ftale, and fo on, another above that, till the ftack or mow is brought near the top. What is further neceffary in order to preferve ftacks from wet weather, will be mentioned on the next particular of this period.

The third branch on the third period of harveft-work. The third branch of this laft period of harveft-work, relates to the covering of ftacks properly, in order to preferve them from external injury, and to the provifion neceffary for that purpofe.

Little needs to be faid to our weft country farmers, upon the method of covering and roping ftacks. Their own method, in both, feems to be commendable. Their mifmanagement is chiefly obfervable, in their being often unprovided with the materials requifite for thefe operations, when they come to be needed ; and, perhaps, in their want of care in building their ftacks, fo as to defend them effectually till their covering is prepared. Something therefore ought to be faid to them upon thefe points ; and after that, a few words fhould ferve with regard to the operations of covering and roping ftacks.

The want of thatch ftraw highly inconvenient. Now, there is nothing, I imagine, that ought to be more ftudied by the weft country farmer, than to have by him at harveft time, a good ftock of old ftraw ; drawn, and ready for thatching his ftacks, as foon as they are built. His ryegrafs, if he has any, comes early, yet affords him nothing to cover itfelf. His bog hay may fpare him a few fpritts and rufhes for itfelf ; and that is, perhaps, all that it will do ; fo that, if he can fpare nothing here, the ryegrafs muft ftand uncovered till it is

black,

black, and perhaps rotten half a foot deep above the eafing: for the end of our fummers, and the beginning of our harveft quarters, are our wetteft times round the whole year. And as there is no poffibility of our being provided, but from the fpritts and rufhes above-mentioned, againft the harveft itfelf; if there are no favings in thefe, e-very thing then put up muft lie at the mercy of the weather, till it is provided by thiefhing part of the crop itfelf: from this very circumftance, I have feen peafe ftacks in the utmoft danger of be-ing wholly fpoiled, by great rains.

But to fpeak precifely to this point; it is not in a variable harveft that the improvident farmer fuffers moft by want of thatch-ftraw. This can only be felt in the very beginning of fuch a fea-fon; for bad weather gives the fervants too much leifure to provide whatever may be neceffary. The want of thatch is commonly moft hurtful in the very beft harvefts. Then it is, that the far-mer is hurried on with his work without; and trufting to the excellence of the weather, the pre-paration of thatch is delayed till all is gathered in, and all needing covering. If the farmer is not overtaken before that, he has reafon to expect that it cannot be long after it; yet the long con-tinuance of good weather tends to increafe his prefumption and fecurity, and it is ten to one that he fhall fuffer at laft: if he does, it muft be moft feverely. In paffing a barn-yard, fometime about the end of October, in company with two country men, we obferved a dozen good ftacks all unthatched, and all as green as a field in braird. We at firft blamed the farmer's negligence; and one of the countrymen, to aggravate his fault, obferved, that he had no excufe, for we had not for many years enjoyed fo good a harveft. The other, as I then thought, very judiciafly checked him; alledging that the goodnefs of the harveft weather might be the fole caufe of the man's ne-glect.

Sometimes hurtful in the beft fea-fons.

At Nether-mains in Cu-ningham.

glect. Upon reflection, the apology feemed to be juft, as well as kind: for the fact was, that moft of the corns had that year ripened together, and the fine weather continuing, every man was hurried in cutting down and gathering in. At the conclufion of the work a deluge of rain fell out, and the weather continued wet for feveral weeks. This farmer, indeed, like many others, was at laft drove into his barn to provide his thatch; but, alas! he was alfo confined to it, till the growing took place; which hurt him much, as it did many others that year, who had been equally unprovident with himfelf.

A caution.

Circumftances of this kind occurring fhould alarm the farmer, and guard him againft an overgreat confidence in the fineft weather. It is a good maxim, long foul, long fair; long fair, long foul. At the fame time, what is more directly to our point, all farmers, from fuch occafional furprifes, fhould be taught forefight and diligence, in preferving, or providing the neceffary covering for their victual, when it can be got in fafe.

The eafieft provifion for thatching, viz. barley-ftraw.

Could not the farmer fet apart all the ftraw of late threfhed barley, for thatching next year's ftacks? Perhaps it may be fhortened a little; but no matter, it can be put on the clofler: for it will do, as we in the weft feldom keep ftacks over fummer. We keep indeed too many cattle, which are partly ftarved from want of both grafs and fodder. This cuftom however makes us put a value on every ftraw. My advice is, therefore, adapted to our tafte and cuftom: for the ftraw of feed bear comes generally after foddering time; befides we efteem it of little ufe for cattle, when threfhed earlier. For which reafon, I am not even fcrupulous of fetting apart for the enfuing harveft, fome of my earlieft threfhed barley-ftraw. For if I were not provided againft the time of need, I fhould think myfelf affronted if I had left a rufh-bufh, or broom-know uncut, in all my poffeffion.

seffion. It is true, fuch as have large farms in the weft are feldom unprovided; and in the eaft, where they have corns of all kinds to threfh through fummer, they fcarce ever can be in want of thatch at harveft time. And what, I pray, would the eaft country farmers fay of our practice, did they know that few of thofe in the weft, have a fingle fheaf of laft crop remaining, to put upon their ftacks of the prefent crop; but that it muft be threfhed out of itfelf, before the crop can be covered from the weather. Might they not afk us, with all our oeconomy, What could be the dif-ference, in providing our thatch from laft crop, or from the prefent, fince fooner or later every crop muft furnifh the quantity required for a year? might they not twit us with the old proverb, That fince we will be faving, it is ftill better to hain the braird than the bottom: for without knowing what a bad winter may require of us, we dip very deeply in that winter's provifion, for the ftraw that in harveft is abfolutely neceffary to fecure the crop. *The folly of not keeping it.*

But in regard that, after all that can be faid up-on the advantages of a proper forefight and pro-vidence, with refpect to our probable wants, many will be more or lefs unprovided when the demand comes upon them; our firft rule here is, that great care be taken in the building of ftacks, e-fpecially above the eafing, in order to keep out the rain till the thatch can be provided. This is done, as was hinted upon hutting, firft, by filling the heart well, and thereby floping the outer fheaves, fo as to drain off the wetnefs readily. This is an eafy work above the ring-gang, where it is moft needful. Below that it is more difficult, efpecial-ly if the ftack is allowed to grow much. Here the fheaves on the outfide flide out, and both dif-figure the building, and endanger its falling with-out fupporters. But a tight rope round the ftack, and an active hand below, to beat in a fheaf as *Care in building ftacks necef-fary on ac-count of the want of thatch.*

The firft rule.

H foon

soon as it flides out of its place, is the effectual remedy.

It may be neceffary to obferve here what will
sometimes happen, to wit, that the building of a
ftack may be interrupted with rain, before it is half
finifhed; which is not only dangerous to the corn
laid out upon the field for compleating it, but
particularly fo to the unfinifhed ftack. We pafs
over at this time the danger in the field, as not to
our prefent purpofe; and only take notice, that
the common prefervation ufed for a ftack in this
condition is, to fill up the heart as quickly as can
be, with whatever corn is at hand, or on the way
homewards. After this, the workman gives the
whole a clofs covering of thatch fheaves, to keep
out the rain. But as this kind of covering is not
always ready on fuch occafions; fo, at the fame
time, when it is ufed, it is but an infufficient
protection under great and continuing rains. It
were therefore to be wifhed, that we had in ufe
both a better and more conftant fecurity.

Of inter-ruptions in building the ftacks.

I have heard that the farmers in Holland ufe a
kind of timber roof, of a conic figure, for the heads
of their ftacks; which, being hung by the top upon
a triangle, can, by the means of pulleys, be drawn
up, or let down at plcafure; as the weather may
either favour, or obftruct their work. Our
countrymen who have feen them, call them Dutch
barns: for the farmer can build up beneath
them, any fmall quantity of his corn which he
finds ready at the time, and letting down his roof
upon it, he can wait with patience till more of it
can be got in. And this work he can repeat from
time to time, till the ftack is compleated, and the
roof fixed down upon it for good.

Dutch barns hinted as a remedy.

This is the only account of thofe timber roofs,
which I can at prefent recollect; it being a long
time fince I heard of them. And as I never faw one,
nor do I remember to have feen any defcription of
them, in the books upon hufbandry, I dare fcarce

The author not fully in-formed of their nature and ufe.

venture

venture to be more particular myself, left I should
mistake my own late conjectures, for the infor-.
mations of my friend. Neither, for the same reasons, can I judge precisely of their advantages or
disadvantages. One however may presume, that
those who use them find some benefit from them.
But whether the advantages of them are superior,
or rather additional, to what we enjoy from our
own barns; or if they are only supplemental, in
making up for the want of such barns as we have,
I cannot at present pretend to determine. In the
mean time, the difference between these two cir- *Wishes for a*
cumstances is important. I should therefore *more full in-*
think, that the public would be indebted to any *formation.*
man better informed, for an accurate account of
their construction and advantages.

After all, if any of our farmers inclines to try *Hints to the*
his genius, upon the imperfect hints above given, *ingenious*
he might use, at a small expence, the common *farmer.*
fir of the country, both for his triangle and cover :
and if he gave his stacks, and also the conic covers
a square form, the trouble and expence of the
workmanship would be less, and the frame itself
more firm than the circular form, adapted to the
common round figure of our stacks. If the
farmer does not choose the triangle and pulleys,
the cover must be made in such pieces as can be
put together with hands, when it is to be used.
Or, if these pieces should be too heavy, and in
windy weather become unmanageable; the frame
of them only might be made of wood, and be
covered when used, with some coarse wax cloth,
or oil cloth, shaped for one side of the cone.
And, if the top of the cone was precisely a
right angle, any two quarters put together by
the base, would make a square winnow-cloth,
when not in immediate use as a cover. The first
of these with the triangle and pulleys will be the
most manageable, if its expence does not affright
the farmer. Lastly, if the farmer pleases, a simple

H 2   wax-

wax cloth could be fhaped to that kind of head, which any ftack builder would choofe to leave upon his work, were he like to be overtaken with rain. This could eafily be thrown over it, and if a fmall weight were appended to each corner, in order to ftretch the cloth properly, the rain would run off it more eafily, and the wind might not be able to raife it from its place. Hearing that fome of my ingenious neighbours were deliberating about thefe temporary coverings, I have thrown out the foregoing hints into their view, merely as materials for their own thoughts ; hoping to hear foon of fome contrivance that will remedy the inconveniences of which they have complained thefe two years paft.

Which he may improve upon.

2*dly*, The builder fhould endeavour to lay all his outfide fheaves fo clofs together, that no vacancy or even flacknefs be left in the whole round, to admit the rain. Above the eafing it is common to fpread the bottoms a little, by which their heads are kept more erect, and the vacancies below are better covered.

The fecond rule.

If before the thatch is prepared, the ftack fhall fuffer from great rains, which threaten a continuance, and the farmer would wifh to have it protected ; inftead of a clofs thatching with ftraw, I would in this cafe advife a broom covering, where it can be eafily had. For, if the root ends of the branches were a little fharpened, fo that they could be eafily thruft into the ftack, this work could be done at any time, without waiting till it was dried on the outfide : becaufe, whilft the broom is a fufficient protection againft fucceeding rains, it admits alfo a fufficient quantity of air among its branches, to dry up the former wetnefs from the fheave bottoms. I once faved a peafe ftack, by putting on this covering in the middle of a thunder fhower, of fome hours duration. The ftack had been juft put up when it began ; it was therefore fo loofe in its texture, that we were foon obliged

In cafe of rain after a ftack is put up, thatching with broom is advifed.

A fuccefsful trial A. D. 1753.

obliged to cover it with winnow cloths, leaft the rain fhould fink into its center: and we only ventured at a time, to uncover half a yard breadth, immediately before the thatchers, till they could put on the broom. Forefeeing that I fhould be fcarce of thatch that year, (1753) I had for my own fecurity brought home a fortnight before the danger, a load of broom, from a place at two miles diftance. Had I not been in poffeffion of it at the time mentioned, I might have wholly loft my peafe ftack; for the weather continued wet and ftormy for fome time after. But as things happened, every fheaf was preferved; and that without any inconvenience, except a wet fkin to the fervants; and without any expence to the mafter, but a little of his dram bottle, which on fuch occafions ought not to be fpared.

3*dly*, He fhould take care to leave no rifings, *The third* nor hollows in the line of the thatch-gang, that *rule in build-* is, from the eafing to the neck of the top fheaf. *ing ftacks.* For thefe purpofes, after the top fheaf was put on, I have feen the ftack-builder come down, and go round, to take a view of his work on all fides; and then mounting his ladder, I have feen him give every part above the eafing a little hand dreff-ing; that is, pulling out the hollows, preffing or beating in the rifings, filling up the vacant fpaces, by fpreading the bottoms of the neighbouring fheaves; and laftly, fmoothing down the ftarted pens of a fheaf bottom, till he gave the whole the neatnefs of a well pulled hay-ftack. This opera-tion, the work of a few minutes, while a hood fheaf or a couple of ropes were a-making below, hath, befides its neatnefs, thefe two advantages; 1*ft*, It needs lefs thatch; and, 2*dly*, It will bear unhurt a confiderable rain, till that little can be got and put on. Neither of which will be over-looked, under a weftern fcarcity, or in a weftern climate.

Our fecond rule in covering ftacks, is, to do it by *Thatching* thatching.

thatching. To fhake on the ftraw from the top of
the ftack, as is done in the eaft, cofts perhaps, lefs,
time. But it is neither neat nor workman like;
nor is it fo good a fecurity in rainy weather, unlefs
the quantity be greater than we could well fpare :
nor laftly, can it be done to any purpofe, but in a
dead calm. At the fame time, while we blame
the eaft country farmers in this particular, they
are alfo intitled both to our apology and com-
mendation. Their weather is fo generally good,
and their corns fo generally clean at bottom, that
they do not require the care which ours do. Befides, they build their ftacks with fo much more
dexterity than we commonly do; that, with their
other advantages of corn and climate, they need
lefs covering, or lefs care in putting it on. I am
ftill, however, perfuaded, that thatching is much
neater, and a better fecurity in cafe of bad weather.
Only obferve, that in thatching ftacks, it is not
proper to fhorten the ftoppel too much, by thrufting its head far into the ftuff. Nor is it neceffary
to overlap greatly the heads of the under row, by
the tails of that above it. The finking of the
ftack through time, tends to overlap them more
than at firft they feemed to do ; and likewife tends
to faften their heads, if they had any hold at all.
At any rate, if they can be kept on till the crofs
ropes are laid over them, thefe will keep them
firm, though they had little other faftening.

. After the thatch is put on, the next operation
is to keep it on with ropes. Before we fay any
thing to this point, we would obferve, that as
the beft ftack ropes are made of fprits, and other
coarfe ftuff drawn out of bog hay, fuch as have
this convenience fhould provide themfelves in
time. The fpritts fhould be drawn from the hay
when it lies in the fwath ; and being tied up in
fheaves, they fhould be fet up fingle to dry ;
and when fufficiently win, fhould be kept in a
dry place till needed. If this provifion has been
neglected,

neglected, fmall oats may be threfhed out to fupply their place. I muft however blame a want of attention and forefight, in fecuring even this trifling convenience, in a time of more leifure. Hours are fometimes loft in dewy mornings, before hay can be turned or fpread out. It would be profitable, if fuch times were employed in drawing out the fpritts and rufhes, from the finer grafs, for the purpofes above-mentioned ; and the cattle would have more pleafure in eating the remainder.

The firft thing to be done towards the roping of ftacks is, to put on fo many upright ropes as are neceffary to divide the ftack properly. A ftack may be quartered, by two ropes put round the neck of the hooding by the middle, and having their ends faftened below the eafing. Thefe ferve to keep the hooding firm, and are put on before thatching. After the ftack is thatched, thefe upright ropes ferve, as a kind of warp, upon which a number of crofs ropes that lie horizontally are wrought, in order to keep the thatch firm and clofs. If the ftack is large, three, or four fuch upright ropes may be put on it, in proportion to its bulk. This done, the workman faftens his circular ropes to one of the upright ropes, making ufe of his fhorteft neareft the top. Thefe he carries round the ftack, putting them about each of the upright ropes, in order to keep both firm in their places ; and before he fhifts his ladder, he ftrokes down the thatch that may be raifed by the wind, or ruffled by his work, that every part of it may lie neat and ftraight, when it is left. But in regard that the frequent fhifting of the ladder, and the carrying it often round the ftack, is both tedious and laborious, the farmer takes care, 1ft, That his upright ropes be not at fo great a diftance from each other; but that he can reach from one to another, without coming down to fhift his ladder. 2dly, He faftens as many of his crofs ropes at once

Of the ropes that faften on the top fheaf.

Ufed as a warp for the circular ropes.

Of expediting the work.

once as will finish the whole, at equal distances
between the hood-sheaf and easing, that he may
carry all of them about with him together, and so
compleat the work in one round of the ladder:
which makes a great saving both of time and labour. When this work is done properly, the
ropes refemble a kind of net-work in one piece,
which finks equally down together, as the stack
itself subsides. And if at a fortnight's distance

The upright
ropes to be
straitened
from time to
time.

the upright ropes were drawn gently downward,
so as they could be straitened a little by a new
fastening below, every inch of the circular ropes
would lie close to the thatch, and keep it on firmly. The fame straitening of the upright ropes may
be repeated as there shall afterwards be occasion.
The neatest way of fastening them below the easing is, by tying them to a strong circular rope
placed there.

Though what hath been already faid upon the
methods of keeping stuff cool, in stack or mow, be
a sufficient fecurity to the farmer, if he will be
instructed; yet in regard all are not provided
with the conveniences recommended, and many
never will provide themselves with any of them,
chusing rather to follow the beaten road, even
though they should mark themselves out by their
own ill fuccess and difappointments. In regard
also that, however negligent and confident fuch farmers may be, bad feafons will happen, corns will
be fpoiled both in stacks and mows, and loffes
and misfortunes will be the confequences to themfelves, and to the public; compaffion to both inclines me to add a fourth particular, to what is

The 4th head
upon recov-
ering heated
corns.

faid above.

It relates to the means of cooling, and recovering fuch stuff as is begun to heat, and in danger
of fpoiling, &c.

This calamity was remarkably the cafe in the
high grounds laft harveft (1772). The long

The year

continuance of the froft had deferred the plowing
still

till near the end of March; the feafon afterwards being cold and late, and the muir lands being naturally fo, all things feemed to concur in making the harveft very late alfo: and, therefore, peculiarly dangerous to graffy corns; especially confidering the long continued wet weather in that feafon.

The common practice, when a barn mow heats is, to throw it down betwixt the open doors, and letting it lie there till it cools, and can be put up again in its place. And when one can fpare the room fo long as it is needed, the work is eafy; and, with a little patience and difcretion, the cure may be effectual. But, alas! in dangerous weather our barns are commonly fo crammed up, that there is either no room left at all; or the little that is, may be allotted for fome bit of a field not yet under cover; and perhaps in as much hazard without, as that within feems to be. If this remedy fhould fail us, the next in common ufe is, to carry the heated corn out into the barn-yard and adjacent fields; where it muft be fet up, and ftand till it is fufficiently cooled and aired. It is eafy to fee, that this cannot be done without a confiderable expence, both of grain and labour; and that every probable mean fhould be tried, before it is done. And would men be but perfuaded by any arguments to think and provide before hand, fuch a picture of diftrefs could be exhibitedupon thofe dangers, as would excite any mind, a degree above ftupidity itfelf. Suppofe, for example, the back mow were heated, as well as the foremoft; that the ftacks in the barn-yard were fuffering by the fame misfortune: fuppofe the weather fo bad, that none of them could be touched; and when a tolerable day came, fuppofe the ftuff without were needing fuch affiftance, that the farmer could not refolve which he fhould begin to: fuppofe him fufficiently affured of the lofs he muft fuftain, by taking down, handling,

1772 a bad harveft for heating.

Of throwing down mows betwixt the barn doors.

Of carrying them out to the fields.

The miferable fituation of the farmer when much of this work is to be done.

I   and

and again putting up his corns; sufficiently apprized of his danger from a change of weather, and scarce daring to trust any thing abroad for fear of it. And yet under all those inconveniencies, contemplate him drove on by dire necessity, to undo all his former labours, to renew an expence already incurred, to expose himself to hazards from which he had but lately escaped, and to suffer the undoubted loss of what he thought perfectly safe. Contemplate the farmer in this situation, and endeavour to conceive what his perplexity, distraction, and regrete must be. Ask him, what he would then give to have been at proper pains, with his barn, and barn-yard, in order to have effectually prevented his present distress and inconvenience? I dare say there are few of you, who in this perplexed situation, would not give more money than what, if well bestowed, according to the above directions, would have afforded a sufficient security, or an adequate remedy. I would willingly put these matters in a strong light to you, because it is in the immediate feeling of such distresses, or in the strong impression that can be made of them upon the mind, that one can know the value of a perfect security, or certain remedy. For when danger is over, we soon forget it, and and therefore incline to banish the fears of it; and with them all the care that may be necessary to provide for it, against the time to come. In short, we never think of past danger, till we are involved in a fresh one; and therefore are as unprepared for the last, as we were for the first.

In the mean time, not to detain you too long upon an argument, that like all other remedies may be unpleasant, while highly necessary and salutary; allow me to observe, that if it be extremely troublesome to carry out our heated corns into the fresh air, it is not very difficult to carry the fresh air into the heated corn, did you once understand how it should be done.

Of taking in the fresh air to the barns.

Amongst

Amongſt the reſt that ſuffered by heated corn in the year 1772, my old acquaintance Thomas Orr was one: not indeed in his ſtack-yard, for that was ſufficiently ſecured by the logies and funnels above deſcribed; it was in his barn, for which he was not ſo well provided. But, even there, did his foreſight and ingenuity fail him? No; Thomas may be in danger, but is not ſo often overtaken by it as ſome others. Let us hear then his own account of the matter; for his ſcheme ſeemed moſt ingenious, and was in every ſtep of it well digeſted and prepared. Thomas ſuſpected his barn from the beginning, for he had eyes to ſee it, and was not diſpoſed to diſguiſe it to himſelf, under any fallacious hopes. Therefore, though he could not mend the matter at that time, in the midſt of very bad weather, he took every ſtep, that a wiſe man could take, to ſecure himſelf afterwards. Having an open ſlit in the wall, near the top of his gavel, in building his mow upon it, he uſed the following precautions. Firſt, He ſet one ſtale above another, and ſo had his corn, eſpecially in the middle, ſtanding all on one end; even at the ſides, and upon the front of his mow, he ſtudied to give every ſheaf ſuch a ſlope, as pointed them all, as much as he conveniently could, towards the above-mentioned ſlit, or opening. For he reaſoned juſtly, that when his mow heated, the warm air, as it aſcended, would naturally take along the line of his ſtraw, towards the ſame place, and ſo get out by the vent hole. Thomas, however, did not wholly depend upon the building of his mow, though his method was rational, and had been recommended by others. He knew he had hazarded much, as all his neighbours had done; he therefore prepared himſelf for the worſt; for he made uſe of all the ordinary means of knowing the real ſtate of his mow, that is, by thruſting in at different places, four or five hand-ſtaves; and by pulling them out at different times, he was

Thomas Orr's plan.

Deſcribed.

His preparation in building his mow.

able

able to judge by their warmth in his hand, where the heat was greateſt, and what progreſs it was daily making. Finding, by theſe trials, that the heat was actually begun, he then took an old gun-barrel, and being a ſmith to his trade, he unſcrewed the dock, and took it out altogether. He next ſhaped for the muzzle a few wooden pins, with ſhoulders upon each, that they might not go too far into the barrel, nor ſtick too faſt in it; and theſe pins he ſharpened to a point at their outer end. His deſign by their points was, to thruſt the whole gun-barrel with eaſe into the mow, as far as he thought neceſſary: and then by drawing it a little backward, he thought that the ſhoulders of the pins, by taking hold of the croſs ſtraws, would aſſiſt him in diſlodging them from the muzzle, and ſo leave it quite open, for the outer air to paſs freely through it, into the heart of the mow. Here again his reaſoning was at leaſt ſpecious; *viz.* That if the gun-barrel wanted altogether the pointed pins, the ends of the ſtraw would get into its muzzle, when thruſt inward, and either cork it up wholly, or by their reſiſtance prevent its entrance, without a very great force. And on the other hand, if the pins wanted the ſhoulder, they might either go too far into the barrel, and ſtick too faſt in it, or even be otherwiſe difficult to diſlodge. Laſt of all, Thomas having ready in his houſe a ſmall pair of hand-bellows in order to throw in the freſh air through the barrel, whenever he ſhould find it neceſſary; he thought himſelf prepared for the worſt, and therefore patiently waited till the mow was ſufficiently heated, that ſo the effects of his preparations might be perfectly aſcertained. Accordingly, in a few days, when the neighbours had begun to caſt out their heated corns, Thomas drew ſome of his hand-ſtaves, to ſee in what condition his own was; and finding their warmth ſo great, that he could ſcarce hold in his hand the end of his poles, he inſtantly began his operations.

Further pre-
parations.

operations. So, fixing one of his wooden pins into the muzzle, he thruft his barrel into the hot- *His attempt* teft of his corn; then drawing it a little outwards, *and fuccefs.* to difengage the wood, he rolled a little tow round the nofe of the bellows, and twifting it firmly into the dock end of the barrel, that no air might return that way, he began to blow: and, in one word, he continued blowing, till by drawing one of his neareft hand-ftaves, he could feel the inner end of it perfectly cooled. This encouraging his hopes, he drew the barrel from that place; and quickly filling the muzzle with another pin like the former, he thruft all into another part of the mow, at fome diftance from his firft hole; and blowing as before, he continued till he was again fatisfied. And thus, by repeating thefe operations again and again, in different places, he was in two hours time, perfectly convinced of his fuccefs. For all his poles and hand-ftaves being quite cold and dry, he was fenfible that all the moift and warm vapour was fled. What indeed contributed a little to Thomas's conviction, and perhaps not a little to his fatisfaction, was a vifit made him by one of his neighbours, during the courfe of his foregoing operations. This man, either informed of Thomas's defign, or fufpecting fome contrivance going on within, as he faw nothing going on without, that was neighbour-like, came to his barn; and obferving as he paft the end of it, that the fare, or fteam of the vapour, was coming out from the flit-hole in the gavel, like the fmoke of kiln-drying, he told Thomas at entering, that if he had not fufpected what he was about, he would have imagined that he had laid ten bolls of corn upon a kiln-head within, and had put a good fire to the tail of it. Since the foregoing operations a more effectual experiment has been made upon the mow. It has been all threfhed out for ufe, and the owner declares to me, that he never had any in better condition than it was.

Thomas,

His modesty.

Thomas, by way of answer to some compliment made upon his ingenuity, tells me that he is no wiser than his neighbours; but that he just thinks a little what he is going about, and how it should be done. If they would but think a wee, he does not doubt but many of them would contrive things better than he.—Is not his sentiment both modest and just,—is it not full of instruction? It is: for what is wanting to rational creatures, in the management of their ordinary affairs, but thought, or the exercise of their rational faculties about them?

His plan recommended.

Such was the success of Thomas Orr's ingenious contrivance, all executed with his own hand, and the full effect of it seen in two hours or so. This no doubt ought to enhance its value, and recommend the trial to others. Indeed the whole of it seemed to me, from the beginning, to be planned out upon such solid principles of reason, and such an accurate attention to circumstances, as could scarce fail of its effect. I have therefore always encouraged Thomas to such trials; and scarce ever had occasion to correct him, if it was not with respect to some of the properties of air, which Thomas could not be supposed to know. I mean the effects of heat in rarifying it, and the effects of a vacuum, occasioned by rarifaction, in attracting the external cold air. But having already explained ourselves on these points, pages 52 and 53, we shall not enlarge upon them here. One, however, from all that has been said, may safely advise farmers in one single word, that if their barns and barn-yards are not accommodated with some of those provisions recommended on the second head of this period, they should at least in threatening harvests provide themselves with a hand-bellows and a gun-barrel. If one has not a hand-bellows, a little more time might answer all its purposes. Or, if the gun-barrel be not at hand, a stick could be bored, or a small rhone could be made,

made, that could be laid in, and corked up, till
the time required its ufe ; or it could be thruft in *Variations*
afterwards, wherever it was found needful. Thefe *in it for the*
are portable conveniencies : they can be carried *farmer's eafe*
out into the barn yard, and applied with equal
fuccefs to a heated ftack, as to a heated mow. And
if a wife man can by any fuch trifling conveniencies, extricate himfelf from the danger and difficulties above-mentioned, or relieve himfelf from
the labours and perplexities there defcribed, they
are furely worth a little of his attention and care.

Few men have however imitated, or even
hearkened to my friend Thomas, though he may *The fate of*
be faid, to have both fought and found out many *fuperior in-*
ufeful inventions. Thomas has plowed his land *genuity.*
thefe ten years paft, with two old mares, and a
plow of his own contrivance, long before we got
the Merfe, or Northumberland chain plow into
this corner. He has often defied his neighbours
to make better work, or to produce better corn
upon the like grounds ; yet I know not if, as yet,
one man has tried the like, though he can have
the wood, the iron, and workmanfhip at half the
ordinary price. He is indeed a philofopher from
native reflection, and the powers of genius ; yet
the fimplicity of his looks, and aukwardnefs of
his air, are too much againft him, to gain him *Neglect.*
any general credit or leading with the bulk of
men. It is too much the difpofition of human
nature, to contemn alike, (if not more) what is *The caufes of*
above their comprehenfion, as what is below it. *it.*
Hence all blockheads are the moft cenforicus of
ingenious men and meafures ; being fcarce able
to approve any thing, but what is perfectly vulgar,
and beneath all notice. A fool is wifer in his
own conceit, than ten men that can render
a reafon. Befides, floth and inactivity hurt many,
that are neither ftupid nor incapable. Hence men
will ftruggle through the whole of life, with yearly,
nay, with daily inconveniencies and difficulties,
rather

rather than beftow one day's labour, or the price
of it, to relieve themfelves from them for ever.
Pride too, an high opinion of ourfelves, and a
fcornful contempt of others; a prejudice alfo
againft new cuftoms, and a bigotted attachment
to old ones; all of them confpire againft inftruction and improvement. Thefe have got into
our worldly employments, as well as our religious
concerns; and equally obftruct the interefts of this
life, as they do thofe of the life to come. Laft of
all, men who, animated by rivalfhips and inter-
ferings, will fight the world for a difputed intereft,
and reckon themfelves capitally injured if they
lofe it, will yet neglect a thoufand opportunites,
by each of which, if duly improved, ten times the
value may be faved or gained. The gradual im-
provementsof an age, which are the gifts of providence, and the fourcesofpublic eafe and opulence,
thofe narrow minded and narrow hearted men will
defpife; wrapt up in their own indolence, ignorance, and felf-fufficiency, they will fcarce pull
their hands from their bofoms, to receive the
offered bounty, that could make them rich or
eafy, wife or happy. None but the wife can be
made much wifer; for to him only that hath
fhall be given. Hence it is, that improvements of
every kind, even thofe of faving and oeconomy,
the moft obvious of any, go on but flowly; and
inftead of encouragement, meet with neglect, or
oppofition, from the far greateft number of mankind.

My GOOD FRIENDS,

*Apology of
the author.*
I have now prefented to your confideration,
a few thoughts upon the fubject of harveft-work,
in bad feafons or uncertain weather. You that
are moft fkilful in the bufinefs, and moft attentive
to the affairs of it, will perhaps imagine, I have
been too minute and particular, in defcribing
things

things generally known. Or it may be, you will observe some particulars, which you think erroneous; and that you yourselves could have suggested better methods of working. Both these indeed may be true enough in part; but you will, I hope, excuse me for the first of these, to wit, the minuteness, when I tell you, that this sketch was drawn up at the desire of an east country acquaintance, in whose neighbourhood the general goodness of harvest-weather, does not perhaps make such frequent demands upon their care and invention, as a west country climate may do : and therefore to many there, some of our west country customs, as being less needed, may be also less known. Besides, the wiser sort among ourselves will even allow, that our farmers are not all alike wise, all alike intelligent, convincible, and careful : and must further acknowledge, that instruction is designed for the ignorant, not for the skilful; argument is designed for the obstinate, not for the candid; and motive is designed for the slothful, not for the vigilant and active farmer. And you all know, that such designs cannot be so well obtained, but by one's being both particular and pressing on some more important points.

For his minuteness.

As to the second thing that may be observed upon this letter, to wit, That some particulars in it may be erroneous, and that you yourselves could have suggested better methods of working. I am not even unwilling to believe that the first may be the case, and should be particularly pleased to find that the last were so too, *i. e.* that you were able to correct the error, as it would shew you had thought upon your business, and were able both to direct and exemplify a better practice than what is common. What I have all along promised myself from the publication of these thoughts, upon a subject which all of you have had access to learn, as much as the writer of them, is 1*st*, That some of you may meet with certain hints among them, to

For his mistakes.

His views and expectations.

K   which

which you may not formerly have given sufficient
attention; but may now apply to your own use
and benefit. Or, 2*dly*, That you may meet with
some things that you can correct, or improve upon; and be thus led to the free exercise of your
own faculties of thought and reflection; especially upon a subject which needs a great deal of
both, and gets but little of either: for I am
confident, that what you learn by your own
thought, will always produce the most solid and
lasting knowledge. 3*dly*, I expect that this slight
essay will occasionally serve to introduce the innocent subjects contained in it, into ordinary conversation: by which means, its rules and instructions may be canvassed and examined, and either
approved or censured as there is cause. Thus,
from the private reflections of individuals, from
the various opinions, and perhaps collisions of
different minds, new light may be struck out upon any point; and even better methods discovered,
tried, and prosecuted. For next to the instruction
of the ignorant, or the animation of the careless;
the design of all such hints and reasonings should
certainly be, to set wise men themselves a-thinking,
observing, and inquiring; that by a thorough consideration of their affairs, they may be fully prepared for every business on hand. Indeed, to
Thinking re- think much may be troublesome, especially to
commended. such as have not been frequently accustomed to
it. Perhaps the most part of the world would rather do any thing than think; and some may have
very special objections against thinking; it gives
them but little comfort to find out their own faults
and blunders. Servants seldom imagine it to be
their duty: as an English writer says, they will
scarce both think and work for the same hire.
The master, whose interest it is, should therefore both plan the general business, and all the particular operations of his farm. If he is not able for
his own part, he must be often at a loss, and not sel-

dom

dom a fufferer: and the more especially fo, if the
prefumption and felf-fufficiency which commonly
attend ignorance, hinder him from confulting
the wife ; or from employing fuch, whofe knowledge and activity deferve his confidence. But
no man needs to be, no wife man will be afhamed,
to afk, and even to take advice, of thofe who are
below him in the world. For tho' it is too common, that a poor man's wifdom fhall be defp:fed,
and his words not heard, by thofe above all others
who need them moft ; yet, in all trades and profef-
fions, wifdom excelleth folly, and knowledge ignorance, as far as light excelleth darknefs.

*A readinefs
to learn the
property of
wife man.*

Your ordinary meetings, my good friends,
are commonly as a fociety, employed about your
funds for charity. It is an honourable defign;
and while I commend your fcheme and views,
I have no reafon to blame your management.
Your ftock, in a very few years, fince I firft met
with you, hath rifen confiderably; and you are
now able, and with difcretion I think willing, to
relieve the needy and misfortunate. Nay, many
have been the better of your funds, who had no
other claim upon them but as they are funds of
charity; having never contributed any thing towards them. Thefe meetings however might be
more ufeful, were they more frequent, and were
fome of them efpecially appointed for converfing
upon the fubjects relative to farming. Thefe
funds too could not be mifapplied, were fome part
of them allotted annually, to encourage ingenuity, and experiment in your own bufinefs; and to
propagate the knowledge requifite to farming, a-
mong your own fraternity. By this means, you
might guard your brethren againft the misfortunes
which arife from ignorance and mifmanagement;
and enable them, by their fkill and activity, to fecure their future independence and eafe. For allow me to obferve, 1/t, That the beft beftowed
charity is that which tends to raife a brother above
the

*The farmers
fociety ap-
proved of*

*More fre-
quent meet-
ings recom-
mended.
As alfo an ap-
plication of
fome part of
their funds
to the im-
provement
of farming.*

*The beft cha-
rity.*

The eafiest bestowed.
The fureft gain to every man.

the need of any. 2*dly*, That as it is much more beneficial, fo it is much more eafy to prevent evils; than to remedy them. And laft of all—That what is got by care and induftry, by wifdom and management, is, to every man, his fureft and moft lafting wealth. I remain, my good friends,

Your affectionate well-wifher,

Feb. 11. 1773.   and fervant,————

P. S. If this letter is acceptable to your brethren, and becomes in any meafure ufeful to the public, you may again perhaps receive a few hints upon fpring-labour, fuited to your cuftoms and climate; fhould the writer's health and leifure permit him to put down and digeft his occafional obfervations on that fubject.

A. Smith Sculp.

The Hand of the diligent maketh Rich.

THE COMPLETE
ENGLISH GARDENER:
OR,
Gardening made perfectly Easy:
CONTAINING,

Full and ⌐˙ ⌐irections for the proper Management

OF THE

FLO⌐ . ⌐RUIT, and KITCHEN Gardens,
' for every Month in the Year.

The whole laid down in fo plain and eafy a Manner,
that all who are defirous of managing a Garden,
may do it effectually, without any other Inftructions whatever.

To which is added,

The COMPLETE BEE-MASTER; o⁻,

Beft Method of managing BEES, both for Profit and
Pleafure. Together with the whole Art of breeding
and rearing FOWLS, DUCKS, GEESE, TURKIES,
PIGEONS, and RABBETS.

Likewife Plain Inftructions for deftroying Vermin,
particulary fuch as infeft Houfes, Gardens, Dairies, Barns, Bees, Poult y, Rules to judge of the
Weather, and feveral other Articles equally ufeful, &c. &c.

By SAMUEL COOKE, Gardener,

At Overton in Wiltfhire;

Who has practifed Gardening, thro' all its branches,
in many counties, upwards of Forty Years.

Here learn to cultivate the PLANT for ufe;
Raife the gay FLOWER, and flavour'd FRUIT produce;
With fkill to manage the induftrious BEE;
And while you profit, pleafing wonders fee.
You may inftructed here, if you take heed;
Fowls, ducks, geefe, turkies, pigeons, rabbets bread;
Your table with delicious foods fupply,
And clear your houfe of vermin by the by.

LONDON:
Printed for J. COOKE, at Shakefpear's-Head, in
Pater-nofter-Row. [Price 1s. 6d.]

INTRODUTION.

THE Art of Gardening may be deemed the moſt uſeful and entertaining of all others, as it expands the variegated beauties of nature, and adminiſters the moſt wholſome food to the body.—It has been the ſtudy and delight of the greateſt men in all ages, as well as employed the ableſt pens : we need, therefore, no other apology for preſenting the world with this compendious ſyſtem, than the utility of attempting to abridge and arrange the whole in ſuch a manner, as to aſſiſt the underſtanding and practice of the reader.

In ſhort, it has been our care faithfully to ſelect the produce and inſtructions relative to the manures of each month in the year, as the moſt approved method of aſſiſting the memory, without perplexing the mind.

Thus

Thus we hope to exhibit a pleafing view of the product of every month in the vegetable creation, to the honour of the univerfal parents of nature, and benefit of mankind in ge eral, many of whom may be thereby pi . .ted to co-operate with a wife providence, in promoting his wife and falutary defigns.

To render our undertaking ftill more extenfively ufeful, we have annexed, *A prefcription for the deftruction of every fpecies of vermin that infeft fruits, plants,* &c. as alfo, *A Concife Treatife on the management of Bees* ; and, *Directions for the breeding and rearing of Poultry.*

Likewife certain Rules to judge of the Weather : grounded on fifty years expérience and obfervations, by an ancient Shepherd on the South Downs, Suff x.

THE

Complete *English* GARDENER:

O R,

Gardener's Monthly Chronicle.

A S the bounties of nature cannot be more beautifully difplayed than in the vegetable creation, and as the utility of gardening amply compenfates for all our labour; we have in th's little treatife laid down in chronological order the manner of conducting, not only the gentleman, who exercifes it for his amufement, but likewife the induftrious gardener, who follows it as a profeffion. In order to effect which we begin, firft, with the month of

JANUARY.

Work to be done in the Kitchen Garden.

YOUR ground muft be thrown up in ridges that it may be properly fweetened for the reception of fpring crops. Near walls, hedges, or pales, you muft fow carrot, radifh, lettuce, and fmall fallading.

Hot

Hot beds muſt be prepared for ſowing of melon ſeed and cucumbers: likewiſe for aſparagus, which muſt be done at two different times,
leaving about three weeks between each.

Muſtard, creſſes, rape, radiſh, and turnep
ſeeds, muſt be ſown on beds covered with mats,
over arches made with hoops. If the weather
ſhould be ſevere, you muſt cover the mats with
ſtraw.

When the weather is open, and the ground
not too moiſt, you muſt earth up your cellery in
order to blanch it. If it ſhould be froſty, cover
the ridges with long litter, or tanner's bark.

Windſor, Sandwich, and Token beans, ſhould
be ſown about the middle of this month ſome
muſhroom beds muſt be carefully covered with
long, freſh ſtraw.

Tranſplant near the end of this month ſome
cabbage plants of the ſugar-loaf kind; but previous to this the ground muſt be ſown with
ſpinnach. Take off all decayed leaves from your
cauliflower plants under frames, and if the weather is temperate, give them as much air as poſſible.

If the ſeverity of the weather ſhould render
your former labour ineffectual, repeat your
planting, not forgetting to take particular
care of the neceſſary defence.

Peas and beans ſhould be now planted in order to ſucceed thoſe in November and December.
Sow parſly in drills; likewiſe chervil about the
end of this month.

Work relative to the Fruit Garden.

The roots of all new planted trees muſt be
covered with mulch, to keep off the ſeverity of
the

the froft. Fig-trees which are placed against walls muft be covered with mats or reeds, firft taking off thofe which were left on the branches in Autumn. Cut the ufelefs branches of your fruit trees clofe to the ftem. Prune your vines, dwarf trees. and any hardy fort of fruit.

If the enfuing month fhould produce moift weather, clear your fruit trees from mofs, and prepare for planting. Begin now to forward your early fruits, by placing dung or fire under your forcing frames. Prepare your decayed efpaliers, and place them regularly at proper diftances.

If the weather be mild, take grafts from early fruits, fuch as cherries, plums, apples, pears, &c. and lay them in the earth as near as you can to a dry wall. If fevere wheather cover them with litter or ftraw. If they are to be removed, cover the ends with clay, and faften them together with a band made of ftraw.

Work relative to the Flower Garden.

In frofty weather the beds of ranunculufes, anemonies, hyacinths, and other valuable flowers fhould be covered, with fome light covering, fuch as mats or peas-haulm. When they rife above the ground, arch the bed over with hoops, covered with mats or cloths. If the weather be mild, you may uncover them. Turn over pour compofition of earth for future fowing pretty often, that the froft may mellow them.

If the feafon be mild, towards the end of this month, take off all decayed leaves from your auriculas ; take fome of the earth out of the pots, but be very careful not to difturb the roots ; then fill them again, but let none of the earth fall upon the leaves.   If

If the weather be frofty, cover them with mats or cloths ; but if it be temperate let them have the benefit of the air, and the refreshment of moderate rain.

You muft defend your tender flowers from heavy rains, fnow, and hard froft ; and your plants muft be properly guarded from the deftruction of vermin.

Management of the different Manures in the courfe of this month.

The moft material thing in the kitchen garden is the hot bed, which muft be fo placed as to avoid the power of the north and fouth-welt winds, and to receive the cherifhing heat of the fun. When you have marked out its extent, drive ftakes into the ground all round it, about a foot diftance between each ; cover the ftakes with a hay-band, and then fill it with wet litter, or new horfe dung, taking care to form the whole of an equal fubftance, by treading it down various times during its being filled.

When you have thus prepared your bed, adjuft your wooden frames in fuch manner as to admit the mold at top, and let them be placed on a flope. Leave fpace enough for the earth, and be careful not to confine the fhooting of your plants.

Take fome earth from an old hot-bed, and mix with it ; after which cover it with ftraw or mats, fupported with fhort props, and let it continue till it be warm, but not hot. This you may know by putting a ftick into the ground, which when taken out will feel warm to your hand ; but if the heat fhould lofe its ftrength, place by the fide of the bed a quantity of frefh dung. After

After your plants have fprung up in the hot-bed, let them have progreſively the refrefhment of the air and fun. When ſtrong enough tranſplant them into a bed not ſo hot as the former; frequently apply moderate wa·ering, and ſecure them from the violent heat of the fun. A little before ſ ſet cover the glaſſes with mats and litter to ｐ ent their being deſtroyed by blaſts or ſharp winds.

The hot-bed formed for aſparagus muſt be a ſpot of ground adapted on purpoſe, well dug and dunged. Form your lines about ſeven or eight inches aſunder, and when they are a year old, plant the roots ſix or ſeven inches apart. In this ſituation they muſt remain two years, taking care to preſerve them from weeds, before they will be fit for the hot-bed, which muſt be made ſtrong, ſurrounded with bands of ſtraw, and covered with earth at leaſt ſix inches deep. Your roots being thus planted as near as poſſible, cover the buds of the plants two inches thick with earth. Let them continue in this manner five or ſix days, after which put on the frames and glaſſes, and cover them at leaſt three inches thick with freſh earth. On the buds firſt ſhooting, give them as much air as the mildneſs of the weather will admit. If temperate weather continues they will increaſe daily for about a month; but if cold weather ſhould enſue, you muſt apply freſh dung to the glaſſes every night; the good effects of which will be ſoon diſcovered.

Strawberries may be produced early if placed on a moderate hot-bed; as may likewiſe, ſallad in a very ſhort time by means of powdered lime laid on each ſide with a track of dung in the middle; the whole muſt be covered over with good

rich

rich mould. Radifhes are likewife raifed on the hot bed, but muft be properly furrounded with mould that they may take deep roots before the dung reaches them ; by this means they may be produced almoft any time in year. The hot-fpur, charlton mafter, and other pea muft be fown in drills about three feet afunde. that you may have the opportunity of going between them, and the lines muft run from north to fouth. After they have rifen near fix inches high put earth on both fides the lines about four inches deep, raifing on the laft fides of them a kind of bank to fcreen them from piercing winds.

Your vines muft be pruned this month, paying proper refpect to the ftrength of the fhoots : you muft cut off all ufelefs branches, leaving the fhort jointed and ftrongeft nine inches, or more ac-cording to the ftrength of the wood ; but if they be old, take off the ftem and fupply its place with a young one. If you intend to circulate the vine, the laft year's branches muft be fhortened in pro-portion to the body.

In order to raife anemonies you muft form your earth on a rich fand well fifted, and of a pliable texture, for they feldom blow in a hard foil. Put a thin layer of willow earth at their firft tranfplanting, and it will further their growth amazingly.

The ranunculus is managed much in the fame manner as the anemony, only be careful to pre-ferve them from the feverity of fharp winds and froft, becaufe if the leaves fhould be once nipped they will foon decay, and the roots follow. They muft be planted in rows about four inches afunder.

The fallads which are produced this month confift of mint, creffes, radifhes, young onions, cellery

cellery and endive; young lettuce, boorcole, savoy cabbage, sprouts of Dutch and Batterfea cabbages, red and Ruffian cabbages, and various foup herbs, together with the tops of bromet and chervil.

Although this feafon is generally attended with fevere w' ;;er, yet we have fome fruit, efpecially the Lugi pear, which, when kept fo long, is efteemed delicious. There are likewife the golden ruffet, leather-coat ruffetin, winter pearmain, golden pippin, whitmill pippin, nonpareil, and monftrous benette. Nuts, almonds, medlars, and fervices. Aloes begin to throw out their flower-ftems, and oranges to bloffom. If the weather is mild, and you have neglected to fow the feeds of auriculas, and polyanthufes in the months of October and November, you may fow them at this time. The winter aconite may be tranfplanted in flower.

The flowers that grow in this month are, the fingle anemonies, winter ciclamens, acacia, fnowdrops, primrofes, winter aconite, couble blue violet, dwarf tithymal, and yellow ficoides.

FEBRUARY.

The Kitchen Garden.

D I G and prepare you ground for the fowing of carrots, parfneps, radifhes, fpinach, beets, beans, peas, parfley and cabbage lettuce. Sow corn falled, large rooted parfley, fummer and winter favory, marygolds, and other hardy plants, but place them in feparate beds or fpots. Moderate

rate hot beds muſt be prepared for ſowing cauliflower ſſeeds for Summer plants ; theſe ſ ldom
ſucceed unleſs the ſoil be moiſt. If the ſhoots
are forward enou h you may ſlip ſome old arti-
choak-ſtocks about the end of the month. Plant
peas and beans every fortnight or th ee weeks,
particularly the large ſort of each. tranſplant
the melon and cucumber plants into new beds,
but not till the violent heat of the bed is abated.
Cover the muſhroom b ds with frames, and place
them under thatched ſheds to preſerve them from
heavy rain and ſnow. Kidney beans for an early
crop muſt be planted on a moderate hot-bed, and
when the weather is mild, give them as much air
as you can.

Plant imperial, Sileſia and cos lettuces at the
cloſe of the month, if the weather ſhou'd be temperate. The ſeed of aſparagus muſt be ſown in
a good bed, in order to raiſe plants for the next
year. Potatoes and Jeruſalem artichoaks muſt be
planted in dry ground trenched deep ; as alſo garlick, ſhallots, and rocambole. Plant hops, dig
the ground, and prune the old roots, but be careful not to injure the buds of the plants. Tranſplant young cabbages for a crop.

In the Fruit Garden.

In mild weather let your fig-trees be open to
the air, but when froſty, let them be again covered. Prune ſuch trees as have been neglected,
and nail them to the wall. Where they are
wanting tranſplant all ſorts of fruit trees, firſt
breaking the clods that the ground may be ſoft.
After rain, clear of the moſs from the trees, and
be careful of bulfinches, who will deſtroy the
hopes of your labour : if the end of the month
ſhould

should produce mild weather, graft cherries, plums, pears, and other hardy fruit.

Draw off all superfluous moisture from the roots of treets, cut and lay quickfets, and earth up the roots of uncovered fruit-trees. Make new plantations of strawberries, rafberries, goofberries, and currents, if omitted in Autumn; likewife refresh with water, and air, the strawberries in hot-beds. Be careful of your early fruits or forcing frames, and give them air or heat as the weather will admit.

In the Flower Garden.

Towards the end of this month, if the weather be temperate, plant your carnations in the pots you intend them to flower; in bad weather let them be covered over with mats and kept warm. Sow auricula and polyanthus feeds in pots of good rich mould, and place them where they may receive the mild heat of the morning fun. Keep your flower-beds clear of all weeds, as they will detriment their growth. On frofty nights cover your beds of tulips, anemories, and ranunculufes with mats. The flowering trees to be tranfplanted this month are jeffamine, honey-fuckle, lilacs, rofes, laburnum, bladder and fcorpion fenas, fpireas and altheas.

The ever-greens muft not be removed till the beginning of April. Carnations that were planted in Autumn muft have frefh earth put to them; and toward the end of the month fow fweet williams, pinks, primrofe trees, larkfpurs, hollyhocks, and Canterbury-bells. On the fide of a fhady bank fix your plantations for the lilly of the valley.

All foreign feeds, efpecially the annual kind,

C

that

that come from warm climates, muſt be ſown in hot-beds ; likewiſe orange and lemon kernels ; the kernels muſt be put in the ground as ſoon as taken out of the fruit. Clean the different diviſions of you wilderneſs, turn and roll your gravel walks and lawns, and keep them clear of moſs. Head orange trees, give them freſh mould, and ſprinkle them with water that have been ſteeped in ſheep's dung two or three days, but be careful it only goes on the root ; if it ſhould fall on the leaves, they will be infallibly deſtroyed. The double larkſpur and China ſtarworts may be now ſown in dry borders on a moderate hot bed, giving them proper air every day.

The flowers that grow this mouth are Perſian iris, crocurſes, ſilver alaturnus, narciſſus dens caninus, hepatica, yellow gilliflowers, prim-roſes and anemonies, mezerion tree, fruit-bear-ing almond, colutea, and double pilewort.

Inſtructions for Grafting.

In this part of gardening there are four diſtinct methods, viz. Whip-grafting, grafting in the cleft, in the bark, and by approach ; the firſt of which is practiſed on the pear, cherry, and plum.

The method to be uſed with ſtocks is as fol-lows : when you have cut the ſtock and ſloped it (if you put but one ſcyon in) cleave it with a pruning knife about two inches deep, and inject a wedge to keep it open till the ſcyon is already to tie and clay it, firſt covering the chink with moſs. The ſide of the wedge in the ſcyon, which is to be next the wood, muſt be cut thinner.

When you graft in the bark, which is gene-rally

rally done on apples, you muſt cut the head of the ſtock ſloping, ſlitting only the bark a little above an inch on the ſouth weſt ſide, and looſen the bark at the top of the ſlit with your knife ; after which, by a ſmooth inſtrument of hard wood, or ivory cut ſloping as the ſcyon, make room for it by thruſting it down between the bark and the wood where it was ſlit. When this is done, firſt uſing your opening inſtrument, take your ſcyon and put it into the ſtock, thruſting the top of the ſlope as low as the top ſurface of the ſtock. The bark on each ſide the ſcyon muſt be ſo ordered as to fall cloſe to the ſtock, after which it muſt be covered over with clay.

The method of whip-grafting, when the ſtock and ſcyon are nearly of a thickneſs, is performed thus. Let them be both ſloped alike at leaſt a full inch ; as ſoon as they will lie true, tie one upon the other ; clay and bind the place, or make a ſlit in the bare place of the ſtock, commencing near the top of the ſlope, ſlitting a little way, and in the ſloped face of the ſcyon doing the like, beginning at the ſame diſtance from the lower end, carrying it upwards ; when that is done, join them by thruſting the one ſlice into the other till they exactly cover, then put clay, &c.

The various tools neceſſary for grafting are a ſtrong knife with a thick back, a neat hand-ſaw, a ſharp pen knife to cut the grafts, a grafting chiſſel, a ſmall mallet ; woolen yarn, or braſs ſtrings ; and clay intermixed with horſe dung.

The method of grafting by approach, or in arching, is performed where a ſtock grows ſo near another tree, the fruit of which you would increaſe, that it may be joined with a branch of

that

that tree, by cutting the sides about three inches
long, and fitting them in such manner that the
paſſages of the ſap may meet ; in this ſituation
let them be clayed and bound.   Take off the head
of the ſtock, when they are well cemented, about
four inches above the binding ; and in the next
month cut off the ſtub that was left of the
ſtock, and the ſcyon underneath ; cloſe the
place which is grafted, that the ſtock only may
ſubſiſt.

Inſtructions for pruning Apricots.

Nail the branches, which ſhoot forth in the
firſt ſummer, horizontally ; and if you have
plenty, take off thoſe which ſprout forward.

The next ſummer proceed in the ſame manner,
rubbing away all foreright ſhoots, and nailing
the other as horizontally as poſſible on the wall.
About a fortnight after Michaelmas prune the
trece again as before.

The third year do the ſame, and be particularly careful not to hurt the ſpurs which riſe
from the wood of the preceding year.   Shorten
the branches in winter pruning, ſo as to ſupply
freſh wood where wanting, and cut off all luxuriant branches.

In pruning of peaches, you muſt be careful
to keep them conſtantly ſupplied with bearing
wood.   Take off all weakly ſhoots, and nail the
others to the wall, fixing them at ſuch diſtance
that the leaves may have room to ſpread without
ſhading the branches too much ; theſe muſt be
alſo nailed ſloping or horizontally.

When your fruit is as big as a ſmall nut, thin
them about the diſtance of four or five inches, by
which means they will much increaſe in their
growth.   The

The Nectarine is in all respects to be managed as the peach ; and other stony fruit in the same manner as these, only requiring less care, as they are hardier in their nature.

There are two things essentially necessary to be observed in pruning the before mentioned fruits. First to furnish every part of a tree with bearing wood ; and secondly, not to lay the branches too close together.

Culture of Flowers and Plants.

For the auricula, a box of oak or deal must be prepared about four feet long, two feet wide, and six inches deep, with holes in the bottom about six inches asunder ; lay cinders of sea coals about two inches thick in the box, cover them over till the box is full with earth taken out of hollow willow trees.

The seeds must be sown on the top, without any earth put over them ; they must be pressed with a flat board into the mould a little below the edge of the box, to prevent the light seeds from floating over the brim in watering.

The box must be placed, from the time of sowing till the beginning of April, in some place where they may receive the heat of the sun ; after that they must be removed to some place that is shady.

If the seedlings fail the first year, they will come up the second, and may be transplanted in July or August.

When you have planted them in beds of light, well sifted mould, about four inches from each other, they must be placed so as to receive the heat of the morning sun.

C 3

In

In April following they will shew themselves, when they must be transplanted into pots of soil, composed of an equal quantity of rotten dung. Be careful to preserve them from the rain, as it will much detriment their colour.

The polyanthus requires very little culture, and may be annually produced from seeds. If the weather is mild, you may sow them the latter end of this month, but it must be in a good, rich soil, under a wall or hedge.

If any particular sort is wanted, they must be taken from a slip, as the seed seldom produces the same kind. When they are out in five or six leaves, place them in shady borders, where they are intended to blow. In order to preserve their beauty, you must transplant them often.

The larkspur may be propagated by letting the seeds of the flowers drop, which will come up the next Spring. Plant them in an open place, and shift them often.

The hollyhock is raised from seeds sown this month on a bed of good earth, and must be planted near walls or hedges. In October they will be fit to transplant.

Of sweet williams there are two kinds, the single and double. The first are raised by sowing the seed in light-earth, and will be fit to transplant about Michaelmas.

The latter are raised by layers, much in the same manner as carnations.

Roses are all produced by layers or suckers, which may be either planted now or in Autumn ; if they are planted this month, be careful they are properly watered.

Pomegranates are raised by laying down the young shoots, either this month or the next, and

may

may be tranfplanted, either in the Spring or at
Autumn. Let them be put into pots, or againft
a fouth wall, that the fruit may have opportunity
to ripen.

The luburnum is raifed by fowing the feeds on
a bed of frefh light earth, fifting mould over them
about the depth of half an inch. They will appear in about thirty days. Two years after coming up they muft be tranfplanted. An open place
is as beneficial to their growth as under the fhade
of trees.

The althea, or Chinefe rofe, is beft propagated
in a light, rich foil. It is a green-houfe plant,
and is raifed in a hot-bed, fowing the feeds this
month, or in March.

Of lilacs there are three forts, the white
the deep purple, and the yellow blotched ; they
are raifed by fuckers, which if taken off in October, you may plant in the nurfery, and in
four years after they will be fit to tranfplant.
They will thrive in almoft any foil that is dry,
fometimes digging up the earth round the
root.

The philirea, which is a beautiful plant, may
be fown this month on open beds of good mould ;
they make fine ornamental hedges, and if properly fupported with rails or ftakes will grow very
quick.

Of laurus-tinus there are two different forts,
the ordinary and the Portuguefe, both of which
are produced from the feed fown as foon as they
are ripe, in good ground, or of fuckers and layers. Though often trainted as a headed plant,
yet it is beft if planted in a wildernefs or againft
a wall. This, like all foreign plants, is inclined to bloffom about Spring in its own climate,
which

which is our Autumn, and therefore this month
is the proper time for pruning it.

The laurel-tree is propagated either by feed or
berries, as foon as they are ripe. Towards the
end of the month you may tranfplant them.

The yew-tree is beft cultivated in a light, barren foil ; the leaves are pliable to any form ; the
moft common are, conic or pyra idal. About
the end of two years you may fet them in the
nurfery, and place them near a foot afunder in
April. Let rotten ftraw be put about their roots.

The moft beautiful of ever greens is the holly.
When the berries of this plant are ripe, they
muft be gathered, and after having laid fome
time to fweeten, they muft be put in fand or
earth, after which they may be fown in the nurfery beds.

The ftriped holly, which only has a place in
gardens, cannot be pruned into thofe nice figures which moft other trees admit of, and are
therefore converted into a ball, a pyramid, or
headed.

The bay-tree is propagated much in the fame
manner as the holly. If moift weather fhould en-
fue, they will come up in about fix weeks ; you
muft fhelter them the three firft Winters, after
which they muft be tranfplanted. Of this kind
there is one with variegated leaves, which, if dif-
coloured by the froft, will fhoot afrefh, if you
cut off the top branch in the Spring.

Directions for the manures of this month.

The beds for raifing mufhroons muft be formed
in the following manner. Dig a trench five or
fix inches deep, lay in it either the dung of
horfes,

horfes, mules, or affes, ridgeways; or dung
from a mill where the horfes tread; this muft be
the laft covering before the earth is laid on.
When the bed is compleated, which muft he
three or four feet high, cover the dung with frefh
earth about two or three inches thick; after this
get fome dry mufhroon earth, and ftrew it over
the bed on the laft covering of dung before the
mould is laid on.

In fevere weather you muft put hoops and
mats over it, and the whole bed muft be covered
with dry litter or ftraw, to fcreen it as well from
the Summer's fun as Winter's froft.

When the bed is thus prepared, twice or thrice
a week you muft water the covering of ftraw,
and in about two months the mufhroons will begin to appear, at which time they muft be cut as
they fpring up.

The different kinds of cabbages are the Dutch,
the Savoy, the Ruffia, the fugar-loaf, and the
Batterfea. They may be produced in any foil, if
kept well watered. The Savoy cabbages are ufed
for Winter, and towards the Spring they fhoot
forth fprouts which are even preferable to the cabbages themfelves.

A light ground mixed with fand is beft calculated for carrots. Dry weather is the beft to
fow them. Keep them as clear from weeds as
poffible after the firft houghing, till they are
full grown; then take them up, and what you
don't ufe for the prefent, lay in fand for the
Winter.

Turneps will grow in any foil, though they
thrive beft in a fandy, loomy ground; when the
plants begin to leaf, they muft be houghed at a
proper diftance from each other.

Parfneps

Parſneps thrive beſt in a rich ſoil, and are to be treated much in the ſame manner as carrots; only a greater diviſion muſt be left between them.

The manner of cultivating ground for ſtrawberries is as follows. Take a quantity of horſe-dung and coal-aſhes well mixed, lay it upon the land, and then dig or trench it; after this borders muſt be made three feet high, and ſlips planted thereon from eight to eighteen inches apart, according to the ſorts.

There are five kinds of ſtrawberries, the Chili, the hautboy, the ſcarlet, and the red and white wood-ſtrawberries. The Chili ſtrawberry, being the largeſt of all, ſhould be ſet two feet aſunder.

Of raſberries there are two ſorts, the white and the red, the former of which is moſt valuable. They thrive in much the ſame ground as ſtrawberries, and are propagated by ſlips taken from the roots about the end of this month, or the beginning of March.

They muſt be planted in ſingle rows about a foot aſunder; between each row muſt be a ſpace of three feet, leaving the heads when planted, two feet high. The Muſcovy cluſtered raſberries will very ſoon ripen, if planted againſt a wall, betwixt the trees, when there is a vacancy.

You muſt be careful to keep them clear of weeds in the Spring, and prune the tops of the ſtrongeſt ſhoots of the laſt year, leaving them about three feet high, and cut away all branches that are dead and weak. This, like the ſtrawberry, will not have its true crop till the third Summer after it is planted:

Gooſeberries are produced either by ſeeds, ſuckers, or cuttings; the ſeeds may be ſown as

ſoon

foon as ripe, and the following Spring they will come up. The fuckers are to be taken from the roots of old trees, when their leaves are fallen in open weather, and tranfplanted in nurferies. If the cuttings are planted in September and October, they will take root.

Currants thrive in much the fame foil as the goofeberry, and are generally planted againft walls, that the fruit may grow larger : but the ftandards produce the fweeteft fruit.

Thofe who are curious may preferve the fruit till Auguft or September, by tying up the bufhes in mats when they are juft ripe. The largeft fruit being always found on the youngeft branches, both of the goofeberry and currant; the tree fhould be kept from old wood, never leaving any fhoots beyond the growth of three years.

Among the various things produced this month are, fallad-herbs, water-creffes, and blanched dandelion. If January's froft has not prevented it, cucumbers will produce fruit towards the clofe of the month, as will likewife kidney-beans, if fown at the fame time. There are alfo cabbages, fprouts, white-beet, turneps, parfneps, potatoes, fkerrets, and fcorzonera ; likewife chardones and young carrots. Afparagus is alfo much improved in flavour.

We have now many kinds of pears and apples. Likewife nuts, almonds, and medlars. And there are, even at this time, cherries and green apricots. The oranges in the green-houfe being now to fhoot forth their bloffoms.

M A R C H.

MARCH.

Work to be done in the Kitchen Garden.

IF the heat of your cucumber and melon beds is declined, you muſt renew it by putting new horſe-dung round the ſides ; give them air in the day, and cover the glaſſes with mats every night. Cabbages, ſavoys, and red cabbages muſt be now ſown for Winter uſe. Plant out your cauliflower plants for the general crop ; and if the weather is mild let them have air.

Sow radiſhes, ſpinach, and ſallad herbs every week. Peas and beans every foitnight.

Cellery muſt be now ſown to ſucceed that in the laſt month. Slip and plant mint, tanſey, tarragon, penny-royal, chamomile, balm, ſavory, ſage, roſemaiy, hyſſop, lavender, wormwood, ſouthernwood, thyme, and moſt plants that are aromatic.

Lettuce plants, which have ſtood the Winter in warm borders, muſt now be planted in a more open expoſure. Sileſia, cos, and imperial lettuces muſt be ſown in an open ſpot of ground, to ſucceed thoſe in February.

About the middle of this month dreſs and rake your beds of aſparagus, and in April the buds will appear. You may now make new plantations of aſparagus, in the natural ground prepared for that purpoſe.

Dreſs your artichoaks, leaving only two or three of the beſt ſituated and cleareſt plants upon each root to bear ; ſlip up the reſt clean off, and

plant

plant the beſt of them to produce heads, the latter part of the year.

Near the end of the month ſow on hot-beds, purſlane, naſturtium, French and African marigolds ; likewiſe marygolds in the natural earth. In ſome warm place ſow young ſallads, likewiſe rape, ſorrel, finnochia and ſpinach. Burnet and endive muſt be ſown very thin to prevent running to ſeed.

Sow leeks, chervil, fennel, beet, and dill. Divide the roots of tarragon, and make young plantations of chives.

You muſt now dreſs up your ſtrawberry beds, and keep them clear of runners till the plants bloſſom ; when neceſſary, let them be watered. Slip and ſet ſage, &c. if the ſoil is clayey, or if over moiſt, mix aſhes to bind it.

The gardener muſt be careful this month that the inclemency of the weather don't injure his plants and trees : all young planted herbs muſt be watered every morning. You muſt be diligent in deſtroying the weeds before they run to ſeed. Your gardens ought to be compleatly cropped by the end of this month.

In the Fruit Garden.

It is now time to make an end of planting fruit-trees, and to fill up all vacant ſpaces ; alſo to finiſh the pruning of apricots, peaches and nectarines, which are to be done agreeable to our former directions.

Such peaches, plums, pears, and cherries as have had one year's growth, ſhould be pruned the beginning of this month. Neither is it too late to cut off the heads of new planted trees againſt

D   a wall,

a wall, and to reduce them to five or fix buds. Prune fix-trees, and what great wood can be fpared mult be cut clofe off to the ftem.

Graft apples and cherries ; the firft take beft on crab-ftocks, and the laft on black cherry ; but the moft curious method is by inoculation.

The heads of thofe ftocks which were inoculated laft Summer, muft be cut off two inches above the bud flopeways, beginning the flope oppofite to the bud ; and the dead wood, by fome called the cock-fpur, muft be cut clean off the following year in March, that the wound may be healed, and the ftock and fcyon the better incorporate.

Layers of the vine and fig muft now be laid, and horizontal fhelters erected over fome of the earlieft bloffoms of fruit-trees to fecure them from perpendicular dews and fevere frofts.

Sow poppies, the venus's looking-glafs, rofe-campion, valerian, foxglove, acanthus, and fuch like other annuals, as you could not venture to fow in February. Likewife the feeds of the various kinds of ftock gilly-flowers, particularly the ten-weeks. Sow a few every fortnight in the common earth, and divide or flip all kinds of fibrous-rooted plants, not in flowering, fuch as the gentianella, cardinal-flower, double white rocket, fcarlet lychnis, rofe-campions, double wall-flowers, perennial fun-flowers, afters, monk-hoods, fweet williams, hollyhocks, &c.

Plant tube-rofes in pots of frefh earth, giving them a gentle warmth, but no water till they have rifen out of the earth. Your tulips muft be fheltered from blights, which may be done by covering them with mats or canvas.

Sow

Sow the feeds of the campanula pyramidalis, and take off flips from the roots; let your pots have frefh air, and place them in fome pit, where they may receive the warmth of the fun, which will much increafe their growth. Your fhelves and places of fhelter for the auricula muft be mended and repaired; they muft be defended on all fides, except the eaft, from the fun, and be careful that no rain comes to them. Your carnation-layers muft be tranfplanted for blowing, if they were not planted the latter end of the year.

Slip and fet box for edgings, or in figured works: fow the feeds of juniper and fir, and tranfplant the yew, ever-greens, philirea and holly. Plant and make layers of the paffion tree, and graft the Spanifh white jeffamine upon the common white Englifh fort. Move your ananas or pine apples out of the ftove in the bark beds, that the fruit may be forwarded.

This month and the next make layers of the vine, which will be fit to tranfplant the Michaelmas following; this tree is alfo propagated either by laying down the young branches as foon as the fruit is gathered, or at that time making plantations of cuttings. It may be likewife raifed by drawing a young branch through the hole at the bottom of a garden pot about Chriftmas, and then filling the pot with earth; they will take root, and may be cut from the mother plant with fruit growing on them the Michaelmas following. Thofe which are thus raifed in pots will preferve their fruit good almoft till Chriftmas, if they are fheltered from the weather in a green houfe, or fome fuch place.

Figs are propagated either from feeds, fuckers, or layers: the fuckers are feparated from the old

roots

roots the beginning of March, and are to be then tranfplanted, without cutting any of their tops. The layers are managed much like the vine, and if the feeds are fown in rubbifh or fuch like foil about March, they will readily come up. It delights in the fame foil with the vine, and may be planted in ftandards, or againft walls. Obfervations have been made that the ftandard fig-trees bear fruit in greater abundance and much better than thofe planted againft walls, becaufe, as they are endangered by pruning, fo they thrive not in confinement.

This tree is different in the manner of pruning from any other ; for as the method is to take away the fmall branches in other trees, in this it is to be avoided, becaufe the fig puts forth its fruit at the extremities of the laft year's fhoots. You muft cut off fome of the weak fmaller fhoots, which do not promife to bear, but be careful you do it clofe to the great wood. Take away all the great wood to avoid confufion, and the branches of the tree muft not be permitted to grow too high, becaufe it will prevent their being full ; therefore the new thick branches muft be fhortened yearly to a foot, or thereabouts ; you muft break off the bud at the end of the branches in Spring, that inftead of a fingle branch it may have two, which will caufe them the ealier to fhoot out figs. Whatever you cut from the fig muft be as clofe to the great wood or roots as you can ; and you may cut down a whole tree to the roots, to recover it from a fickly ftate, if the winter has been unkind. It puts forth fuckers, which muft be kept down, in great abundance.

When

When your figs have shot six or seven inches, cut or stop the shoots, and continue so to do all the Summer, by which two crops in a year will ripen.

Now is the time to plant beans, leaving a distance of three feet betwixt the rows, and the large sort of peas four feet. Set them about five inches apart in a stiff soil, without any manure : keep them clear of weeds, and water them about the time of their blossom. Beans in the Winter are commonly sown in single lines, under a south wall or hedge.

Mint and balm will grow any where, and are propagated by parting their roots any time in the Spring, as well as by sowing. The mint is more generally cultivated than the other, being of itself a good sallad, of use in soups and sauces, and proper for distilling. When 'tis about a foot high you may cut it in bunches for Winter use, observing to dry it in the shade ; which should be attended to as a general rule for others herbs.

Thyme is raised either by seeds sown in this month or April, or from slips planted at the same time : there are several sorts of this herb, one whereof has variegated leaves, and is proper for edgings.

Sage is likewise propagated from seeds or slips, but most commonly from the latter, taken from the roots at the end of this month, or the beginning of April, and planted in light earth a foot asunder.

Rue is a plant which delights in shady places, and is multiplyed by slips set in a light soil : this plant has been thought to prevent the plague, for which, in times of pestilence, it was much valued.

D 3

Penny-

Penny-royal and camomile are propagated from flips planted in March or April ; they grow best in a stiff soil, and should be fixed in a shady place. Fennel, dill, parsley, &c. are raised from seeds sown in the natural ground this month.

There are two forts of marjoram ; that which is called Winter sweet marjoram will last some years ; the other sown annually on hot beds is not so durable. The first is increased by planting the slips in moist ground about March or April.

Tansey is increased by parting the roots in the Spring, and is a plant which, for its valuable qualities, should be always kept dry in the Winter. It is extremely useful for people who are affected with the gout in the stomach. That disorder has been removed by boiling half a handful of it in a pint of strong white wine, and drinking it hot.

The seed of cellery may be sown this month and the next in such part of the garden as is open to the air. It must be planted about six weeks after it comes up, in beds, allowing six inches distance between the plants : they must remain there till the middle of June, when some of the first sowing will be fit to plant in trenches for blanching. A light rich soil is best, and the trenches must be cut eight or ten inches wide, and of the same depth, in which the plants are to be put as soon as made, after having pruned off their tops and roots ; they are to stand at five inches distance, and as they increase in growth, are to be earthed up to within four or five inches of their tops.

Endive loves a light rich soil, and though it may be sown in this month, yet it is better to leave it till the next. When it has been come
up

up about fix weeks, plant it in beds, as directed for cellery, and, about the middle of July, plant it in rows about fix inches apart. As foon as it is well grown you may tie up fome of it to whiten, which work fhould be continued every fortnight.

Purflane is a very cooling herb, and admired by fome in Summer fallads. If it is fown this month it muft be covered with glaffes; if not till the next, the heat of the fun will be fufficient. Sorrel is fown in rows or drills, like other fallading.

Spinage, in March, April, and May, is to be fown in feveral parcels of ground at different times, about a fortnight from one another, as a conftant fupply for the table, till there is plenty of other greens. There are two forts of it, the prickly and the round : this, like moft other plants of the like nature, thrives in a light, rich foil. Spinage-feed is fown for the Winter in the beginning of Auguft.

In this month fow feeds of the cabbage lettuce of all kinds in the open ground among the crops; they delight in rich light ground and a warm expofure : to preferve a fupply they fhould be fown every month from March to Auguft.

The feeds of artichoak are fown at the beginning of this month, and planted out in April. The middle of this month is the moft proper feafon to flip the roots for new plantations ; they are generally raifed by fuckers. When the flips are cut, you muft leave three heads growing upon every old root. The flips muft be planted in lines two feet afunder, and four feet diftance from each other. After planting they muft be well watered. A ftrong rich foil, well expofed to the fun, is the moft proper for them.

Sow

Sow your cauliflower feed this month in fome corner of the garden, where the plants may be sheltered. Near the middle of the month, when they are in their firft leaf, plant them in a nurfery about five or fix inches afunder, and continue them there till the latter end of May or June, when they are to be tranfplanted abroad for your crop. Rainy. or moift weather is the belt. If it be a dry feafon; make holes in the ground about three feet apart, and before you fix the plants, water the earth. You muft afterwards water them very often.

The Autumn following they will bear large flowers ; but fome of them will not flower till after Michaelmafs, and fuch plants muft be taken up with the earth round their roots, and fet together in a green houfe, or fome fuch place, where they will enlarge themfelves, and be fit to ufe in the Winter.

To have Summer cauliflowers you muft fow the feed the beginning of Auguft, upon fome decayed hot bed, and tranfplant them about three inches diftance, as foon as they have put out their firft leaf, upon fome other bed ; the middle of September draw out every other plant, and fet them fix inches apart under a fouth wall, to ftand there till Spring, when they are to be planted out for flowering ; or you may fet them in the places where they are to bloffom, covering them with glafs bells in the Winter.

If the weather is open, Afparagus may be fown the beginning of this month ; the February or March following the feedlings will be fit to be planted out.

In order to obtain a natural crop, you muft proceed thus ; firft meafure out your ground, allowing four feet for breadth of each bed, and
two

two feet for the alleys between the bed; then open a trench at one end, and lay in the bottom of it horfe-dung, about fix or eight inches thick. Then trench the fame quantity of ground, lying next to the firft trench, throwing the earth of the fecond trench upon the dung in the bottom of the firft; and thus continue till the whole is done.

This being over, in lines at eight or ten inches diftance, plant the afparagus, taken frefh out of the nurfey, fpreading their roots, and covering their buds with earth about four inches thick. Each bed takes up four rows; when all the beds are planted, fow the whole with onions, and rake it level, for the alleys will not be of any ufe till after Michaelmas, when the onions will be off, and the fhoots of the afparagus plants made that fummer are to be cut down. Then dig up the alleys, and throw part of the foil upon the beds, to raife the earth about five or fix inches above the buds of the plants, fupplying the alleys with dung or fome rich foil.

In March following, the earth muft be raked down, and the alleys are to be turned up every Winter, and now and then enriched with dung. After Michaelmas cut down the haulm, and give them their Winter dreffing; and you are not to be later than the middle of March without raking and laying down the beds.

It is a general rule not to cut any of the afparagus till the fourth year after planting; but where the plants are ftrong, a few may be taken here and there, in very fmall quantities, the third year.

About the beginning of April, the afparagus appears above ground, and may be cut till the

begin

beginning of June, when they have stood five years; but if they are younger, you must not cut them after the middle of May.

In the Flower Garden.

The poppy is an annual plant, sown in spots, and of various colours; it is a beautiful but not lasting flower, and is commonly found in borders under walls. The venus's looking-glass is likewise sown in much the same manner. White hellebore is propagated from off-sets parted in March, in a soil that is light and rich.

Primroses will grow in almost any soil. The seed is sown in the natural ground about the latter end of this month; and the seedling plants, which will not blossom till the second year, must be sown in a nursery, and the young plants removed to proper places the August after they are come up.

The stock gilly-flower is a shrub raised from seeds sown in this month, and transplanted the Autumn following. It loves a light dry soil; and the double kinds of them, which we find amongst the seedling plants, may be increased by slips or cuttings planted in May, June, or July; which being transplanted into pots, are, for their grateful smell, a proper ornament for the nicest places in the garden, and to adorn chimnies.

The several sorts of double wall-flowers may be raised from slips planted in shady places, either in March, April, May, or June; but the bloody wall-flower may be more easily propagated from seeds sown in March

The sun-flower is raised from seeds sown in large borders, where it will grow six feet high;

it

it will grow in the shade, and almost any soil.
Everlasting double and single sun-flowers are
raised by parting the roots in this month, or at.
Michaelmas.

The passion-tree is raised either from layers or
seeds sown this month; and if you plant the
cuttings in May or June in fine earth, they
will take root: it must be fixed in a place that
is moist and cool, and be often watered. It will
bear fruit shaped like lemons, and of the same.
colour. You cannot fail of fruit if you lay
plenty of cow-dung about the roots, and water
them often during the flowering season. It is
called the passion tree by the contrivance of some
Spanish friars, who, by adding some things wanting in the natural flower, made it as a representa-
tion of our Saviour's Passion.

The juniper tree is a plant so pliable, that
it may be brought to any form whatever: a
barren soil is best; the berries must be sown
in rich ground without watering. They will
come up in about two months, and they must
remain in the seed-bed two years before they will
be fit to transplant.

The palm-tree is a green-house plant, but.
might be made to stand abroad, after being sheltered three or four years. It is produced by
setting the stone of the fruit in light earth this
month, and giving them the assistance of a
hot-bed.

Produce of the month.

We have now, exclusive of the sallads the
preceding month, some purslane, with young
tops of tarragon. Sprouts of cabbages, young
cabbage

cabbage plants, or coleworts, and Winter fpinach.
Carrots fown in July, radifhes of Michaelmas,
red beet, and fome late fown turneps.

In the hot-beds we have kidney-beans and
fome peas : and cucumbers upon the plants raifed
in January ; we have alfo afparagus upon the hot-
bed made in February, preferable to thofe of the
preceding months. And, towards the end of this
month, the radifhes fown upon the hot-bed in
February will be fit to draw.

At the end of this month we have fome fcarlet
ftrawberries ripe upon the hot-beds ; and alfo
fome few beans, if we forward them by artificial
heats. Fruits yet lafting, are pears and apples of
feveral forts, with nuts, almonds, &c.. We
have in fome gardens ripe cherries and green
apricots.

The flowers that blow this month are crocus,
daifies, violets, wall-flowers, ftock gilly-flowers,
iris's of different forts, hepatica's, crown imperial, primrofes double and fingle, fome kinds of
fritillaria, and near the end of the month a few
auricula's. Anemonies double and fingle, hyacinths, jonquils, narciffus, fome precope tulips,
violets, and the white polyanthus.

A P R I L.

Work to be done in the Kitchen Garden.

IN the early part of this month plant kidney-
beans in fome warm fpot ; likewife garden-
beans for a latter crop : fow marrow-fat and
other large kind of peas : continue to fow all
forts

forts of young falled herbs, alfo cos, Silefia, and cabbages lettuces; young cellery plants muft be fhifted into beds of rich earth, and, till they have taken root, muft be watered every day. Draw up the earth to the ftems of your peas and beans, keep them clear of weeds, and hough the ground between the rows. Prepare your dung to make ridges for melons and cucumbers, and fow fweet marjoram, thyme, and other aromatic plants. The ftems of your cabbage and cauliflower plants, which were planted in Autumn, or early in the Spring, muft be earthed up clofe; let this be done after a fhower of rain.

Plant cuttings or flips of rofemary and lavender, efpecially after rain. Near the end of the month hough carrots, parfneps, and onions, leaving the two firft above five or fix, and the latter about three or four inches diftance. Continue to make plantations of ftrawberries till the middle of the month.

In open borders fow fmall fallads, fuch as creffes, muftard, turnep, or rape and radifh: fow feeds of thyme, and other aromatic herbs, which muft not be delayed longer than the latter end of this month: fow fmall feeds fhallow in the earth if the foil is heavy, if it is light, fandy ground, they muft be fown deeper.

Make ridges for cucumbers and melons for a full crop, and prune the melon plants upon the forward ridge from all fuperfluous branches; but this is to be done very carefully, without lifting up the runners from the ground, which might bruife the tender branches, and endanger the whole plant. They may be raifed under bell-glaffes, or oiled paper, covered over with two hoop-

E   ' fticks,

sticks stuck in the ground, one across the other, the size of a bell-glass.

If the weather be dry and windy, you are to stake up all new-planted trees, if that work was neglected in the preceding month, watering them well once in eight or ten days. Defend trees and plants from snails and slugs, which in this month make great destruction in the kitchen-garden.

In the Fruit Garden.

All suckers must be removed from fig-trees, which are now apt to send forth plentifully. The apples that remain to be grafted may be compleated this month, which is the best time for grafting between the bark and the wood.

You must watch the new planted vines, and not suffer above one shoot, or two at most, to remain. The only thing you are to endeavour to accomplish is, to get large bearing wood as soon as possible, which may be effected by a taking a-way the smallest shoots; the head being disburdened, the root is strengthened of course. Rub off such young shoots of new-planted trees against walls as direct themselves forward, leaving only those which shoot sideways.

New planted trees should be often refreshed with water, and have either a semicircular paving of small stones round their roots, or a small heap of weeds or grass laid to keep them moist and cool.

The binding of all trees that are not thriving should this month be taken off. Let your garden be kept clean, and dig borders half spit deep. The most effectual method to destroy the weeds,
and

and preferve a good culture to old trees, is by repeatedly ftirring up the earth.

The reafon why the bloffoms of young fruit
fall off from vigorous peach-trees in this month,
has been compared to a nurfe overmuch abound-
ing with milk, by which means the child is frequently in danger of being choaked. It is on
this principle that thofe who are experienced in
gardening have directed the laying the branches
of trees horizontally, and keeping them free
from great wood, and perpendicular fhoots in
the middle, that the fap may be carried in that
due proportion and quantity which is neceffary.
It is more eafy to be effected by horizontal than
perpendicular fhoots.

Pear and apple-trees that are barren muft be
managed thus ; take off the ftrongeft branches
about a quarter of an inch, according to the bignefs of the branch, cutting it entirely away to the
wood. They will continue to bear fruit for
fome years ; and when they die, you will always
find in the pear-tree a fufficient number of others
to fucceed them.

Cherry-trees that are not in a thriving way
muft be dealt with thus ; flit down the tree per-
pendicularly with the point of a knife, juft entering the bark of the ftem to prevent their being
hide-bound, becaufe the grain of the bark, contrary to moft other trees, runs horizontally. If
this operation is not executed, it will remain in
an unthriving ftate for ten or fifteen years ; but
after they have been thus dealt with, they will
thrive and profper amazingly.

The gardener muft now be particularly careful
to deftroy all fnails and flugs, which are very
detrimental to the young wall-fruit. The only

E 2   means

means to effect this is to wrap about the stem of a tree two or three rounds of line, or rope made of horse-hair, such as are generally used to hang cloaths on ; these are so full of stubs and straggling points of the hair, that neither a snail nor slug can pass over them, without being killed ; so that the head of the tree, if it be a standard or dwarf, can receive no hurt, if the bottom of the stem is properly secured.

When the hair is very short that forms these lines it is by far the best ; for then they will be full of points, and compleatly armed against any attempts of these destructive vermin. In espaliers of fruit-trees it is only necessary to wrap these hair-lines about the stems of trees near the root, and about the bottom of every stake, which is to be done in the Winter when the snails are laid up in close quarters. In order to preserve plants and herbs, which are liable to be destroyed by slugs or snails, the hair-lines are to be fastened about the edges of the beds in which they are planted.

In the Flower Garden.

This month and the beginning of the next, sow the seeds of the carnation, a flower of all others the most delightful as well for its agreeable smell as beautiful colours. The compost proper for this flower is made of sandy loam, and well consumed melon earth, one load of the latter to two of the former ; they must be well sifted together, and let them lie in a heap for some time to mellow ; then sift it a second time, either to sow the seeds in, or to plant your layers on. When you have filled your pot

with

with this earth, and fmoothed the top, fprinkle
on your feeds, and after having covered them
with the fame compoft, prefs it gently with a
board, and let them ftand open to the air ; the
feed will come up in about three weeks, and the
young plants be fit to tranfplant into beds the
July following, where they muft be fet about
ten inches diftant from each other, and fhaded
from the fun with mats for about three weeks,
uncovering them every night, that the dews may
refrefh them.

The different kinds of this flower are divided
into five claffes, and are diftinguifhed by the
names of piketees, painted ladies, beazarts, flakes
and flames : the piketees are of a white ground,
fpotted colour, or pounced with red or purple ;
the painted ladies have their petals tinged on the
upper fide, either with red or purple, and the under fide of the leaves is plain white ; the beazarts
are ftriped with four diftinct colours ; the flakes
are of two colours or more, always ftriped ; and
the flames have a red ground ftriped with black
or very dark colours. Each of thefe claffes is very
numerous, but the piketees abundantly fo. As
tulips are the glory of the Spring, fo thefe flowers
are the pride of the Summer. The feeds of this
flower are gathered the latter end of September,
in dry weather, with the ftalks they grow upon,
and they muft remain expofed to the fun through
a glafs for a month or two, without opening any
of the hufks till the time of fowing the feeds.

Now fow in the natural ground all foreign
feeds, and fuch flowering feeds as have been
omitted the preceding month. Sow fcarlet beans,
and when they are grown up faften them properly

to a wall, where the branches will advantageously spread. The feed is annually fown this month in good ground well expofed to the fun. Sow fcabious and marygolds, and part and fet all fibrous rooted plants.

About the beginning of this month your auricula feeds will appear above ground, and are to be carefully watered ; and thofe auricula which are now in their bloom, fhould be refrefhed with moderate waterings every three days ; but they are to be guarded againft the fun and rains.

After rain clip your edgings of box. Sow pine and fir feeds, covering them with a net to keep them from the birds : this is the beft time of the Spring to remove all forts of ever-greens. If the weather be moift it is not yet too late to make layers of jeffamine, honeyfuckle, rofes, and fuch like fhrubs.

Inftruĉtions relative to the manure of the month.

Melon feeds are fown on the hot-bed for ridge plants the beginning of March, and about a week after fowing they are fit to plant out four inches apart, where they are to remain till their firft leaf is about the bignefs of a crown piece ; when the fecond or third joint appears, you muft cut off the prime leader from each plant near the ear-leaves, and they will each of them quickly put out three other runners, which will produce fruit in abundance ; thofe are commonly pruned at every third or fourth joint.

About the latter end of April, the plants they raife will be fit to plant on ridges, which are thus made : cut a trench about two feet and a
half

half wide, and fixteen inches deep, in which lay horfe-litter, prepared as for a hot-bed, about two feet thick, fpread equally and trod gently ; then at the diftance of about four feet, in the middle of the ridge, you are to make holes ten inches over and fix deep, which are to be filled with earth prepared for that purpofe. When this is done, the whole muft be covered with the fame earth, about five inches thick ; and the beds are to be made four feet wide and flat. Two or three days after the ridges are made, plant two melon plants in each hole, and cover them with glaffes and mats.

Of kinney-beans there are two forts ; the one bears early and near the root, without running high, called the Batterfea bean ; the other grows near fix feet high. Thefe beans muft be fown the firft week in this month, in a light frefh foil, making drills from north to fouth, and laying the beans in them about four inches afunder, covering them with earth, raifed in a ridge, to keep the wet from them. The lines of the Batterfea bean fhould be two feet apart ; and the other kind are to be fowed in rows, like the rounceval peas, having alleys between them two feet and a half wide : the Patterfea kind need not be ftaked : but the others will not bear well, unlefs they are ftaked. From the firft fowing in this month, we may once every three weeks, till the middle of July, continue to fow frefh ground with kidney-beans to fucceed one another ; obferving, that when the ground is very dry, as in June and July, and the weather hot, we muft water the drills as foon as we have opened them, before we put in the feed, which will contribute to their vegetation ; but

after

after they are fown, we muſt avoid watering
them. The Batterſea beans, out of curioſity, may
be fown in hot beds the firſt week in September, and they will produce beans fit to gather in
January.

It is the buſineſs of a gardener, if he has
ground enough, to provide ſo many crops of
peas as may furniſh a table throughout the whole
Summer : about November or December is fown
the firſt crop; and the Charlton, or maſter
hotſpur, are the moſt proper for that feafon,
fown in drills about two or three feet afunder,
the lines running from north to fouth : in February a fecond crop of the fame kind of peas ·
ſhould be fown ; and in March we may put in
a third of the fame fort : about the beginning of
April ſome ground may be prepared for the
dwarf-peas, which feldom rife higher than half
a foot, and are fet four or five inches apart, in
lines about eighteen inches diſtant from one another : there is a fort of dwarf peas may be fown
in May or June, to have a conſtant ſupply of
young peas ; the ſmalleſt fort are fown in edgings, and being fown upon a gentle hot bed the
firſt week in September, will produce peas in the
Winter.

Rofemary and lavender grow beſt in a light
fandy foil, and are raifed from ſlips planted in
this month, which quickly take root if they are
ſhoots of the laſt year, but if older, they will
not grow : thefe herbs are apt to ſuffer by froſts,
and ſhould be planted in the dryeſt and warmeſt
part of the garden.

The products of the month.

Upon natural beds in gardens near London, we have plenty of afparagus, but in the more fouthern parts of England it is cut fooner by a fortnight. We have plenty of cucumbers and mufhrooms, that were fown on hot beds made the beginning of February. Young radifhes are now very plentiful ; and towards the end of the month fome of the Dutch brown lettuce, which have ftood the Winter, will begin to cabbage. Sallads on the natural ground are, crefles, radifh, turnip, and muftard ; and the other herbs proper to mix with them are, young onions, terregon, and burnet. There are fcallions, leeks, and fweet herbs, growing of all forts. Young carrots, fown in Autumn, and fome fprouts from the old ftems of cabbages and coleworts, or young cabbage plants : radifh tops are at this time a very good fallad.

There are feveral forts of fruit that are now ripe ; cherries and large green apricots are to be found in plenty in fruit gardens ; alfo ripe ftrawberries, upon thofe plants which have been affifted by hot beds.

Be careful to water your pine apples often, in the heat of the day giving them air, and if they want larger pots, tranfplant them.

The flowers that blow this month are, auriculas, polyanthus's, tulips, daifies, hepatica, iris's, wall flower, rofemary, tanfies, ranuncula, gentianellas, crown imperial, double cuckow flower, fea pink, double paradife, fyringas, fritillaries, laurus tinus, ftar of Bethlehem, marfh marigold, paliurus, and lilly of the valley.

M A Y

M A Y.

Bufinefs of the Kitchen Garden.

TAKE out all the plants from the roots of
your artichoaks, which have been produced fince the old ftocks were flipp'd, and cut
off all the fmall artichoaks from the fides of the
ftems. If it is likely to rain fow turneps, hoe
thofe fowed laft month, and in open ground
fow cucumbers for pickling. Towards the latter end of the month, if the weather is favourable, tranfplant the tomatos for foups, and the
capfieum for pickling, which have been raifed
upon hot beds ; and it the weather is dry, water them often. You may forward the cabbag-
ing of your early cabbages, by tying their leaves
together with a withy or bafs mat. Deftroy all
manner of weeds in your garden-beds, before
they fhed their feed. Sow peas and beans in a
moift foil for a latter crop. About the middle
of the month plant cauliflowers for Winter ufe ;
keep the ground moift, and fhade the beds every
day with mats. Plant out the red and white
cabbages and favoys for Winter ufe. Tranfplant
the firft fown cellery into drills for blanching ;
draw the earth about the ftems of the cauliflowers, cabbage plants, beans, or any others crop.
In the heat of the day fhade the cucumbers under frames with mats, but let the melons in
warm weather have air. Tranfplant Silefia, cos,
and imperial luttuces, to fucceed thofe of the laft
month.

In the Fruit Garden.

You muſt be very careful to thin peaches and apricots of their ſuperabundant fruit, for too many on a tree make the whole inſipid ; and therefore two upon one branch are eſteemed ſufficient. You muſt now take away all dry, withered branches from wall trees, and be careful to cleanſe them from ſnaile, cankers, &c. Cut off the extremities of the ſhoots of goofberries, which will in a great meaſure prevent or kill the canker-worm.

Tie up the ſhoots of the vine to the props, leaving only three or four of the ſtrongeſt ſhoots. Looſen or diſengage ſuch branches of the vine as will be obſerved ſometimes to be bound between the joints of the wall, and behind the larger wood. About the latter end of the month begin to nail the moſt forward branches of the vine, where fruit is cloſe to the wall, and be carful to pick off all fruitleſs ſhoots.

In the Flower Garden.

Your choice tulips muſt he ſhaded from the heat of the ſun, and defended from rain ; when they have done flowering break off their ſeedpods.

·The ficoides, which is propagated by the cuttings being planted abroad in a natural bed of earth in this month, will be fit to put in pots in Auguſt, where it may remain in the open air till the latter end of September : ſome kinds of this plant are annual, and therefore muſt be raiſed from ſeeds every year ; and one ſort of it will

will ſtand the Winter, if we raiſed young plants of it about July or Auguſt, that do not bloſſom three or four months. The ſhrub kinds which have their ſtalks woody will bear moderate watering, but the others, which are more ſucculent, muſt have very little water. Theſe plants muſt have the benefit of the ſun to open their bloſſoms, unleſs two kinds, which only flower in the night. The cuttings of theſe plants ſhould not be planted till the ſun has dried up the wounded parts.

The torch-thiſtle bears no leaves. It is a ſucculent plant, propagated from cuttings, planted between May and the end of July ; they muſt be planted upon a little hill in the middle of the pot, for they can hardly endure water ; they muſt ſtand abroad about twenty days to take root, before put into the hot-bed, obſerving to water them at their firſt putting in pot ; and during the Summer months they may now and then be gently refreſhed : the beſt compoſt for theſe plants is the rubbiſh of old walls, mixed with about one third of ſandy ſoil.

The myrtle tree is increaſed by layers in this month ; the youngeſt ſhoots that are tender muſt be bent into the earth after it is well ſtirred, and being often refreſhed with water, will take root, and be fit to take off from the mother plants the Spring following. The cuttings of this tree are planted in July, ſtripping off the leaves two inches from each cutting, and ſetting that depth about an inch apart, in pots of fine light earth, watering them frequently till they have taken root, which will be about the latter end of Auguſt : this young plantation is to remain till the ſecond of March before they are tranſplanted

into

into fingle pots. Near the middle of April fuch old trees as are in a bad ftate may be pruned about the roots, and have frefh earth put to them; their branches muft be cut within three or four inches of the ftem.

The pyracintha is an evergreen plant, raifed from cutting, planted in this month or June; the cuttings, which are to be frefh tender twigs, are to be planted in pots of fine earth, and wa. tered frequently, keeping them from the fun till the following Winter, at which time a warm expofure will cherifh them, and prepare them to make ftrong fhoots in the Spring. It may alfo be raifed by feeds and layers. A light gravelly foil, unmixed with dung, or other rich manure, is by far the beft.

Manure of the month.

The induftrious gardener will now be daily vifiting the kitchen and fruit garden, not only difciplining the barren, but encouraging the weak plants. All new planted trees are to be watched, left fome of them, for want of feafonable help, fhould pine and languifh; therefore fuch as are found in a declining ftate muft be fheltered with boards and mats; for though the fun gives life and motion to vegetable nature, yet thofe that are weak are apt to be overpowered with its heat, and on its too frequent and fudden returns will certainly die away. The analogy between plants and animals is fufficiently fhewn in this obferva-tion, and particularly the human race; for we frequently find, in a fevere feafon, the bodies of fome men will be fenfibly injured by a too fudden approach to a large fire.

F   An

An operation muſt be performed towards the
latter end of this month, which is, by ſhorten-
ing luxuriant branches in all fruit-trees, except
vines, to two inches of the place from whence
they ſhoot : Winter pruning, inſtead of taking
from, gives vigour to a tree; but this operation
now, when Nature is in its full career, gives a
great damp and check to its courſe. The ſhort-
ening luxuriant branches this month reſpects not
only ſuch branches as are intended to be left to
fill a void place, but alſo all vigorous ſhoots made
from the place of inoculation in the nurſery, as
well as the ſame made from new planted trees,
eſpecially apricots and peaches, which are apt,
from too much vigour, to be in very great danger.
In the Summer trees of all kinds may be thus
tranſplanted.

Produce of the month.

We have this month great plenty of aſparagus,
and cauliflowers are now in perfection. The
imperial royal Sileſia, and others ſort of cabbage
lettuces, are in their prime, and very proper ſallads for this ſeaſon, mixed with young burnet,
purſlain, the flowers of the ſmall naſturtium, and
cucumbers.

Carrots which were ſown on hot beds in February are now very good ; but thoſe remaining
of the crop ſown at Michaelmas are paſt uſe ; we
have ſtill ſome kidney beans on hot beds. This
month produces plenty of artichoaks ; and peas
and beans which were ſown in October may be
now gathered.

Pears and apples of different ſorts ſtill remain
eatable. We have now green gooſeberries for
tarts,

tarts, and towards the end of the month we have ripe scarlet strawberries in the natural ground ; likewise the common May cherry, with some few of the May duke cherries against walls, and green apricots for tarts.

The flowers that blow this month are, columbines, tulips, peonies, double jonquils, ranuncula's, asphodels, yellow lily, lychnis orchis, pinks, roses, rockets, veronicas, stock gillyflower, starflower, chalcedons, crowfoot, martagon, double catchfly, Venetian vetch, arbor judæ, bee flowers, campanellas, honeysuckles, buglos, moly, cyanus, cytisus, and iris's.

J U N E.

Work of the month.

PLANTS of all sorts must be carefully preserved from the violent heat of the sun ; those that have been already transplanted must be moderately watered about their extreme fibres : the evening is the best time to do this sort of work. You must not cut asparagus after the first week of this month, as it will very much impoverish the roots. In dry weather gather seeds of all sorts that are ripe, and spread them to dry before their husks or pods are rubbed or beaten. This is the proper season for distilling most sorts of herbs. Shade your melon plants in the heat of the day, and water the alleys between the beds. Destroy all snails and weeds. Plant the late crop of kidny beans, lettuce for a late crop, and likewise endive. The business in the kitchen garden is little this month, except weeding and watering.

F 2

In

In the Fruit Garden.

The shoots of peaches, whose leaves are infected by blights, and begin to appear curled at the extremities, are to be carefully pruned off. Peaches, apricots, and plumbs, expect their Summer nailing, and likewise pruning, to let the fun come to the fruit, and avoid too much confusion.

You muſt now check the luxuriant growth of vines by a Summer pruning, wherein the branches muſt be ſhortened at the fourth or fifth bud beyond the fruit; but if a vigorous branch be wanted to fill a void place next year, it is beſt to let that particular branch alone till October. Nail or otherwiſe faſten thoſe branches of grapes which project too much, and thoſe unprofitable roots which were not before diſcovered, muſt be taken off.

In the Flower Garden.

We have this month the ſaffron crocus, a plant of great uſe as well as beauty; the leaves appear as ſoon as the flower is paſt, and remain all the Winter, which in the Spring ſhould be tied together in knots, to help the increaſe of the roots. About Midſummer they will be fit to remove or tranſplant: it chiefly delights in a chalky ground, but it will alſo proſper in a ſandy ſoil: the piſtillum contains the ſaffron uſed in medicine. The roots of the ſeveral kinds of this plant may be taken out of the ground in this month, and replanted with other bulbs; they love a light ſoil, and may be increaſed by off ſets.

This

This is a proper time to clip edgings of box, ever-green hedges, &c. especially after rain.

Let your pine-apples be frequently watered, and in the heat of the day give them air ; those that want larger pots may be transplanted.

Mow grass walks early in the morning after rain, and continue to roll your gravel walks.

Transplant the roots of cyclamen, saffron, and colchicum. After rain continue to transplant annuals, and sow others to succeed those sown in the former months. Gather choice aquatick plants from rivers, ponds, ditches, &c. and transplant them into your water-tubs, where they make a pretty shew among other curious plants.

Such of your carnations as are strong enough to bear it, may be laid, but be careful to pick off their most tender flower buds. Large podded carnation, which generally burst, are now to be helped, by opening the other side of the pod with a fine penknife, without touching the flower leaves : earwigs, which infest these flowers, may be destroyed with ox-hoofs and tobacco-pipes.

Produce of the month.

Battersea and sugar-loaf cabbages are now fit to cut. You may draw young carrots and onions sown in February, and some young parsneps. The pot-herbs in use the preceding month are still good : and the flower-stems of burrage and burnet are good in cool-tankards. We have now melons of the first ridges.

The sallads of this month are composed of purslain, burnet, the flowers of nasturtium indi-

F 3   cum,

cum, and cabbage-lettuces of various forts, with
fome blanched endive and cucumbers. Artichoaks, garden-beans, peas, kidney-beans and
cauliflowers are in great perfection the beginning
of this month.

Till about the end of the month you may gather green gooseberies for tarts. The ripe fruits
are ftrawberries, rafberries and currants ; we have
likewife cherries of many kinds, as the duke,
white, black, and red hearts. We have alfo
codlings fit for ufe, and near the end of the
month fome genettings and the mafculine apricot, peaches and nectarines, together with grapes,
are now ripe in the forcing frames. Winter pears
and apples are yet lafting. In the barks beds ananas or pine-apples. Obferve to net your cherries
againft the walls, or dwarfs, to prevent their being deftroyed by the birds.

The flowers that blow this month are, campanula, convolvulus, lychnis, fnapdragons, amaranthus, antirrhinum, pinks, nafturtium indicum,
fraxinella, jafmines, carnations, honey-fuckles,
panfies, rofes, campions, poppies, marygolds,
ftock gilliflowers, cornflag, fatyrions, candy-tufs,
monkfhood, tube-rofes, digitalis or foxglove,
and hollyhocks.

J U L Y.

The bufinefs of the month.

THE exercifes in the garden are now for
the moft part gathering in the fruit of our
labour beftowed in the Winter and Spring months;
for we are arrived at that happy feafon which.

affords

affords us almoſt every variety the kitchen garden can produce. In order to preſerve a further ſupply, you muſt now ſow the laſt crop of kidney-beans, in a ſituation defended from morning froſts in Autumn. Plant cellery into drills for blanching, and continue to ſow all ſorts of ſmall ſallad herbs. On dry evenings, water ſuch plants as have lately been tranſplanted, and carefully deſtroy the weeds in every part of the garden. Give no water to your melons, which now begin to ripen. Repair your young aſparagus beds, and plant in moiſt weather freſh plants, where any have failed : water, duly in dry weather, the cucumbers brought up under hand-glaſſes ; tranſplant the cellery into beds, which was ſown in May, and ſome endive, to ſucceed that planted the former month. Clear your artichoaks from weeds, and break down cloſe to the ſurface of the ground the ſtems of thoſe fit for uſe on the old ſtocks ; make a bed for muſhroons as directed in February, and cover it very thin with earth. About the cloſe of the month, ſow ſpinach for Winter uſe ; coleworts, carrots and onions for Spring uſe ; tranſplant broccoli and cabbages for Spring uſe ; and plant out cauliflowers for the Autumn crop : tranſplant all kinds of lettuce ſown laſt month ; deſtroy the different ſorts of pernicious inſects, which abound this month.

In the Flower Garden.

In the vineyard carefully tie the fruit branches to the props or eſpaliers, and diligently remove all weak and fruitleſs ſhoots, either by pinching or the knife, and keep them free from weeds all

the

the Summer ; the much better way in Winter is to fork up the ground inſtead of digging it. The vines are now in their full ſtrength, and puſh with the utmoſt vigour ; inſomuch that the greateſt confuſion imaginable will enſue, if they are neglected and left unpruned.

Apricots are now to be expoſed to the ſun, by taking off ſome of the leaves, that the fruit may take its proper beauty and colour ; and the latter end of the month the peaches muſt be treated in the ſame manner. If any ſtrong wood or water ſhoots puſh from the apricot or peach-tree this month, unleſs a void place wants to be filled, they ought to be entirely taken away ; but their young ſhort branches are to be carefully preſerved by nailing them to the wall.

You muſt now pay attention to the pear-tree, which, if over vigorous, muſt be properly diſcipined ; and all branches that puſh forward are ſtill to be cut off two inches. You may continue inoculation, eſpecially after wet weather.

A plentiful application of water to a peach-tree full of fruit is a great advantage to the ſwelling and ripening of the fruit. The fruit-trees that are in pots muſt be now daily watered, otherwiſe their fruit will drop off : but with this care they will perform wonders. Fruit near the ground (if not too near) have a double advantage, and may be expected to be large and firſt ripe.

Snails, waſps, flies, earwigs, &c. being this month the great enemies to wall-fruit, particularly nectarines, the moſt effectual methods for their deſtruction are to be put in practice. In this and the preceding month, weeding ought to be be diligently minded, that the borders of fruit-trees, &c. and alleys may be kept clean.

Lay carnations as they gather ftrength, and often refrefh them with water. Sow tulip-feeds, which are now ripe, in cafes of light earth ; fow alfo fome anemony feeds and annuals in edgings, to blow in September.

Continue to make cuttings of the torch-thiftle, Indian fig, hythimals, fedums, and other fucculent plants. Raife myrtles of cuttings, according to the directions given in May. Lay down young fhoots of the Arabian jeffamine. Set coffee-tree berries, which are now ripe ; and the fruit of the ananas. Roll you gravel walks well after rain.

In the Fruit Garden.

The management of the vine being a very principal concern this month, we fhall fay fomething farther relating to it.

It has been obferved, that, from a vigorous fhoot of a vine already once pruned, there will pufh again feveral Midfummer fhoots weaker than the former, from the firft, fecond, and third bud, towards the extremity ; which fhoots are to be taken off, only remembering that it is proper to fpare the laft of fuch fhoots, fo far as to leave one bud upon it, from whence nature may exert itfelf a third time in Autumn : for if thofe fhoots were all entirely removed, the vine would pufh at thofe bearing buds which lie at the bottom of the fhoots ; the effect whereof would be either the want of fruit at thofe places next year, or a neceffity of pruning the branch fhorter than was intended, or is covenient in the Winter.

Grapes

Grapes being expofed to the fun this month will not receive any danger ; for though the vines appear thin of leaves and wood, that fault will be recovered by the fhoots in Autumn.

In order to deftroy wafps and other injects, which now devour the peaches, apricots, and other fruits, place phials of honey and ale near the trees, and you will foon catch a large quantity of them. Renew the bottles once every week. Cover your grapes with nets, to prevent the birds getting at them.

Water, having a large quantity of walnut tree leaves fteeped in it a fortnight or three weeks, being poured on the ground, will deftroy worms, and make them quit their holes ; and they may be taken by a candle and lanthorn in a Summer's evening after rain.

In a dry feafon, if you take lime and brine, and pot-afhes decocted in water, and caft it on your grafs-plats, it will not only deftroy the worms, but improve the grafs ; and a decoction of tobacco refufe will deftroy worms in gravel walks.

Produce of the month.

The fallads for this month are cabbage-lettuces, purflane, tarragon, burnet, young onions, cucumbers, flowers of the nafturtium indicum, and fome endive blanched.

We have now great plenty of melons, artichoaks, cauliflowers, cabbages, young carrots, turneps and beet, peas, garden beans and kidney-beans. And alfo all forts of herbs for the kitchen ; which are now very good, efpecially if the gardener has remembered from time to time to cut them down for fhooting afrefh.

Small

Small cucumbers for pickling are in their prime ; and this is the beft month for the pickling of them.

The different fruits we have this month are, goofeberries, currants, rafberries, cherries, early plums, jenetting and codling apples, apricots, peaches and nectarines ; and towards the end of the month we have figs and fome of the July grapes. The peaches are good for little yet, but the apricots are in full peifection.

There is one fort among peaches peculiar, called the bourdine, which fucceeds very well in a ftandard, as the apricot ; and if it be fituated in a warm place, and not carried up too high in the ftem, will bear very well : this and the ftandard apricot-trees require only the fame management with orchard fruit-trees. The wall peaches muft be treated with a great deal of care, for the quantity and excellence of their fruit will be in proportion. Thefe kinds of peaches, like the feveral apricots, are all varieties from one original ftock or kind : they have been raifed by planting the ftones of fine peaches, for thefe trees vary from feed like flowers. The firft ftock may be from a nurfery, but it will be worth while to raife new kinds this way afterwards. The peaches which ripen in the beginning of Auguft fhould be chofen for this purpofe, and fuch as have a thin fkin, a yellowifh, juicy flefh, and a fmall ftone, fticking to the flefh, not parting from it. Some of the choiceft of thefe fhould hang on the tree till they drop off, and the ftones of thefe fhould be planted in a fmall bed of the nurfery fix weeks afterwards. The young plants are to be managed in the fame manner as tender fhrubs or plants of other kinds,

and

and at two years growth are to be planted in the
places defigned for them, with the fame care,
and in the very fame manner, as directed for
apricots. They muft remain in their new places
till they have borne fruit ; and after the fecond
year of fruiting their value will be difcovered ;
thofe that are bad muft be pulled up, and the fine
ones propagated by inoculating them on ftocks in
the general manner. The beft ftocks for the
early kinds are the almond, and for the others the
mufcle plum. Thefe ftocks are to be raifed from
the ftone, and trees planted at one year old, to
prevent their fending down great top roots ; and
after two years more growth in the nurfery they
will be fit for this purpofe. When the trees are
to be brought to the places where they are to
ftand, they muft be take up with care early in
Autumn, the roots trimmed, the trees carefully
planted, and all the branches nailed flightly to the
wall : they are to be defended during the Winter,
by laying turfs at their roots the wrong fide upwards.

The flowers that blow this month are, bafils,
geraniums, gladiolus, clematis, or virgin's bower,
African marygolds, thlafpi creticum, veronica,
lark-heels, lupines, fcabious, marvel of Peru,
lobels, catch-flies, lillies of all forts, apples of
love, marygolds, female balfams, dittany, paffion flower, cardinal-flower, fun-flower, and valerian.

AUGUST.

Work to be done in the Kitchen Garden.

AS the firft part of this month is generally hot and dry, frequent waterings are neceffary, which muft be carefully attended to, as well as the deftruction of vermin.

About the middle of the month, or towards the latter end, fow fome common cabbage-lettuce, and brown Dutch lettuce, to be planted under frames, to come up early in the Spring ; alfo cos and Silefia lettuces. Sow cauliflower feed for the early crop under bell or hand-glaffes. Weed your beds of coleworts fown laft month ; if the plants are too thick, draw fome of them out and tranfplant them. Sow your early Batterfea and Yorkfhire cabbage feed. Earth up your cellery in dry weather ; tie up your full grown endive, manage your artichoaks as before directed ; gather your cucumbers for pickling ; fow turneps for a latter crop ; hough your fpinach fown laft month, and gather your feeds as before directed. In moift weather cut off the flowering branches of thofe aromatic plants which are paft flowering, that they may make new fhoots before Winter.

In the Fruit Garden.

We are now to review the laying peaches and apricots open to the fun to perfect their ripening. Continue the pruning of thofe vines that were neglected the laft month, and keep the

G

fruit

fruit as clofe to the wall as poffible ; but the grapes are now to be difcreetly fhaded with leaves, and fufficiently defended againft the cold nights, at the latter end of the month.

In gathering apricots this and the other months, great care is to be ufed that you do not break the branch whereon they grow ; becaufe from thence we are to expect another bearing branch the fucceeding year.

The borders are now to be reviewed and kept clean ; and at the latter end of this month give them a ftirring, the better to receive the autumnal rains.

Give the ever-green hedges and pyramids a fecond clipping, which in a wet feafon will be much wanted. Make layers of all forts of fhrubs and trees, which remain abroad all Winter, obferving always to lay down the moft tender fhoots.

There being little more to be done this month in the fruit garden than what has been directed in the former months, we fhall proceed to the works.

In the Flower Garden.

The tulip-tree is a plant of the wood, and fhould be fet among fuch trees as are defigned for groves, where it will rife to a great height ; its leaves are fomewhat like thofe of the maple, and the flowers have fome refemblance of a tulip, which gave name to the tree. The feeds of this tree, which are brought from Virginia, are to be fown in pots this month, and fheltered all the Winter, and the Spring following they will come up. The young plants may be tranfplanted into pots, at two years growth, and muft have fhelter in the Winter

for

for the firft nine years at leaft, till they have gathered ftrength enough to reíift the feverity of our frofts, and they may then be planted in the natural ground ; a fandy foil is the beft. This time of fowing of feeds muft be obferved, becaufe experience has fhewn they are not to be raifed in the Spring.

The bufhous violet, or fnow-drop, is reckoned amongft the daffodils It is one of the moft early flowers in the Spring, generally blowing in January.

The hyacinth will bear the feverity of our frofts, and blows early in the Spring ; it is increafed from off fets of the roots, planted the latter end of this month, or in September, in beds of fandy foil. The tuberous hyacinth is a plant of an afpiring head, and a very tender nature ; the roots of it muft be taken up in April, and being carefully parted, are to be replanted in pots of prepared earth, and have the affiftance of a hot-bed like other tender fhrubs. In September you may take up the bulbs of this plant, and preferve them in dry fand.

Lillies are propagated by parting their roots when the leaves are fallen about July, or Auguft, and delight in an open fandy foil : they are very proper flowers for the middle of borders in great gardens, or to be planted under hedges in long walks ; and the ftriped white lilly is fo great a rarity as to deferve place in the niceft garden. The orange lilly is very ornamental in gardens, and an agreeable companion for the white lilly. The lilly of the valley delights in fhady ground, and is eafily increafed from plants.

Produce

Produce of the month.

We have now fallads compofed of cabbage lettuces, creffes, muftaid, cucumbers, radifh, with a mixture of tairagon. We have horfe-radifh, plenty of cucumbers for pickling, all forts of kitchen herbs, and towards the end we cut cellery.

There are artichoaks, cauliflowers, beans, peas, and kidney-beans cabbages and cabbage fprouts, beets, carrots and turneps, but other boiling roots muft not yet be ufed. We have likewife mufk-melons in great abundance.

Although the prefent produce is very extenfive, yet we have feveral roots and herbs of the laft year, fuch as rocambole, fhalots, onions, gar-lick, &c.

We have variety of fruit this month, fuch as apricots, peaches, and nectarines; feveral forts of grapes, figs, Summer pears and apples, mul-berries, and fome filberts. Morella cherries are now ripe, and plums of various kinds. Goofe-berries, rafberries, and currants are ftill very good.

The flowers that blow this month, are colchi-cum, Autumnal hyacinths, belvederes, ranuncu-las, cyclamens, amaranthus, ftarwort, nigella monthly rofes, hellebore, jeffamines, and the mallow tree.

SEPTEMBER.

Bufinefs of this month.

MAKE plantations of Dutch and brown lettuce to ftand the Winter. Plant out cauliflowers fown the laft month, upon old cucumber or melon beds, and fow Spanifh radifh fpinach. In dry weather hough and clean turneps, weed the beds of fpinach, onions, carrots, cauliflowers, cabbage plants, and coleworts.

About the middle of the month you may fafely tranfplant moft forts of annual aromatic plants. Continue to fow fmall fallad herbs; gather all feeds as they ripen, and preferve them as before directed.. Blanch endive, tranfplant lettuces, cut down the haulm of afparagus, and be careful to dung and hough the beds. Preferve your young cauliflower plants from rain, prepare the ground of your Summer crops for frefh ones, or trench it up to lie till Spring free from all weeds.

Near the end of the month plant fome beans and early peas in warm borders. Let your latter crop of cellery be tranfplanted into drills, and the laft crop of broccoli where it is to continue. Seeds in general muft be dried in the fun before they are laid up, to preferve them properly for future ufes.

In the Fruit Garden.

Gather such fruits as are ripe upon the trees, and others that are full grown, and in good condition to be laid up for the use of the following months. Such pears or apples as are fit to gather will easily quit the tree; therefore use no violence if they do not come off easy. A room where very little air comes is the best place to keep them for Winter use.

Before you eat Winter pears, let them be warmed by the fire as you do red port, which will very much heighten their flavour.

You may still inoculate pears; but a vegetative nature has now made a considerable stop in its circulation of sap, and the growth of most trees, and all kinds of delicious fruits are now ripe, we have little to do in this and the former month, but to collect and enjoy what the gardens so abundantly produce.

Be careful to preserve your fruit from wasps; earwigs, and ants.

In the Flower Garden.

Let your tall flowers be staked to prevent injury from the winds, which at this time blow hard. Sow the seeds of bulbous rooted plants, as tulips, ranunculus, crocus, &c.

Take off your carnation layers; transplant flowering shrubs of all sorts, and make layers of them, such as the honey-suckle, jessamine, virgin's bower, Virginian dogwood, periwinkle, &c. Plant your jonquil roots, and let them stand two or thee years in the same place. Sow stock-gilliflowers

liflowers for a fupply in the Spring. We may
yet plant ever-greens, fuch as hollies, yews, box,
&c. if they rife with good roots, but the beft feafon is Auguft. Sow poppies, larkfpurs, annual
ftocks, candy-tufts, and Venus's looking-glafs,
to bloffom early in the Spring.

Manure of the Month.

As the tulips is a beautiful flower, and requires
paiticular care in its cultivation, we fhould defcribe
it at large. It is propagated as follows: the ftems
of this flower being left remaining upon the root,
will perfeft the feeds about July, which will be
fit to gather when the feed-vefkls begin to burft;
then they are to be cut clofe to the ground in a
dry day, and laid in fome dry place till September, which is the moft propcr feafon for fowing
them.

They love a foil compofed of fand and natural
black earth, or the rubbifh of old buildings and
natural earth, but may be fown in a natural foil,
and the firft year their roots will be very fmall,
but after their fecond appearance above ground,
they may be taken from the pots or cafes they
were fown in, and put in a bed of natural fandy
foil well fifted, where the thicknefs of half an inch
of the fame earth fhould be fpread over them; and,
thus they are to continue, without any other culture
than adding half an inch of the earth for the covering every year, till they begin to blow, which
will be in five or fix years time. In this manner
tulip feeds are to be fown every year for new varieties.

It is good to plant all the forward blowers in
a bed together; and of the late flowering tulips
to

to place the talleft forts in the middle line of the
bed, with two rows of the fhorteft blowers on
each fide.   When they are planted in this month,
they need no fhelter till the March, that the flower-
buds appear, and then they ought to be defended
from blights with mats or painted cloth ftrained
upon hoops ; which covering will ferve alfo for
fheltering the flowers from the heat of the fun and
rain, when they are blown.

There are two different claffes of tulips ; the
præcore, or early blowers, and the ferotine, or
later blowers : and thefe are diftinguifhed by their
double and fingle flowers.   They have alfo different denominations from their colours and fta-
ture ; as bagats, which are the talleft flowers,
commonly purple and white marbled ; agates,
which grow fhorter than the other, whofe flowers
are veined with two colours ; and beazarts, which
have four colours, tending to yellow and reds of
different kinds.

The cultivation of violets in gardens is increafed
by tranfplan ing their runners either in this month-
or in February ; they will take root of themfelves
at every joint, without the affiftance of any art.
They fhould be planted in the moft rural part of
the garden, or near the edges of garden beds ; a
binding foil and fhady fituation is by far the beft.

Annuals ftocks are fown in fpots, or may be
ufed for edgings, their flowers being of a pink colour.   You may increafe daifies by parting their
roots either in Spring or Autumn, they make
pretty edgings for flower beds.

The honeyfuckle or woodbine is a twining plant,
proper to be placed about trees in avenues, to in-
termix its bloffoms among their branches ; or it
may be trained up into a ftandard as a headed
plant

plant in the moſt remote part of the garden. Theſe plants, and indeed all flowering ſhrubs, are beſt managed as headed plants, and planted in pots, by which means, when in flower, they may be agreeably mixed with ever-greens, and removed as ſoon as the bloſſom is over, to make room for others. They are raiſed from layers or cuttings, ordered like thoſe of the jeſſamine, in this month or October: they love ſhade, and are the natural inhabitants of the woods, where they prefume the air with their fragrant odours.

The Virginia myrtle, which bears berries, from which is drawn the green wax whereof candles are made, is propagated by ſowing the berries in pots of black ſandy earth, in this month, being kept continually moiſt.

The box-tree is valuable for its wood, and for the continued verdure of its leaves. This plant will make delightful hedges in gardens: but it delights in chalky mountains, where it will grow much quicker than in our gardens. It is raiſed by layers, ſlips, or ſeeds; and the beſt time to make layers or ſlips of it is in this month; the ſeeds of it may be ſown ſo ſoon as ripe, or laid in ſand during the Winter to be ſown the Spring following.

Produce of the Month.

The ſallads of this months are compoſed of creſſes, radiſhes, chervil, young onions, burnet, tarragon, ſome blanched cellery and endive, and lettuce.

There are yet melons and cucumbers, plenty of muſhroons upon beds and in paſture grounds, young garden peas and beans, and ſome kid-
ney-

ney-beans. Cabbages and fprouts of cabbages in great abundance; carrots, turneps, fkirrets, beets, onions, fhalots, rocambole, and horfe-radifh.

We have in this month good flowers and fuckers from artichoaks planted in Spring; and in our kitchen garden we have ftill plenty of cauliflowers.

The fruit-garden affords us this month grapes, peaches, and nectarians in great abundance. The old Newington peach, which is fo much valued, is now in its greateft perfection. There are blue and white figs, blue and white perdigran plums, the Summer bon cretien, bergamot, and other forts of pears. Some apples, walnuts, and filberds.

The method of preferving ripe grapes till Chriftmas is thus: let them be gathered when they are full ripe, and dry; cut the branches off with three or four joints of the branch, and wax each end of the joint with fealing wax: then hang them in a room where there is generally a fire. Melons that are full grown and not ripe, will ripen, if put in a net and hung up in a warm room.

The flowers that blow this month are, love-apples, moly, colchicums, Guernfey lilies, fun-flowers, hollyhocks, tube-rofes, double violets, faffron-crocus, poppies, ftock-gilliflowers, carnations, Indian pinks, Æthiopic apples, and mufk-rofes.

OCTO-

OCTOBER.

Bufinefs of the Month.

IT is now time to make plantations of lettuce for Winter ufe : tranfplant cabbages and cauliflower plants ; take up thofe cauliflower plants which begin to flower, tie their leaves together, and bury their roots and ftalks in fand in a cellar, or fome cool place. Cut artichoaks with long ftalks, and preferve them in the houfe by fetting their ftalks in fand. Drefs and earth up fuch artichoaks as have done blowing, and continue to earth up cellery for blanching. Draw up fome full grown endive, to plant down on the fides of the ridges to blanch. Tranfplant lettuces upon warm borders, and keep your fpinach, carrots, onions, &c. fown in July and Auguft, clean from weeds. Plant beans and peas at the beginning and end of this month upon dry grounds, and in warm fituations. Tranfplant cauliflower plants into the places where they are to abide the Winter. Break down the inner leaves of your cauliflowers fown in May, to defend them from froft or wet, and earth up the ftems of your broccoli plants : make fome moderate hot beds to plant mint and tanfey upon. Guard your mufhroonbeds from wet and froft : fpread fome rotten dung on the beds of feedling afparagus plants, and make hot beds for afparagus, if required at table in December. Lay on the quarters of the garden the dung of your melons and cucumber beds, alfo the dung of the lay-ftall.

Sow

Sow kidney-beans in baskets under a south-wall, to be afterwards forwarded by hot-beds, for early beans : and hotfpur-peas, and Spanish beans, in some well expofed border under a wall or a hedge. Sow alfo radifhes in fome warm place to draw early in the Spring ; and crefles, let uce, muftard, fpinach, &c. upon a decayed hot-bed : put likewife fome roots of mint upon a gentle hot-bed for Winter fallads.

In the Fruit Garden.

This is the moft proper feafon for planting of peaches, apricots, and other fruit-trees, which is beft done in untryed earth, nothing being more prejudical to them than dung.

If the weather fhould be moift or wet this month, the borders muft be raifed, and the trees planted high ; for it is certain death to peaches and apricots to ftand where water ftagnates in the Winter. Vines fhould be planted againft walls feven or eight feet afunder. The beft foil for vines is the rubbifh of old buildings, fea-coal afhes, or drift fand with rotten dung, mixed with an equal quantity of natural earth.

Preferve a good ftick of untryed earth to be ready, on all occafions, for fruits-tree, ever-greens and flowers.

In the Flower Garden.

Continue to tranfplant and lay rofes and fuch like flowering fhrubs ; and to plant the cuttings of jeffamines and honeyfuckles in fhady borders : Sow the berries of yew, holly, and other ever-greens, prepared in earth or fand, and if the feason be mild, thefe kinds of plants may be pruned.

Let the time of watering your houf'd greens be in the morning, when the fun fhines upon them; but after the middle of the month you are to give no watering to your tender fucculent plants. Be careful to keep your walks clean from autumnal leaves.

Manure of the Month.

With refpects to foils for plantation of fruit-trees, it has been obferved that vines thrive beft in dry light ground : that peaches, plums and cherries delight in a fandy loam ; and figs, pears and apples agree with all forts of foils, provided the ground be near three feet deep. For the diftance to be obferved in planting of fruit trees, a wall of feven or eight feet high will require the trees to be planted about ten or twelve feet afunder ; and if the walls be ten feet high, eight or ten feet afunder ; but in either cafe the peach and nectarine fhould be planted at a much lefs diftance than the apricot, plum or cherry.

Before you begin your plantations be careful that the ground is properly enriched for that purpofe; the border fhould be dug two feet deep the whole length of it, and four or fix feet over, filling it up with a fandy loam half a foot higher than the level ; be careful to preferve fome of the fineft mould near the top, to plant your trees in. Experience tells us that untryed earth dug from a wafte or common fed with cattle is the moft agreeable for all manner of young fruit-trees.

Produce

Produce of the month.

The herbs which form fallad this month are crefles, chervil, muftard, radifh, turnep, rape, fpinach, lettuce, burnet, tarragon, young onions, blanched cellery, and endive.

For kitchen ufe we have now parfley, beets, and all forts of aromatic herbs : likewife cauliflowers, artichoaks, peas and beans, and kidney beans fown in July ; and we have yet cucumbers, and fome melons, with plenty of mufhrooms.

This month produces the following roots for boiling ; carrots, turneps, parfnips, potatoes, fkirrets, fcorzonera, and beets. To ufe raw, we have onions, garlick, fhalots, and other roots. Likewife fome chardons.

The fruits of this month are, fome of the late peaches and plums, grapes, figs, and mulberries, with fome filberds and walnuts, and great variety of pears and apples.

The flowers that blow this month are, panfies, amomus, heliotropes, arbutus, fingle wallflowers, carnations, flock-gilliflowers, double violets, and the faffron crocus.

NOVEMBER.

Bufinefs of the month.

DRAW up the roots of carrots, parfnips, potatoes, beets, large rooted parfley, &c. lay them in fand, defended from wet and froft,
pick

pick off decayed leaves from your cauliflower plants, and draw earth up to the stems of those under bell and hand glasses. Weed your spinach, onions, and other crops sown in July and August.

Sow peas and beans to succeed those of the former month, and draw up earth to the stems of those which are come up. If the weather is mild your cauliflowers and lettuce plants that are in frames, or under glasses, may have some air given them. The ground between your artichoaks must be trenched, laying a large ridge of earth over the roots, equal on their sides and tops.

In the Fruit Garden.

It is now proper time to begin pruning pears and plums, especially the dwarfs and those on the espaliers ; the vine, of all other works, is the most material to be observed this month. Lay down the branches, particularly such as you would have fruit upon the following year, to be set growing in pots upon a table at great entertainments. The branches for this purpose must be shoots of the same year, and so drawn thro' the hole at the bottom of a garden pot, that when it is filled with earth there may be a reasonable number of eyes or buds above ground. Eight or nine bunches of grapes will grow on a strong branch.

Nurseries for stocks of all sorts of fruit-trees may be made this and the preceding month, as well as in February and March. You cannot easily chuse or make the soil of your nursery for wall-trees too rich, because stocks should be

H 3

vigo-

vigorous. Plant the beft plum-fuckers, or fow the ftones and kernels whereon to raife peaches and apricots, pears and apples.

Trees that are unhealthy may be refrefhed by applying new mould to their roots. Let your moft delicate ftone fruit be covered, to defend them from the feverity of the piercing winds. In planting and fowing it is a general rule to fow moderately dry, and plant moift.

Nail the tender branches of fig-trees clofe to the wall, before the great frofts come on. If the weather be open continue to plant and remove fruit trees.

In the Flower Garden.

Preferve heaps of earth for your ferveral forts of flowers, and make the proper mixtures for exotics ; obferving that where the ground is too ftiff it may be brought to a ftate of loam, by adding to it a fufficient quantity of drift or fea-fand. Tie up all trees and fhrubs to ftakes, otherwife, by their being loofe and at liberty, they will be deftroyed by the winds. Cut down the ftalks of tall blowing flowers that have done bloffoming, within three inches of the root. Rofes, jeffamines and honeyfuckles may be yet tranfplanted if the weather is open.

Lay down your auricula pots upon their fides, the plants towards the fun, to drain them from moifture, and preferve them from frofts. Give your feeding bulbs daily airings, and keep them fheltered from the froft. Plant hyacinths, and jonquils, and plunge them into hot-beds, to bloffom about Chriftmas.

Manure

Manure of the Month.

Plant currants, goofeberries, apricots, cherries, early peaches, nectaries, &c. againft a paling of five feet high, made after the following manner: the ftakes to fupport this paling muft be fet about four feet diftance from each other; to which you muft nail whole deal boards of twelve feet long, well jointed to one another, and ploughed on the edge, fo as to fet in laths, that thereby the fteam of the dung, which is to lie at the back, may not get among the plants; becaufe wherever fuch fteam comes it will caufe mildews. The deals are to be an inch in thicknefs; for if they are not quite fo thick, the trees will be apt to be fcorched upon the firft application of the firft dung; and if they are thicker, the artificial heat applied to their backs, upon the time it begins to decline, will not be powerful enough to warm them thorough, and then the dung muft be often refrefhed.

When the pailing is up, you are to mark out a border on the fouth fide of it about four feet wide; and on the outfide of the border, faften to the ground in a ftraight line, fome fcantlings of wood about four inches thick, to reft glafs-lights upon, which are to flope back to the pailing for fhelting the fruit, as occafion requires; between thefe glafs-lights muft be bars cut out of whole deal, about four inches wide, fo made, that the glafs-lights may reft in them: thefe bars muft always remain fixed, as in a frame for a hot-bed.

H 3   At

At the end of this frame moſt be a door ſhaped to the profile of the frame, to be opened, either the one or the other, as the wind happens to blow, always obſerving that the door be opened on that ſide only which is freeſt from the air.

If a frame of this nature be made in the Summer ſeaſon, you may plant it the ſame Summer with fruit-trees, and the trees will take veιy good root before Winter, and be ſo well ſtoɪed with ſap againſt the follcwing Spring, as to ſhew no ſign of their remoʋal, but bear extremely. Beſides, by this Summer planting, the trees ſeldom or never throw away their ſtrength in Autumn ſhcots, or make any atrempt towards it, till September and October, when the froſts prevent their deſign.

The trees planted muſt have time allowed for the juices to digeſt, before you b gin to force thɪm: therefore the hot dung is not to be applied to the back of the paling before November. About the middle of this month, or towaɪds the end, is time enough to bring ripe cherries in February; at the ſame time likewiſe heat may be uſed for apricots, ſo as to make the maſculine apricots as large in February as duke cherɪies, and ripen them the beginning of April. Apricots, tho' forced in the uncommon ſeaſon, will thrive and proſper well for many years; but our cheeries do not bear this alteration in nature ſo well. Some forward ſorts of plums will ripen about the end of April; and the Anne-peach at the ſame time. The early nectarine being thus forced, would ripen with the maſculine apricot. And as to gooſeberries, we may have green fruit

fit

fit for tarts in January and February ; and ripe goofeberries and currants in March and April.

In this frame you might alfo plant a row or two of ftrawberries, which would ripen at the end of February or beginning of March. And amongft the fruit you may mix here and there a monthly rofe-tree ; and have a border planted with early tulips, hyacinths, jonquils, narciffus, and other flowers, which by the forcing heats would make a kind of Summer all the Winter.

The trees planted in thefe frames muft be clofe to the paling, contrary to the methods of planting again walls ; for the roots will run under the pales, and draw nourifhment equally from the earth about them, but with walls it is otherwife. The trees need not be planted at a greater diftance than four or five feet : and thofe that have ftood feven or eight years againft walls, may be removed to thefe forcing frames without any danger : As to pruning thefe trees, the fame method is to be followed as re-commended for other trees in February ; but the feafon for doing it is not the fame ; for in the forcing frames our Spring begins in Novem-ber, but in the other cafe it does not begin till the end of January or February. The trees are to be pruned and nailed to the pales (every branch as clofe to the pales as may be) about a week before the forcing heat is applied ; and all the glaffes, to be put up as foon as they are pruned.

The hot dung to be laid to the back of the pales, ought to be toffed up in an heap fome days before it is ufed, that it may yield a heat

every

every where alike : and when it is fit to be applied to the pales, you muſt lay it four feet wide at the baſe ; and let it ſlope to two feet at the top, the heighth in all being at firſt with-in four inches of th top of the pales, and in ſix weeks time it will ſink to about three feet, when you are to apply freſh dung. The firſt heat does li tle more than ſwell the buds of the trees, and bring them to a green colour ; the ſecond forwards their bloſſoming, and the third brings the fruit to maturity. It helps very much the bloſſomin of the trees, to cover them with the glaſs-lights, when froſt happens : but no opportunity of ſhowers ſhould be denied them, if the weath r be tolerable mild, till the buds begin to ſtir ; after that, the glaſſes are to remain over them conſtantly till the ſun begins to have ſome power. When the ſun ſhines warm, and the wind is not too ſharp, give air at the front of your frame ; and if this does not happen during a fortnight's ſpace, then give air at the end, and put up mats or canvas to correct the winds, and cauſe the air to circulate in the frames.

About three changes of dung will ſuffice to bring your cherries to ripeneſs in February, allowing each parcel to remain a month at the back of the pales : but if April proves cold, the forcing heat is to be continued till May, for plums, peaches, nectarines and apri-cots. Where theſe forcing frames are kept, the dung, when it has loſt its heat, may be laid in heaps to rot for the improvement of land.

Produce

Produce of the Month.

The fallads of this month are compofed from the fmall herbs on the hot-bed, with burnet, cabbage-lettuce, cellery, and endive blanched, and young onions. If the cucumber plants that were fown in July have been properly guarded from rain and frofts, they will produce fruit this month. We have cauliflowers and fome arti-choaks in the greenhoufe.

The roots we have this month are, carrots, parfneps, turneps, beets, fkirrets, horfe-radifh, potatoes, onions, fhalots and rocambole. The herbs and plants for boiling are, cabbages and the fpinach.

The dried herbs are, mint, fweet marjoram, and marygold flowers. The pot-herbs are cel-lery, parfley, forrel, thyme, favory, beet-leaves, and clary.

Apples and pears of feveral forts are now ripe, fuch as the St. Germain, la chafferee, the ambret, colmar, criffan, and fwain's egg ; there are wal-nuts, medlars, and fervices. We have likewife fome grapes and figs.

The flowers that blow this month are, fingle anemonies, gentianella, polyanthus, ftock gilli-flower, and double violets. We have likewife fome carnations in the green houfe.

DECEMBER.

Bufinefs of the Kitchen Garden.

SAVOYS and cabbages which are defigned
for feed, muft be hung up by their ftalks
in a dry room for a week or ten days : after
which plant them down in a warm border almoft
over their head. Plant each kind at a diftance,
and cover them with dry ftraw or peas-haulm if
the weather be frofty.

Sow radifhes, carrots and lettuce on warm
borders for an early crop. Carry dung into the
quarters, and fpread it on the ground ; trench up
the quarters, laying the earth in ridges, that it
may be mellowed by the froft. In mild weather
uncover your cauliflower plants under frames every day. Earth up cellery as near the tops of the
plants as poffible.

On the approach of hard froft, cover ceilery
and endive with fern or ftraw. If the weather be
mild, fow early peas in warm borders about the
middle of the month, and in frofty weather cover
them with reeds or ftraw.

In the Fruit Garden.

The principal bufinefs to done in the fruit
garden this month is the pruning of vines, and
thofe other works which were left unfinifhed the
preceding month.

About the latter end of the month prune and
rail wall fruit trees and ftandards that are hardy ;

dy ; and you may yet fet moft fort of kernel ftones.

Moft fort of hardy trees, that fhed their leaves in the Winter, may be removed or planted.

You muft be attentive to fruit trees in orchards, and fuch branches as make confufion muft be taken away. Cover every confiderable wound with a mixture of bees-wax, rofin, and tar, in equal quantities, and of tallow about half the quantity of any of the others ; which are to be melted together in an earthen veffel well glazed, and with a painting brufh dipped into it, the wound is to be covered over.

You muft now be careful to deftroy fnails, which harbour in moft parts of the garden. but particularly behind the ftems of wall trees, where they will be found in great abundance.

In the Flower Garden.

Provide fhelter for your tender flowers in the green houfe, fuch as choice anemonies and the ranunculus. Take off dead and rotten leaves from your exotic plants. Let your green-houfe plants have but little water ; and be fure to obferve this rule, that aloes, euphorbiums, Indian figs, torch-thiftles, and fedums, have not any water given them till the latter end of March.

You muft not be over hafty in warming your green houfe with artificial hearts, but admit as much fun as poffible, becaufe as that is a natural heat, they will be better cherifhed. The principal matter is to keep out frofts, which may be done by covering the windows of your greenhoufe with mats.

A

As no plant can live without air, it is adviseable, that at the end of your green-house there should be an anti-chamber, through which you are to pass to the house; which chamber will have fresh air from abroad every time you go into it, and on opening the door of it into the green house, the air will there mix with the other that has been pent up, and impregnate it with new parts, by which means it will contribute to the vegetation of plants, without affecting them too suddenly.

The weather being generally severe at the close of this month, those gentlemen that have water-works in their gardens must cover their fountain pipes, and the stone of those works, with stable litter, to preserve them from frosts, which will occasion the stone to crack, and consequently destroy it.

This is the proper time to turn up gravel walks into ridges, in order to destroy the weeds; in which manner they are to continue till April, when they must be laid afresh.

This method of managing our walks at this time of the year, is by many objected against; because, besides being deprived of the benefit of them all the Winter, it doth not answer the end of the practice, but rather the contrary. Turning the walks up in ridges kills indeed the present weeds; but for the very same reason that the husbandman stirs and tills his land, to enrich and fertilize it, so this turning and ridging of walks is a real tillage, and adds fertility to them, to the future increase of grafs and weeds.

This considered, if constant rolling, after rains and frost will not effectually kill the mofs and

weeds

weeds of your gravel walks, the beſt way if
they muſt be turned, is to ſtay till April, and
then turn and lay them down at the ſame time.
But the better way is, inſtead of turning the
gravel-walks, to run the top over with a Dutch
hough, in the ſpring of the year, after a froſt:
then let them lie ſome time before they are raked
and rolled, and that will kill the moſs and weeds,
or where the walks are very large, a garden har-
row will anſwer the ſame end.

Work of the month.

A very principal part of the buſineſs of this
month conſiſts in its being eſteemed a greater ex-
cellency to produce a ſingle cucumber or cherry
at Chriſtmaſs, than to bring to maturity loads of
them in their natural ſeaſon.

In December and January we may have ſome
green peas, by the help of the forcing frame mentioned in the preceding month, or otherwiſe by
the aſſiſtance of hot-beds ; and we may have cucumbers fit for the table every month in the
year : the common natural cucumbers laſt tolerable good till the end of Auguſt, tho' they run
upon the ground ; and if we take care to let
ſome cucumber vines run up ſticks againſt walls,
they will have very fair fruit till the end of October, but eſpecially if they are covered in the night
from froſts ; and in November and December a
gardener among his cucumber plants, of various
ages and degrees of growth, may have fruit ſet ſo
as to be brought to perfection, and cut down on
New-year's-day.

I

The

The time for fowing cucumbers for Winter
ripening are to be thus obferved ; begin to fow
feed on the natural ground, to tranfplant them
upon a moderate hot-bed the latter end of July,
and continue your fowing every week till the latter
end of Auguft ; and thofe plants that are fown a-
bout the latter end of Auguft, will begin to fhew
fruit the beginning of October : in September,
fow three times, viz. about the ninth, the nine-
teenth, and the twenty-fifth days of that month ;
and thofe fown on the laft of thofe days, will
bear fruit fit to be cut the firft of January :
then you may fow in October, and have a
good crop in February, with good management.

To bring cherries in December, it has been
practifed to pull off all the bloffems of a tree
as foon as they were budding out in the Spring,
and the tree kept very dry from rains all the
Summer ; and about the end of July, or in Auguft, giving it gentle waterings, by little and
little, about the end of September it has been in
full bloffom, when glaffes are to be kept over
it ; and at the end of October, if the weather
is cold, or beginning of November, dung is
to be applied at the back of the pales, and re-
newed as directed in November for your forcing
flames. The morello cherry, which is apt to
come late, will hold a long time upon the tree,
even till the end of October ; and if fuch trees
were fheltered from frofts with mats or glaffes,
there is no doubt but the fruit will remain a
month longer upon the tree, and perhaps till December.

Currants will remain good upon the trees till
October, if the bufhes are well matted up as
foon

foon as the fruit is coloured, but the mats are to be put up in a very dry feafon. And it is the opinion of many gardeners, that we have many forts of fruits which will hang upon trees all the year about, and be fair to the eye all that time, if they are kept from the forft : but as it is natural for trees to difburden themfelves of the loads of fruit, you are to begin to cover them before they are ripe, otherwife they will be in danger of dropping from the trees.

Befides the paling and frames for ripening of fruit in the Winter, defcribed in the preceding month, fome curious gentlemen advife the building of walls with fire-places at the back, at twelve or fourteen feet diftance from one another; the flues thereof to be made with various turnings, till you come near the top of the wall, by which means the whole wall may be regularly warmed at once ; and thefe walls are to have frames and glaffes in the fame manner as ufed againft the paling already treated of. The walls of this kind feem to be juftified in the obfervation I have made, that a vine, or other fruit tree, planted againft a chimney, where a fire is conftantly kept, or againft the back of an oven frequently ufed, will fhoot and ripen its fruit much earlier than in any expofure to the fun againft a common wall ; which plainly fhews fruit may be forced by fire.

Black and white grapes, with other forts of fruit, have been ripe in April, by being planted. againft a fire-wall.

And not only fruit, but plants of all kinds, may be forced by fire as well as dung : for there is a way for making a hot-bed by means of fire ; for

the

the ufe of thofe gardeneis who have not an opportunity of getting horfe-dung. This hot-bed
is thus managed ; you are to make a frame of
brick-work of any length, but as wide only as a
common hot-bed, to have a fire-place at one end,
to pafs into a flue, which is to wind from fide to
fide, till it reaches the other end, and difcharges
its fmoak by a chimney ; the top of thefe flues
may be covered with fquare tiles, and when the
intermediate fpaces between the flues are filled
with coarfe fand, cover the whole with fquare
tiles, and raife the wall about ten inches above
the pavement, fo that you may cover the pavement as deep with fand, if there be occafion ;
then upon the fand place fuch frames as are generally ufed for hot-beds, to hold the earth in
them, and that the earth may receive the heat of
the fand. This bed, by the heat of the flues,
when the fire is lighted, may be made as ufeful
as any hot-bed, and may be lefs troublefome, and
more lafting.

Produce of the month.

We have this month in the green-houfe feveral
trees and fhrubs in flour, viz, laurus tinus,
Glaffonbury thorn, geranium, thlapfi, femper-
birens, jeffamines of feveral kinds, ficoides, and
aloes. The following are now in fruit ; the
arbutus, or ftrawberry tree, amonum plinii, o-
range, lemon, citron, olive, and the pomegra-
nate.

We have in the confervatory fome artichoaks
preferved in the fand. There are feveral forts of
cabbages, and their fprouts, for boiling ; afparagus upon hot-beds ; and if diligence has been
uled,

ufed, you may find fome cucumbers. or the plants which were fown in July and Auguft.

We have this month on the hot-bed fallads of fmall herbs, with mint, terragon, burnet, cabbage-lettuce preferved under glaffes, and fome creffes and chervil upon the natural ground, with which high tafte helps the fallads of this feafon. To thefe may be added blanched cellery and endive.

There are variety of herbs for foups and the kitchen ufe, fuch as fage, thyme, beet-leaves, parfley, forrel, fpinach, cellery, and leeks tops of young peas, &c. Likewife fweet marjoram, dried marygold flowers, and dried mint. The roots are, carrots, parfnips, turneps, and potatoes.

The fruit garden produces little this month, except pears and apples ; of the latter we have but few, tho' there are yet plenty of the former, particularly of the St. Germain, ambret, and the colmar.

The flowers we have this month are fingle anemonies, ftock-gilliflowers, fingle wall-flowers, primrofes, fnow-drops, black hellebore, Winter aconite, polyanthus ; and in hot-beds, the narciffus and hyacinth.

I 3   The

The Compleat Bee-Mafter ;

O R

Beſt Method of managing BEES, as well for profit as pleaſure.

THESE little infects are no lefs to be valued for the profits of their labour, than the trifling expence and trouble attendant on them, there being no wood nor foreſt, no fruit nor flower, but what contributes to their daily toil : nor are they at any time idle, but in very cold or wet weather.

The moſt convenient place to make choice of for your apiary, or bee-garden, is near the houfe, that you may the better look after them in fwarming time. It muſt be fecurely fenced from all forts of cattle, efpecially hogs, and from all forts of fowl, whofe dung is very prejudicial to them.

They muſt be well defended from high winds on every fide, with fuch fences as may let the fun come to them : but they fhould be fheltered with a brick wall that is folid, in order to keep the wind from coming thro' it, as well as over it ; that place being beſt for them which is moſt expofed to the fouth, and where they have the beſt opportunity to fettle at their hives, when they come laden home.

You fhould likewife plant feveral trees and fhrubs at a reafonable diſtance, near home, for
them

them to pitch on at their fwarming, that they may not be in danger of being loft for want of a light-place. Limes, phillyreas, fycamore-trees, and firs, are particularly good to be planted near them, becaufe they draw a great heal of honey and wax from their flowers.

Having fitted the place, the feats to fet the hives on are to be provided, which muft be fet a little fhelving, that the rain may neither run into the hive, nor lay about the door.

It is better to avoid fetting any hives on a bench; becaufe in Winter it may caufe the bees to fight, by going in each other's houfes, which they may fometimes miftake for their own; and therefore fome efteem fingle ftools beft, which are to be fet at about two feet diftance from one another, and to be fupported with four legs, about twelve or fourteen inches from the ground. They fhould not be above half an inch, or an inch, bigger than the hive, fave only before, where there ought to be the fpace of three or four inches, that the bees may have room enough to light upon it. The beft ftools are of wood; thofe of ftone are too cold in Winter, and too hot in Summer. The ftools fhould be fet towards the fouth, or rather a point or two to the Weft, that the hive may fomewhat break the eaft wind from the door, and ftand in ftraight rows from weft to eaft.

There is another method made ufe of, which is, to make for every hive of bees you intend to keep, a cot or houfe of about two feet fquare, and two feet and an half high, fet on four legs, about ten inches above ground, and five or fix inches within the ground,
and

and covered with boards or tiles, to cast off the
rain ; the back, or north side, being closed up very
close, and the east and west sides to have doors
to open and shut at pleasure, with hasps to them,
and at the face, or south side, to have a falling
door, that may come about half way down,
which is to be elevated at pleasure, and serves in
Summer for a penthouse, not only to beat off the
rain from the hives, but to defend them from the
extreme heat of the sun, which is apt to melt
their honey. The other lower half should have
two small doors to open to either hand, which
will serve to defend the holes of the hives from
injurious winds. When the Winter approaches,
and the cold winds are like to injures the bees,
you may then fasten all the doors, which will defend the bees from the extreme of heat and cold,
both which are injurious to them.

If you find them to stand too cold in Winter,
you may put straw within the doors, to keep
them warm ; but the extremity of cold don't
injure them so much as wet, which these cases
best preserve them from. They likewise prevent the bees getting abroad upon every sun-
shine day, because the hives stand six or eight
inches within the door which make them dark,
and the bees insensible of the small heat ; when,
after the common way of stools or benches, the
sun casts its rays to their doors ; which light and
warmth together excites them forth, to the expence of their provision, and the loss of their
lives, as is evident by frequent experience ; the
mildest and the clearest Winters destroying, or
starving, the most bees ; whereas the coldest and
most frosty Winters best preserve them.

As

As foon as the willow bloffoms appear, you may open the under doors, that the light, and warmth of the fun and air, may encourage them to work, or elfe you will hinder their early breeding, and make them flothful.

There are various forts of hives ufed in feveral countries, but thofe moftly ufed in England are wicker hives, made of previt ; willow or harl, daubed with cow dung, tempered with duft, afhes, or fand ; or hives made with ftraw bound with bramblets ; fome out of curiofity, that they may fee the bees work, have them made of wood or glafs, but they are fo cold that the bees do not thrive well in them. Others have placed double hives one by another, and fome upon the tops of others ; that fo, by the taking of one of them away, they may leave the other for the bees, without driving or killing of them ; but as thefe experiments are feldom brought to perfection, 'tis needlefs to fay much about them.

The warmeft and beft hives are thofe made of ftraw, the bignefs of which fhould be of between five or feven gallons, of a round form, rather broad than high : but you ought to have of each fize, that you may fuit your fwarms to them according as they are bigger or lefier ; and where you defign to multiply your ftock, make ufe of fmall hives, and of the larger where you defire a great deal of honey. Having thus made your hives, you muft drefs them after the following manner ; take off all the ftaring ftraws, twigs, and jags, that are offenfive in the hive, and make them as fmooth as poffible. If you need but few hives, you may prune them with a knife ;

if

if many, finge and rub them with a peice of brimftone.

Having pruned your hive, put in your fpleets, three or four of them, as the largenefs of your hive fhall require : the upper ends whereof fet together at the top of the hive, and the lower faften about a handful above the fkirts. Befides thefe fpleets, the ftraw hive fhould have four other fpleets driven up into the fkirts, to keep the hive from finking when it is loaded ; two of which are the two door-pofts, the other two are hind pofts, fet at a equal diftances.

The hives you intend to ufe in fwarming time muft be rubbed with fweet herbs, as thyme, balm, favoury, marjoram, fennel, hyfiop, bean-tops, &c. and when the fwarm is fettled, take a branch of the tree whereon they pitch, and wipe the hive clean with it, and wet the infide of the hive with honey, mead, falt and water, fmall beer, or honey, and milk, or fugar and milk.

Again, your hives muft be kept clofe for defence of your bees, firft, from the cold, by mixing of cow dung with lime or afhes, and with fand, with which you muft ftop up the edges of the hive round, and againft Winter put a wicket of a fmall piece of wood, in which are three or four notches, cut juft big enough for the bees to go in and out at, that no vermin may get to them.

If the Spring be mild, calm, and fhowering, it is good for fwarms, and they will be the earlier ; but if it proves a cold, dry, windy Spring, then there will be but few fwarms, and thofe alfo backward. There are the moft

fwarms

swarms and greatest plenty of honey in dry weather.

You must begin too look after them, about
the middle of May in an early Spring, and observe what you can of the usual signs that pre-
cede their swarming, that you may be the more
watchful over those that require it. When
the hives are full (before which they will never
swarm) they will cast out their drones, although
they be not quite grown, and the bees will hover
about the doors. In cold evenings and mornings, there will be a moisture or sweating upon
the stool, and they will continually be running
up and down hastily, and lie out in sultry evenings and mornings, and go in again when the
air is clear.

In warm and calm weather, the bees delight
to rise ; but especially in a hot gleam, after a
shower or gloomy cloud hath sent them home
together. Then sometimes they gather together without at the door, not only upon the
stool, but the hive also ; where when you see
them begin to hang in swarming-time, and not
before, you may be sure they will presently rise,
if the weather holds.

When the bees lie forth continually under
the stool, or behind the hive, especially towards the middle of June, 'tis a sign or cause
of not swarming : for when they have once
taken to lie forth, the hive will always seem
empty, as though they wanted company, and
they will then have no inclination to swarm.

It is stormy and windy weather also that
will not suffer them to swarm, when they are
ready, and that makes them lie out ; for the longer

ger they lie out, the more unwiling they are to fwarm.

In order to make them fwarm, fome keep the hives as cool as may be, by watering and fhadowing both them and the place where they ftand, and then enlarging of the door to give them air, they move the clufter gently with their brufh and drive them in.

If yet they lie out and fwarm not, then the next calm warm day about noon, while the fun fhineth, put in the better part with your brufh, and the reft gently fweep away from the ftool, not fuffering them to clufter again. Thefe rifing in the calm and heat of the fun, by their noife, as though they were fwarming, will make the others come forth perhaps unto them, and fo they may fwarm.

Many other ways have been attempted to caufe bees to fwarm, as by placing a large pewter-platter under the clufter of bees as they hang out in the heat of the fun, fo that it may ftrongly reflect the heat upon them, which will provoke them to fwarm.

If neither of thefe methods fhould fucceed, but that they lie forth ftill, then rear the hive enough, to let them in, and cloom up the fkirts all but the door : if this has not the defired effect there is no remedy.

The figns of after-fwarms are more certain. When the prime fwarm is gone, about the eight or tenth evening after, when another brood is ready, and again hath over filled the hive, in the morning before they fwarm they will come down near the ftool, and there they call one another, and at the time of fwarming they defcend to the ftool, where anfwering one

ano-

another in more earnest manner with thick and shriller notes, the multitude come forth in great haste, &c.

If the prime swarm be broken, the second will both cast and swarm the sooner; it may be the next day, and after that a third, and sometimes a fourth, but all usually within a fortnight; sometimes also a swarm will cast another that year.

When the swarm is risen, 'tis the usual custom to make a noise with a pan, kettle, mortar, &c. but some reckon it an insignificant ceremony, and others esteem it prejudical. But if they are like to be gone, cast dust or sand among them to make them come down.

When they have made a choice of a lighting place, you will quickly see them knit together into a cluster; when they are fully settled, and the cluster hath been a while at the biggest, then hive them. And having in store several hives of various sizes, make choice of one that the bees may go near to fill it that year, but rather under-hive a swarm than over-hive them, and rub the hive with sweet herbs, as it is before directed.

The man that hives them must drink a cup of good beer, and wash his hands and face therewith, or being otherwise defended; if the bees hang upon a bough, shake them into the hive, and set the same upon a mantle or cloth on the ground, as is usual; or you may cut off the bough, if it be small, and lay it on the mantle or cloth, and set the hive over it, which is the better way.

If they light near the ground, lay your cloth under them, and shake them down, and place

K the

the hive over them ; and such bees as gather together without the hive, wipe them gently with
your brush towards the hive ; and if they take to
any other place than to the hive, wipe them off
gently with your brush, and rub the place with
wormwood, nettles, may-weed, &c. Then set
the swarm as soon as you can to the lighting place
till all be quiet, every one knowing his own
house.

If the swarms separate, and light in sight of
one another, let alone the greater, and disturb
the lesser part, and they will fly to their fellows :
but if not in sight, hive them both in two sepa-
parate hives, and bring them together, shaking
the bees out of one hive on the mantle whereon
the other hive stands, and place the other full hive
on them, and they will all take to it.

If your swarm should happen to come late
after the middle of June, and that they are
small, under the quantity of a peck ; then put
two or three of them together, whether they rise
the same day, or in divers ; for by this uniting
they will labour carefully, and gather store of
honey, and stoutly defend themselves against
all enemies. The manner of uniting them is
thus.

When it grows dusk in the evening, having
spread a mantle on the ground, near unto the
stool, where this united swarm stands, set a
pair of rests, for two supporters for the hive ;
knock down the hive out of which you intend
to remove your bees upon the rest : then lift up
the hive a little, and clapping it between your
hands to get out the bees, set the stock to the
swarm to which you would add them, upon the
rest or supporters over them, and they will
forth

forthwith afcend into the hive ; thofe that remain in the empty hive, by clapping it, will
haften after their companions. When you
have got them all, either that night, or
early the next morning, place the hive on the
ftool, &c.

Many people think it better to place the hive
wherein you have newly put your fwarm you
intend to drive into another, in a place that the
fkirts may be uppermoft, and fet the other
upon it, binding them about the fkirts with a
towel. Then let them ftand till the morning,
and the bees will afcend, that you may the next
morning fet the receiver on the ftool : and
thus you may put three or four fwarms together ; but obferve to unite them the fame evening, or the next at fartheft, left having made
combs, they are the more unwilling to part from
them.

It is good in all refpeḉts, to defend one's felf,
as well as may be, againft their ftings ; the fureſt
way of doing which is to have a net knit with
fmall meſhes, that a bee cannot get through ;
and of a fine thread or filk, large enough to come
over your hat, and to lie down to the collar of
your doublet, through which you may perfectly
fee what you do, without any danger, having alfo on your hands a good pair of gloves ; if wool-
len the better.

If a bee fhould happen to catch you unawares,
pull out the fting as foon as you can, and take
a piece of iron, and heat it in the fire ; or for
want of that, take a live coal, and hold it as near
and as long to the place as you can poffibly endure it, and it will attract the fiery venom ; and
afterwards anoint it with fome honey or mithridate

or

or if you take a little fpittle and wet it, it will cure it.

When a fwarm has entered its hive, they immediately (if the weather will permit) gather wax, and build combs ; and in a few days time there will be compleat combs. They lie fo thick about them, that it is impoffible one quarter of them can be employed at once, untill the combs are brought to a confiderable length, and then a great part of them may be employed in filling them, and the reft in finifhing their cells or combs.

Towards the end of Summer, their number begins to leffen ; for in their profperity at fwarming time ; and fhortly af er, they are far more in number than in the Autumn or Winter, as you may eafily difcern between the quantity and number of a fwarm, and thofe you kill when you take th m ; for the bees of the laft year's breed do now by degrees wafte and perifh by their extraordinary labour, their wings decay and fail th m ; fo that a year, with fome advantage, is the ufual age of a bee, and the young only of the laft Spring furvive, and preferve the kind till the next.

There aie feveral things that are injurious to bees, and will much hinder their profperity, if not prevented.

1. No.fe, which may in part be remedied by the fituation of the apiary, free from the noife of carts, coaches, bells, echoes, &c.

2. Smoak, where land hath been burn-beaten near unto an apiary, and the wind hath brought the fmoak towards it, a great many of the bees have been killed ; which is the reafon they will not thrive in or near great towns.

3.

3. Difagreeble fmells are very offenfive to
th m.

4. Bad weather, as wind, rain, cold, heat,
&c. which is prevented by the fituation and fenc-
ing of the apiary, and ordering the ftock as before.

5. The mice, birds, and other devouring creatures, which are to be deftroyed.

6. Noifome creatures, as toads, frogs, fnails,
fpiders. moths, ants, &c. which you muft endeavour to keep from them, and cleanfe alfo the hives
ever anon from thefe vermin.

7. Hornets and wafps, in fuch years wherein
they abound, prove great enemies to the bees,
by robbing them of their honey : they are deftroyed by placing near the door of the hive a
glafs phial half, full of beer, cyder, or any fuch
thing ; if fome fugar be added to it, it will do the
better.

8. Bees themfelves prove the greateft enemies
both by fighting and robbing. Several occafions
provoke the bees to fight : which, if the battle be
only newly begun, may be hindred by ftopping
up the hive clofe ; but if they be gone fo far that
moft of the bees are out, the cafting of duft a-
mong them was the ancient way.

The beft time to remove an old ftock is a little before, or a little after Michaelmas ; or, if
you have overflipt that time, then about the end
of February, or beginning of March, before
they go much abroad, left it prevent their fwarming. You may remove them at any time in the
Winter, but not fo well as in the forementioned
feafon.

The beft time of the day to do it is in the
evening, next after hiving, if the weather be

fair

fair, and do it in the evening when the bees are quiet ; the beſt way of doing of which is thus :

Take a board about the breadth of the bottom of the hive you intend to remove, and in the evening, or two or three evenings before, lift it up, and bruſh the bees that are on the ſtool forward, and let the board be a little ſupported by two ledges, to prevent the death of the bees on the ſtool. On this board ſet the ſtock, and ſo let them ſtand till you remove them. When you come to move them, ſtop up the door of the hive, and ſet the board whereon the hive ſtandeth, on a hand barrow, and carry them to the place you intend.

The feeding of bees is of little uſe ; firſt, becauſe the bees that have not a profitable ſtock of honey to ſerve them over the Winter, are not fit to keep ; and then, becauſe they that are beemaſters, and have not care enough of them, to keep them from ſpending of that ſtock they have in Winter-time, muſt not expect to reap any conſiderable advantage by them ; and it may be preſumed will never take ſo much pains and care as is required in feeding of them. But as

There are ſome ſtocks of bees in the ſpring time, that may ſeem worthy of our care to preſerve, viz. ſuch as have but a ſmall ſtock of honey, and a good quantity of bees, by means of a cold, dry, unſeaſonable Spring, cannot make ſuch timely proviſion as in other years they might have done, yet in all probability may prove an excellent ſtock, and may be worth our aſſiſtance.

Food may be afforded to them ſeveral ways,
- but

but the beſt is by ſmall canes or troughs conveyed into their hives, into which you may put the food you give them. The chief time of feeding them is in March, when they begin to breed, and to ſit on their young ones, which muſt be daily continued till the Spring ſeaſon afford them eaſe and proviſion abroad, becauſe at that time their combs are full of young bees.

About the middle of Auguſt weigh your hives, and take the heavieſt ; and the lighteſt, if they do not weigh 14 pounds, will hardly maintain themſelves over Winter.

Of all food, honey is the beſt and moſt natural, which will go farther, if it is mixed well with a moderate proportion of good ſweet-wort. Some preſcribe toaſts of bread ſopped in ſtrong ale, and put into the bee-hive, whereof they will not leave one crumb remaining. Some alſo adviſe to put in the hive dry meat, or flour of beans ; others, bay ſalt, roaſted apples, &c. which are very good, eſpecially ſalt ; which, if ſome were mixed with water, and always ſet near them, it might do well, it being certain, that bees near the ſea always thrive the beſt ; which ſome attribute to their drinking of ſalt water, they flying (ſay ſome) many miles to get it.

It is again propoſed for the improvement of bees, to take a handful of baum, one dram of camphires half a dram of muſk diſſolved in roſemary, as much yellow bees-wax as is ſufficient, oil of roſes much, ſtamp the baum and camphire very well, and put them in the melted wax with the oil of roſes, and ſo make it up into a maſs, letting it cool before you put in the muſk, for otherwiſe the heat will fume away moſt of the ſcent.

Take

Take of this mass so much as a hazle-nut, and leave it within the bee-hive ; it will (as he says) much increase the number of the bees, and you will also find both honey and wax, three times of more profit than otherwise you would have had.

A great thing to advance your bees is the having of fields near you sowed with brand, cole-feed, or turneps, from which they will draw great quantities of honey. Beans also are very good for them.

As the chief aim of the keeper of bees is an advantage by their honey and wax : so many have endeavoured to find out some way to reap the profits of bees without destroying them. One way that has been used for this purpose is driving them after this manner.

In September, or in any other time after they have done breeding (else the honey will be corrupted by the young bees in the combs) place the hive you intend to take with the bottom upwards between three or four stakes, and set the hive you intend to drive the bees into, over the same, as before directed in the uniting of swarms ; then often clap the under hive between your hands in the evening ; and so let them stand till morning, and then clap it again, and get as many bees out as you can, which will repair to the other hive.

This way is something troublesome to the unexperienced, yet beneficial in such cases where you have a great stock of honey and few bees in one hive, and a small stock of honey in another, by which means you save the lives of your bees, which will gladly exchange their hungry habitation for a more plentiful.

But

But thefe ways have altogether failed the defigns of the undertakers, as I faid before ; and,
therefore I fhall at prefent only defcribe the common ufage, which is the taking of combs by
killing the bees, which certainly muft be the only way of ordering them, becaufe it is impoffible for them to live, if you deprive them of their
food ; and therefore, about the latter end of Au-,
guft, confider with yourfelf what ftalls you will
keep, and what you will kill. The beft fwarms
to keep are thofe of one or two years ftanding ;
and thofe of three or four, which, by reafon of
their fwarming the laft Summer, are full of bees,
and are the moft likely to be beft ; but thofe of
that age which have caft hives, not being likely
to continue, are to be taken, as are alfo poor
fwarms not worth their feeding, and all light
ftocks, and fuch as do not carry out their drofs,
and drive away the drones in good time ; alfo
thofe whom the robbers eafily affault, are to be
fufpected ; and if their combs be once broken,
delay not their taking : and alfo all ftalls of three
years old, or upward, that have miffed fwarming.
two years together, efpecially thofe that have lain
out the Summer before, and did not caft the
laft Summer, for fuch do feldom profper ; and
therefore it is better to take them while they are
good, than in a vain hope of increafe to keep
them till th y perifh.

It is not fafe to truft to any after they have ftood
five years and upwards, that have miffed fwarming two years together, unlefs it be fome fpecial
fort of bees, which always keep themfelves in
heart ; fuch may be kept nine or ten years.

Likewife, if you have any that are very full
of honey, as in fome years they will be, even
down

down to the stool, such stall is worth three or four, and therefore take them in their season.

Having made choice of your stalls to be taken, two or three hours before sun-setting dig a hole in the ground about nine inches deep, and almost as wide as the hive skirts, laying the small earth round about the brims, then having a little stick slit at one end, and stripped at the other, take a brimstone match five or six inches long, and about the bigness of your little finger, and making it fast in the slit, stick it in the middle or side of the hole, so that the top of the match may stand even with the brim of the pit, or within one inch of it, and then set another by it dressed after the same manner, if the first be not sufficient. When you have fired the matches at the upper end, set over the hive, and presently shut it close at the bottom with the small earth, that none of the smoak may come forth, so shall you have the bees dead in a quarter of an hour.

The hive being taken and housed, lay it softly on the ground upon the sides, not the edges of the combs, and loosen the ends of the splints with your finger, and the edges of the combs where they stick to the sides of the hive, with a wooden slice, take them out one after another, and having wiped off the half dead bees with a good feather, break the combs presently, while they are warm, into three parts.

The honey which first flows of itself from the combs is called Virgin honey, as is also the honey which comes from the first year's swarm. This is the best and finest honey, being more chrystalline, and of a finer taste, than that which is squeezed out of the combs, and so may be kept for particular uses, or for making of the finest mead.

I

I shall conclude at present with giving you some account of the way of ordering your honey and wax, with the virtues of them, that you may be the more sensible of the advantages that accrue to mankind by this small insect.

When your combs have run out as much as they will, put it up warm into pots by itself, this being the finest honey, as I said before, and it will for two or three days work up a scum of coarse wax, dross, and other stuff, which must be taken off. The other honey, which is the coarser sort, you must get from the combs by pressing them, which you may also pot, except what you design for the present to make metheglin with ; which being done, what remains put into a hair bag, and wash in a trough, or other vessel, to make mead or metheglin ; and when the sweetness is all washed out, being crushed dry, try the balls for wax.

The manner of ordering, which is as followeth.

Take the wax and dross, and set it over the fire in a kettle, or other vessel, that may easily contain it, and pour in as much water as will make the wax swim, that it may boil without burning, and for this reason, while it is gently boiling over the fire, stir it often ; when it is thoroughly melted, take it off the fire, and presently pour it out of the kettle into a strainer of fine thin linnen, or of twisted hair, ready placed upon a screw or press, lay on the cover, and press out the liquor (as long as any wax comes) into a kettle of cold water, but first wet both the bag, and the press, to keep the wax from sticking ; at the first cometh most water, at the last most dross, and in the middle most wax.

The

The wax growing hard, make it into balls, squeezing out the water with your hand; which when you have done, break all the balls in o crumbs, and in a kettle or skillet set it over a gentle fire; while it is melting, stir it, and skim it with a spoon wet in cold water, and as soon as it is melted and scummed clean, take it off, and pour it into a pan or mould, besmearing the bottom and side, first with honey (the wax being as cool as it will run thro' a linen strainer:) when you come near the bottom, pour it gently, till you see the drofs come, which strain into some other thing by itself, and when it is cold, either try it again, or (having pared away the bottom) keep it for use.

When the wax is in the pan or mould, if there is any froth remaining on the top, blow it together at one side, and skim it off gently with a wet spoon. This done, set not the cake abroad where it may cool too hastily, but put it in a warm house not far from the fire, and if it be a large cake, cover it warm, to keep the top from cooling till the inward heat be allayed, and so let it stand, not moving it till the cake be cold; if it stick, warming the vessel or mould a little will loofen it, so that it will presently slip out.

The properties of good wax are, that it is yellow, odoriferous or sweet, fat, fast or close, light, pure, being void of any other matter. 'Tis always a ready money commodity, especially English wax, which is much better than foreign, and commonly sells for about five or six pounds a hundred, it being of extraordinary use both in chirugery and physic, besides the use that is made of it for lights, the clearness and sweet-
nefs

nefs of which makes it preferred before all other forts.

As to its chirurgical or phyfical virtues, it is reckoned a mean between hot and cold, between dry and moift, being the ground of all fearcloths and falves; it mollifies the finews, ripens and refolveth ulcers; the quantity of a pea being fwallowed down by nurfes, diffolveth the milk curdled in the breaft.

Its oil is of excellent virtue to cure wounds, be they never fo large or deep (being before ftitched up) in ten or twelve days at the moft, and healeth fmall wounds in three or four days, by only anointing the wound therewith, and applying a cloth wet in the fame, ftayeth the fhedding of hair, either to the head or face, by anointing therewith. And it is good for inward difeafes, if you give one dram at a time in white wine, it will provoke urine, help ftitches and pains in the loins, the cold gout, and all other griefs coming of cold.

Honey is little inferior, either as to its benefit or ufefulnefs; it is of fubtil parts, and therefore doth pierce as oil, and eafily paffes the parts of the body; it hath a power to cleanfe, and therefore it openeth obftructions, and cleareth the breaft and lungs of thofe humours that fall from the head: it loofeneth the belly, purges the foulnefs of the body, and provoketh urine; it nourifheth very much, and breedeth good blood: it prolongeth life, and keepeth all thing uncorrupted, which it is put into; and therefore phyficians do temper therewith fuch medicines as they defign to keep long.

It is good for fuch as have eaten mufhroons, or drank poppies; it is an eminent ingredient in

L
the

the great antidotes of treacle and mithridate, and is good againſt pleuriſies, phthiſicks, and other diſeaſes of the lungs. But it is for any diſtemper much better to be taken clarified than raw, it being thereby made more nouriſhing, lighter of digeſtion, and leſs laxative, as alſo leſs ſharp. &c.

The whole Art and Method of breeding and rearing FOWLS, DUCKS, GEESE, TURKIES, PIGEONS and RABBITS.

FOWLS.

THE country yard cannot be ſaid to be compleat, till well ſtocked with fowl, whoſe advantage will appear to every one who keep them. The pooreſt villager may reap the ſame benefit from the products as the moſt ſubſtantial farmer, they being able to ſhift for themſelves the greateſt part of the year, by their feeding on inſects, corn, or any thing almoſt that is edible by any ſort of animal.

I ſhall not enter into a minute deſcription of the ſeveral ſorts of cocks and hens, only adviſe you to chuſe thoſe that are the beſt breeders, and the beſt layers ; the oldeſt being always reckoned the beſt ſitters, and the youngeſt the beſt layers ; but no ſort will be good for either, if they are kept too fat ; the beſt age to ſet a hen for chickens, is from two years old to five, and the beſt month to ſet them is February ; though any month between that and Michaelmas is
good.

good. A hen fits twenty days, whereas geese, ducks and turkeys, fit thirty. Obferve to let them have conftantly meat and drink near them while they fit, that they may not ftraggle from their eggs and chill them.

One cock will ferve ten hens.

If fowls are fet with buck or French-wheat, or with hemp feed, it is faid they will lay more eggs than ordinary ; and buck wheat, either whole or ground, made into pafte, which is the beft way, is a grain that will fattin fowls or hogs very fpeedily ; but the common food ufed is barley meal with milk or water, but wheat flour is better moiftened.

A good hen fhould not differ from the nature of the cock ; fhe fhould be working, vigilant and laborious, both for herfelf and her chickens ; in fize the biggeft and largeft are the beft, every proportion anfwerable to thofe of the cock, only inftead of a comb, fhe fhould have upon her crown, a high thick tuft of feathers.

She fhould have many and ftrong claws ; but it will be better if fhe has no hinder claws, becaufe they often break the eggs, and befides, fuch as have, do fometimes prove unnatural.

Crowing hens are neither good layers nor good breeders.

The elder hens are rather to be chofen for hatching than the younger, becaufe they are more conftant, and will fit out their time ; but if you chufe for laying, take the youngeft, becaufe they are lufty, and prone to generation ; but do not chofe a fat hen for either of thefe purpofes ; for if fhe be fet, fhe will forfake her neft ; the eggs fhe lay will be without fhells, and befides, fhe will grow flothful and lazy.

L 2

Thofe

Those eggs that are laid when the hens are a year and a half, or two years old, are the best; you must at that time give the hens plenty of victuals, and sometimes oats with funegreek to heat them, if you would have large eggs; for those that are fat commonly lay but small ones; mix some chalk with their food, or mix some bruised brick with their bran, moistened with a little water; and give them their belly full of half boiled barley, with vetch and millet.

Some hens have the ill faculty of eating their eggs; to prevent this, take out the white of an egg, and put moist plaister round about the yolk, and suffer it to grow hard; and when the hen attempts to eat it, and finds she cannot do it, she will soon give over breaking her eggs.

You may likewise pour a clear plaister upon the yolk of an egg, and let it harden, so that it may serve for a shell, and put it into the nest; or you may shape an egg of plaister, or chalk, and let that be for a nest egg.

Those hens that have spurs often break their eggs, and generally will not hatch them, and they will sometimes eat them; these must be scoured as well as those that scratch and crow like a cock; first, by plucking their great quills out of their wings, and by feeding them with millet, barley and paste, cut into bits, pounded acorns and bran, with pottage, or crumbs of wheat bread, steeped in water or barley meal.

Keep them in a close place, and at rest, and pull the feathers from their heads, thighs and rumps. If a hen be too fat, or has a looseness, she will lay windy eggs.

A

A hen will fit well from the fecond year of her laying, to the fifth : the beft time to fet a hen, that the chickens may be large and moft kindly, is in February, in the increafe of the moon, that fhe may difclofe the chickens in the increafe of the next new moon, being in March ; for one brood of this month's chickens is worth three of thefe of any other month.

Hens may fet from March to October, and have good chickens, but not after that time, for the Winter is a great enemy to their breed-ing.

A hen fits juft twenty-one days, and if you fet a hen upon the eggs of ducks, geefe or turkies, you muft fet them nine days before you put her own eggs to her, of which a hen will cover nine-teen ; but always fet an odd egg, what number foever you fet her with.

It will alfo be proper to marke one fide of the eggs, when you put them under the hen, and to obferve whether fhe turns them from the one fide to the other, and if fhe does not, then take an opportunity when fhe is from them to turn them yourfelf. But a hen that does not turn them her-felf is of the lefs value.

Take care that the eggs you fet a hen on be new, which may be known by their being heavy, full and clear, which may be known by looking through them in the fun ; nor do you choofe the largeft, for they have oftentimes two yolks, and tho' fome are of opinion that fuch will produce two chickens, it proves commonly a miftake, and if they do, they generally prove abortive and monftrous.

A hen muft not be taken off or difturbed from

L 3.   her

her neft, for that will make her utterly forfake it.

While fhe is fitting, you may place her meat and water near her, that her eggs may not cool, while fhe is gone to feek her food. If fhe fhould be abfent from her neft, ftir up the ftraw, and make it foft and handfome, and lay the eggs in the fame order fhe left them.

It is very neceffary to perfume her neft with rofemary or brimftone, and you maft take care that the cock does not come at the eggs and fet upon them, for he will endanger the breaking of them, and caufe the hen not to like her neft fo well as before.

When hens are laying, the old ftraw fhould be taken away, and frefh put in, that it may not breed fleas, or other vermin, which much incommodes them.

The maladies incident to hens are as follows ;

Setting hens are fometimes troubled with lice and vermin : for the cure, pound burnt cummin and ftapnifgar, of each equal quantities, and mix it with wine, and rub the hens with it, or wafh them with a decoction of wild lupines.

If hens are troubled with a loofenefs, mix a handful of barley meal, and as much wax, in fome wine, make it into a mafs, and give it them in the morning before they have any other meat, or elfe let them drink a decoction of apples or quinces.

Hens, by laying too many eggs, fometimes exhauft their ftrength and languifh : the fame likewife happens by hens fitting too long ; to remedy this, take the white of an egg, which you muft roaft till it looks as if it was burnt ;

burnt ; mix this with an equal quantity of dried raifins, alfo burnt, and give the hens this fafting.

Your hen-houfe muft be large and fpacious, with a pretty high roof and ftrong walls, to keep out both thieves and vermin ; let there be windows on the eaft fide, that they may enjoy the benefit of the rifing fun, ftrongly lathed and clofe fhut ; upwards and round about the infides of the walls upon the ground, fhould be made large pens of three foot high, for geefe, ducks and large fowls to fet in, and near unto the evings of the houfe fhould be long perches, reaching from one fide of the houfe to the other, on which fhould fet cocks, hens, capons and turkies, each on feveral perches, as they are dif-pofed.

At another fide of the houfe, at the darkeft part over the ground pens, fix hampers full of ftraw for nefts, in which hens fhould lay their eggs ; but when they fit to hatch chickens, then let them fit on the ground, otherwife it will be dangerous.

Alfo let there be pins ftuck in the walls, that the poultry may climb to their pearches with the greater eafe.

The floor muft not be paved, but made of earth fmooth and eafy. Let the fmaller fowl have a hole made at one end of the houfe, to go in and come out at when they pleafe, or elfe they will feek out roofts in other places ; but of larger fowl, you may open the door morning and evening.

It would be the better if this hen-houfe was fituated near fome kitchen, brew-houfe, bakehoufe, or kiln, where it may have the

heat

heat of the fire, and be perfumed with fmoak, which is to pullets both delightful and wholfome.

As foon as your chickens are hatched, if any be weaker than the reft, wrap them in wool, and let them have the heat of the fire ; it will alfo be very good to·perfume them with rofemary ; the firft hatched chickens may be kept in a fieve till the reft are difclofed, for they will not eat for two days ; fome fhells being harder than others, they will require fo much more time in opening ; but unlefs the chickens are weak, or then unkind, it will not be amifs to let them continue under her, for fhe will nourifh them kindly.

When they are two days old, give them very fmall oatmeal, fome dry, and fome fteeped in milk, or elfe crumbs of fine white bread ; and when they have gained ftrength, curds, cheefe parings, white bread, crufts foaked in drink or milk, barley meal, or wheaten bread fcalded, or the like foft meat, that is fmall and will be eafily digefted.

It is neceffary to keep them in the houfe for a fortnight, and not fuffer them to go abroad with the hen to worm. Green chives chopped among their meat is very good, and will preferve them from the rye or other difeafes in the head, and never let them want clear water, for puddle water will be apt to give them the pip.

Nor muft you let them feed upon tares, darnel, or cockle, for thefe are very dangerous to young ones, nor let them go into gardens·till they are fix weeks old.

If you would have them crammed, coop them up when the dam has forfaken them, and cram
them

them with dough made of wheaten meal and milk, which dip in milk, and thuft down their throats, but let them not be to big, left they choak them ; they will be fat in a fortnight.

To diftinguifh whether a chicken is good or not. After a chicken is killed it will be ftiff and white, and firm in the vent, if new killed ; but tender, and green in the vent, if ftale.

If you rub your finger on the breaft of a fcalded chicken, if it be new killed it will feel rough ; but, if ftale, flippery and flimy.

A crammed chicken, if it be fat, will have a fat rump, and a fat vein upon the fide of the breaft of her, like a pullet.

In order to fatten chickens, you muft put them into coops, and feed them with barley meal ; put likewife a fmall quantity of brick-duft into their water, which they ought never to be without : this laft will give them an appetite to their meat, and fatten them very foon ; for, in this cafe it muft be confidered, that all fowls and birds have two ftomachs, as they may be called, the one is their crop, that foftens their food, and the other the gizzard, that macerates the food, in the laft we always find fmall ftones and fharp fand, which help to do that office, and without them, or fomething of that kind, a fowl will be wanting of its appetite to eat ; for the gizzard cannot mafticate, or, as it may be faid, grind the food faft enough to difcharge it from the crop, without fuch fand or ftones ; and in this cafe the brick-duft is affifting.

DUCKS.

D U C K S.

DUCKS are very neceſſary for the huſbandman's yard, in that they require no charge in keeping ; they live on loſt corn, worms, ſnails, &c. for which reaſon they are very good for gardens. Once in a year they are very great layers of eggs, eſpecially a ſort of duck that turns up the bill more than the common kind ; and when they ſit they need little attendance, except to let them have a little barley or offal corn and water near them, that they may not ſtraggle far from their neſt to chill their eggs.

In general it is found more profitable to ſet a hen upon the duck eggs, than any kind of duck whatever, becauſe the old one leads them when hatch'd, too ſoon to the water, where, if the weather be chill, ſome will be loſt. They follow the hen a good while upon the land, and ſo get hardy before they venture to the water.

About thirteen eggs is the proper number to let a duck ſit upon ; the hen will cover as many of theſe as of her own, and will bring them up well ; ſo that every way ſhe is more profitable for that purpoſe.

When the ducklings are hatch'd they require no care, if the weather be tolerably good ; but if they happen to be produced in a very rainy ſeaſon, it right to take them under cover a little, eſpecially in the night ; for, though the duck naturally loves water, it requires the affiſtance of its feathers, and, till they are grown, is eaſily hurt by the wet.

The fattening of ducks at any age is very
eaſy,

eafy, and whether it be the duckling, or the grown duck, the method to be ufed is exactly the fame. They are to be put into a quiet dark place, and kept in a pen, where they are to have plenty of corn and water ; any kind of corn will do, and with this fingle direction, they will fatten themfelves extremely well in fifteen or tweny days ; and will bring a price that very well repays their feeding.

G E E S E.

THE benefits arifing from geefe are, for food, their feathers, and their greafe. They will live upon commons, or any fort of pafture, and need little care and attendance ; only they fhould have plenty of water. The largeft geefe are reckoned the beft, but there is a fort of Spanifh geefe that are much better layers and breeders that the Englifh, efpecially if their eggs, are hatched under an Englifh goofe. Geefe lay in the Spring, the earlier the better, becaufe of their price, and of their having a fecond brood. They commonly lay twelve or fixteen eggs each. You may know when they will lay, by their carrying of ftraw in their mouths, and when they will fit, by their continuing on their neft, after they have laid. A goofe fits thirty days ; but if the weather be fair and warm, fhe will hatch three or four days fooner. After the goflins are hatched, fome keep them in the houfe ten or twelve days, and feed them with curds, barley meal, bran, &c. After they have got fome ftrength, let them out

three

three or four hours in a day, and take them in again, till they are big enough to defend themselves from vermin. One gander will serve five geese.

If you would fat green geese, you must shut them up when they are about a month old, and they will be fat in about a month more. Be sure to let them have always by them in a small rack some fine hay, which will much hasten their fatting. But for fatting of older geese, it is commonly done when they are about six months old, in or after harvest, when they have been in the stubble fields, from which food some kill them, which is a good way; but those who have a mind to have them very fat, shut them up for a fortnight or three weeks, and feed them with oats, splitted beans, barley meal, or ground malt mixed with milk, the best thing to fatten them with being malt mixed with beer. But in fatting of all water fowl you may observe, that they usually sit with their bills on their rumps, where they suck out most of their moisture and fatness, at a small bunch of feathers, which you will find standing upright on their rumps, and always moist, with which they trim their feathers, which makes them oily and slippery more than other fowls feathers are, that the water may slip off them, which, if cut away close, will make them fat in less time, and with less meat than otherwise. Geese will likewise feed on and fatten well with carrots, cut small, and given them; or if you give them rye before or about Midsummer, it will strengthen them, and keep
them

them in health, that being commonly their fickly time.

In fome countries they fhear the geefe for their
feathers, and fome pull them twice a year ; but
this latter way is more injurious to them, and
therefore it is better ftaying till moulting-time,
and till their death, for their feathers.

T U R K I E S.

TURKIES are fowls that profper very
well in open countries, where there is
not much fhelter to harbour vermin to deftroy
them ; for they are naturally inclined to ram-
ble. The hens likewife are fo negligent of
their young, that whilft they have one to follow
them, they never take any care of the reft ;
and therefore there muft be a great deal of care
taken of them while they are young, to watch
them, and to keep them warm, they being a
bird that cannot bear the cold. But fome,
where they have a conveniency of a fmall cover near the houfe, let them take their liberty,
and feek their own nefts ; but it is only in fome
particular places that they do well with fuch
management. I knew a gentleman that had a
hen turkey of the wild kind from Virginia, of
which, and an Englifh cock, he raifed a very
fine breed, that bred wild in the fields, and
always became tame when grown up ; they
were a very hardy breed, and much larger than
ours, and reared their young ones without any
care or trouble, breeding much better than our
Englifh.

If you keep them with corn, they are very
great feeders, and will devour a great deal ;

M   but

but if left to their liberty when grown up, they will get their own living, without either trouble or charges, by feeding on herbs, feeds, &c.

Turkies being very apt to ftraggle, will often be laying their eggs in fecret places, and therefore the common fort of them muft be often watched, and made to lay at home. They begin to lay in March, and will fit in April. Eleven or thirteen eggs are the moft they fhould fit on. They hatch in between twenty-five and thirty days; and when they have hatched their brood, you muft be careful to keep the young ones warm; for the leaft cold kills them. Feed them either with curds, or green frefh cheefe cut in fmall pieces. Let their drink be new milk, or milk and water. Some give them oatmeal and milk boiled thick together, into which they put wormwood chopped fmall, and fometimes eggs boiled hard, and cut in little pieces. You muft feed them often, for the hen will not take much care of them, and when they have got fome ftrength, feed them abroad in a clofe walled place, where they cannot ftray; you muft not let them out till the dew is off the grafs, taking care to have them in again before night, becaufe the dew is very prejudicial to them.

For the fatting of turkies, fodden barley is very excellent, or fodden oats for the firft fortnight, and for another fortnight cram them as you do capons. They are only to be crammed in a morning, which muft be given to them warm, and let out all day, being fometimes fed with corn while out; becaufe, being a fullen bird, they are apt elfe not to fat fo kindly.

Their

Their eggs are reckoned very wholfome, and a great reftorer of nature.

PIGEONS.

WE come now to treat of a fowl fmaller in its fize than any of the before-mentioned kinds, but fuperior to many of them in value ; the pigeon. The management of this bird is alfo different in a great meafure from that of the others, fo that it naturally falls under confideration fingly.

The proper pigeon for the dovecoat, which is the only kind the farmer is to regard, is able, the greateft part of the year, to provide for itfelf ; and when it requires his affiftance, the food is not of any dear kind. Befide the common advantages of the breed, there is that great article their dung, which is of fuch fervice for manure, that it muft be the intereft of every farmer to provide it for his own ufe, efpecially as that is to be done with great eafe, and the fame method that affords it will yield him alfo many other advantages.

There are two forts of pigeons, the tame, and dovecoat. The tame pigeon is valued not only for its beauty, but for the largenefs of its body ; the common pigeon, which is the kind ufually kept in dovecoats, and thence called the dovecoat pigeon, is fmaller, and lefs beautiful.

The tame kind generally have but two young ones at a brood ; but they make fome amends for the fmallnefs of the number by the frequency of their hatching ; for, if well fed and tended, they will have young ones every month.

M 2　　　　　　　For

For the choice of thefe the beauty is generally moft regarded; but there fhould be care taken to pair them well, and this is the more worth while, becaufe they are not apt to feperate afterwards.

They muft be kept clean, for they diflike dirt, though they make a great deal of it. But their food is fo dear, that few, but thofe who know very well how to manage them, care to meddle with them. Their beft food is tares or white peas, and they fhould have befide this fome gravel and clean water fcattered about, at all times: a great deal of care muft be taken to preferve them from vermin, and their eggs from the ftarlings and other birds, which always haunt the places where they are kept, and will fuck them.

In order to the perfect thriving of thefe pigeons, it will be proper, befide their food, gravel, and water, always to let there be falt, clay, or fome other thing with fea falt in it, for them to peck at their pleafure.

We have faid thus much with refpect to the management of the tame pigeon, for the information of fuch as may chufe to breed them, and have not had opportunities of feeing it done; and it will be proper to add here, that although the expence and trouble they occafion, be more than is worth the hufbandman's while in general to give himfelf, yet there is this advantage, that their dung is richer than that of the common pigeon as a manure, which is owing to their food.

We come now to the confideration and management of the common or dovecoat pigeon,
which

which is a subject that demands, and deserves the husbandman's utmost regard.

There are some counties where the husband-men sow great quantities of horse-beans and grey peas, and in these particularly the pigeons feed to a great advantage. These sort of pulse are sowed earlier than other kinds of grain ; and their early feeding upon them makes them healthful and strong at those times, and is an occasion of their breeding earlier than they do elsewhere, which is a consideration of great importance.

The common blue pigeon is properly the dovecoat breed ; and it has the advantage of many other kinds, in that it is hardier, and will live in the worst Winters.

If it be too small for the farmer's purpose, he may mend the breed by putting in a few tame pigeons of the most common kind, and the least conspicuous in their colours, that the rest may the better take to them by finding them more like themselves ; this, however, is to be done with caution, and never without a due consideration ; for tho' the bigness of a pigeon's body is a plain advantage, yet it is very well known in the kinds in general, that the smallest bodied are the best breeders.

The ringdove has been by some introduced into the dovecoat, by setting the eggs under a common pigeon ; they will in this case live, and take their chance among the pigeons ; and they have two over them, the one in their largeness, and the other in their hardness ; for they will endure any weather, and live upon any food.

The

The hufbandman fhould have a very careful eye upon the proportion of the fexes among his pigeons ; for there is nothing fo hurtful as the having too many cocks, efpecially if they keep the larger, or tame kind. It is his bufinefs to keep his dovecoat well flocked ; and moft people who keep them make their confciences eafy about deluding away thofe belonging to their neighbours ; but this abundance of cocks thins the dovecoat, for they grow quarrelfome, and will beat others away, till by degrees a very thriving dovecoat fhall be, by this fingle miftake, reduced to a poor condition.

A very cheap and eafy way of making a dovecoat, is to build the wall with clay, mixed with ftraw ; they may be made four feet or more in thicknefs, and while they are wet it is eafy to cut holes in them with a chiffel or other inftrument.

Of whatever materials the coat be erected, it fhould be white-wafhed frequently on the outfide. The pigeon, as has been faid already, is a cleanly bird : it loves the appearance of neatnefs ; and befide the white colour renders the building more confpicuous.

As to the food of pigeons, befide the peas and tares already mentioned, barley is very proper, heartening them very much, and making them lay ; and for the fame purpofe buckwheat alfo is an excellent as well as cheap food.

For the greateft part of the year, however, the common pigeons in a dovecoat take care of themfelves, and need no food from their keeper. There are only two feafons at which it is neceffary or proper to feed them. One of thefe times is the depth of Winter, when the ground

is

is covered with snow, or hardened so by frost, that nothing is to be got; and the other is, the middle or latter end of June.

The reason of feeding them in the first of these seasons is obvious; the latter, the farmers when they speak of this fowl call benting time. There is a grass called bent grass, the seed of which is ripe about this season, and is the only food of that kind the pigeons can easily get, the peas being not yet ripe. This is a very poor food, and the pigeons at this season usually have many young broods; so that they will be starved if they are left to this poor diet; and the farmer will always find his account in giving them food at this season, as well as the other. This lasts however but a small time; and the other is only necessary at the severest days of winter; so that the pigeon is at the utmost, but a small expence, and that for a very short time.

Beside the food, the breeder of tame pigeons has been advised to give them a lump of salted clay, and the same indulgence must be shewn to these. But as they are more numerous, there is to be a larger allowance. A large heap of clay should be laid near the dovecoat, and the brine of the family continually beaten in among it. Another way is to make a kind of mortar with lime, sand, clay and salt, which they will peck with great satisfaction. The pigeons themselves have pointed out this method, for they are continually pecking at the joints of walls to get out the mortar. When it is thus made on purpose for them, it is best to make it thin, and keep it so by often beating it up with brine.

In

In fome places they lay what is called a falt cat near the dovecoat. This is a large lump of falt made for the purpofe at the falt pans ; and is the method commonly taken where there are works in the neighbourhood, but the way of ufing falt in a mixture with clay is better.

What I have found by experience to anfwer beft of all is this. A heap of loam is to be laid near the dovecoat, and beat up to a kind of pap with brine or water ; into this is to be thrown a large quantity of bay falt, and a little faltpetre, and with it a fhovel full or two of large coarfe fand. When brine is ufed to beat up the loam, lefs falt is to be ufed ; and when water, there muft be the more of it in proportion. And in the fame manner, if the loam contain a great deal of fand, the lefs is to be added to it. And if it contain lefs, the more is to be given. Where loam is not to be had, clay will do ; but then a much larger quantity of fand muft be put in ; and the beft fand for this purpofe is large coarfe fea fand, which is already impregnated with falt water ; or that which is got in fcreening of gravel.

It is a very fingular thing that the pigeon loves falt in this manner, and its fondnefs for faltpetre, which is very great, is not fo well known ; tho' this might have been difcovered by obferving the liking this bird has to the mortar in old walls, which contains a falt very nearly allied to the common faltpetre.

Salt is not only ufeful in this manner to pleafe the pigeons, when they are in health, but nothing recovers them fo readily from ficknefs. A
mix-

mixture of bay falt and cummin feed, being with them a univerfal remedy.

A great many contrivances have been publifhed, and many more are handed about among the country people as great fecrets, for making the pigeons love their habitation, and tempting fuch ftragglers from their neighbours as chance to come to the coat to fettle in it. Some have advifed the ufe of afafœtida, and others of cummin feed before mentioned for this purpofe ; but the beft method of all others is to keep up conftantly fuch a heap of falted loam as I have before defcribed ; this is what they love, and they will therefore ftay where they can have it in plenty. This contrivance, with the addition of keeping the dovecoat neat and clean, and not fuffering them to be difturbed in it, will be fure to keep the ftock in good number, and too likely to increafe it at the expence of the neighbours.

The profit of pigeons is very confiderable, and very certain, for they breed faft, and there is a conftant demand for them. Near great towns it may be worth while to keep fome of the large tame kind ; becaufe, although they cannot be fed but at a large expence, yet their young come fo early, and are fo fat and fine, that they command a price, which very well returns it. But in the country the common pigeon is the proper kind ; for though the price that the birds fetch is not nearly fo great, their number and fmall expence of keeping, very well make amends.

I have fpoken often to the farmers to recommend their fetting up dovecoats, but have found it in nothing fo difficult to make them liften to me. While they have bought pigeons dung at

a

a great price, and fetched it from a great diſtance, they have ſtill been backward to think of keep-ing pigeons themſelves for their own ſupply. There is a ſuperſtition among them, that it is un-lucky to ſet up a new dovecoat ; this has come down from father to ſon, and they perſuade them-ſelves it would certainly be followed by death in the family. Nothing can be ſo ridiculous, or ſo weak, as ſuch a ſuppoſition : but there never was an old woman's tale ſo deeply rooted.

R A B B E T S.

RABBETS are very profitable creatures for their great increaſe, and their being kept on dry barren ſand, or gravel that will maintain nothing elſe, which the dryer it is the better for them ; this ſort of lands they muſt improve by their dung for rye. Beſides which many make great profit of them, by keeping of them in hutches near great towns, and ſome keep great quantities of them in pits to catch when they want them, they being a very diſh upon any oc-caſion ; but they muſt be in a very dry warm ſoil ; if they are any thing deep ; they will be elſe too cold, or too damp for them. I ſhould rather prefer for them a large barn made very tight after the way of making of barns for preſerving corn in, to keep vermin out of ; for the tame rabbets muſt lie dry and warm, or elſe they will not breed in Winter. which is the chief time of their pro-fit, and what makes them preferred before the wild ones, they are much better meat, if they have their liberty, eſpecially the white ſhock Turkey rabbet.

A

A rabbet begins to breed at a year old, will kindle at leaft five times a year, if it litters in March ; it carries its young in its belly for thirty days, and as foon as the doe has kindled, they are to be taken from her at about fix weeks old, then put the doe to buck ; or you may put her to buck when her young are about a month old.

The males are of a cruel difpofition, and frequently kill the young ones, if they can come at them ; and therefore the females, after they have kindled, hide them, and clofe up the holes in fuch a manner that the buck cannot find them.

The huts in which tame rabbets are to be kept, fhould be about two feet fquare, and a foot high, and that fhould be divided into four partitions or fquares, one quarter with an open grate or wire window, through which the rabbets may feed, and a lefs apartment with an out light, in which the doe may kindle or kennel, and under this window fhould be a box or trough, in which may be put her meat ; and thus may be made hutch over hutch, three or four ftories high, keeping bucks and does a part from one another.

In the chufing tame rich rabbets, it is more material to regard the richnefs of them, than their fhapes ; but let the bucks be as large as you can get them ; and thofe coats are efteemed the richeft, that have the equalleft mixture of black and white hair together, but fo that the black may rather fhadow than the white ; a black coat, with a few filver hairs, being much richer than a white coat with a few black ones.

The

The increafe is more in the tame than the wild, the former bringing forth oftener than the latter.

The beft food for them is the fweeteft, fhorteft, and beft hay that can be got. This hay muft be put to them in little cloven fticks, that they may with eafe reach and pull it out of the fame, fo as not to fcatter or wafte but as little as may be ; and fweet oats and water fhould be put for them in the troughs under the boxes, and this fhould be their ordinary and conftant food, all other being to be ufed phyficially, giving it them two or three times in a fortnight, to cool their bodies, fuch as mal-lows, clover-grafs, four docks, blade of corn, cabbage or colewort leaves, and the like, all which do both cool and nourifh them greatly ; but you fhould but feldom give them fweet grains, becaufe nothing brings them to the rot more.

If they have any grafs cut for them, you muft be very careful that there be no weeds nor hem-lock amongft it ; for tho' they will eat it very greedily, it is prefent poifon, killing them fud-denly.

In general, the advantage of their dry meat is, that it prevents difeafes ; and thofe who commonly keep them upon frefh and moift food, as many do, giving them carrots and other eat-able roots among it, would do well to change it for dry meat in wet weather : for moift food is the great caufe of thefe creatures having the rot, and they are moft of all fubject to this in damp feafons.

Their hutches muft alfo be kept fweet and clean, for the fcent of their pifs and dung is fo ftrong, that it will be a very great annoy-ance

ance both to themfelves, and thofe that look after them.

As to the wild rabbets, there is properly but one breed of them, and all the direction that is needful in the choice is, that fuch as are taken to begin a ftock, be large, and big bodied, with a good deep fur, that hangs faft upon their backs, and with ftout limbs. The hufbandman who has watle ground in his hands, that is fenced well, and not with live hedges, fhould never omit this part of his ftock, for the worft of his ground will do, and the advantage he receives from them will be very great.

A fmall number is fufficient to be firft turned in, for of all creatures ufeful to mankind, they are the greateft breeders.

Experience fhews that the wild rabbet fucceeds better in fome places than others ; the young growing up much quicker, and the flefh being finer, and better tafted. The reafon of this is to be fearched in the foil and the produce, and this may teach the hufbandman on which of fuch grounds as feem proper, it will be moft to his benefit to breed them.

In general, the fhorter and fcantier the grafs, the better is the tafte of the rabbet ; the drier the ground the better they fucceed ; where there is much water they never are well flavoured.

Of all creatures water is the leaft neceffary to the rabbet, for we fee the tame ones will live very well altogether without it, on moift food. Where the foil is drieft, the air fineft, and the water that there is in the way is running and clear, there the rabbets may reafonably be expected to fucceed beft.

N   As

As I have obferved that the common wild rabbet will very freely be kept tame, fo it has been found, many years fince, that thofe which we ufually underftand as tame rabbets, will live very well wild, efpecially the hardier kinds. This is a confideration of fome confequence, becaufe there is one of the tame kind that is, in every refpect, better than the common wild one. This is that which is known by the name of the filver haired rabbet. It will live and thrive as well wild as the common fort, and it is always better tafted, and fair to the eye, fo that it brings a larger price. The fkin alfo is of much more value, and the demand for it among the furriers is conftant and certain.

For thefe reafons it is, in many cafes, advifeable to breed this fort wild inftead of the other ; for though it often is fo, it is not always. This, though as hardy as the other, requires a better fupply of food, and is poor, and of little value, upon thofe barren and heathy lands, on which the common wild rabbet fucceeds very well.

The proper place for this kind is a park, where they may run at liberty among the deer, and other cattle, and where there is good grafs, though not rank, upon the ground ; the other is the proper kind for the moft miferable and poor lands.

Plain

---

*Plain Inſtructions for deſtroying Vermin,
particularly ſuch as infeſt Houſes,
Gardens, Dairies, Barns, Bees, Poultry, &c.*

For *deſtroying of* B U G S.

TAKE a quantity of unſlacked lime, put it
into a quart of water, and let it ſtand three
or four days, then pour off the water, and add
a quantity of common ſalt, the ſtronger both of
lime and ſalt the better ; waſh the ſides of the
wall and bedſtead with this liquor two or three
times a week, and it will kill them. Or,

Take a handful of wormwood and white hellebore, boil them in urine till it is half waſted,
and waſh the joints of your bedſtead with it.

The gall of an ox mixed with vinegar, or the
dregs of oil and ox gall mixed ; rub the joints
and cracks of the bedſtead with it, and it will
kill them. Or,

Old oil and brimſtone powdered and mixed together, then anoint the bedſtead with it. Or,

Boil gule and vinegar together, then rub the
bedſtead with, and it will kill them. Or,

Take a handful of rue and wormwood, and
mix them with common oil, and as much water
as will cover the rue and wormwood ; let it boil
till the water is all boiled away, then ſtrain out
the oil from the herbs, and mingle with ſheep's ſuet

as

as much as the oil ; then anoint the bedstead with it, and it is an infallible remedy. Or,

Take the rind of green walnuts bruised, and steeped in water three or four days, then wash the room and bedstead with it often. Or,

Get a trap about a yard and a half long, or more, if your bed is broad, and about half a yard in depth ; put it at the head of your bed, to the bottom of the pillow, and in the morning they will creep into it ; take it into your yard, knock it, and they will drop out, so you may kill them. They are made of wickers by basket-makers. To conclude ;

Let your rooms be kept clean, set open the windows when you rise, and lay your bed-cloaths open four or five hours, and it is the only way to prevent your having bugs.

For *destroying* F L E A S.

TAKE lavender and wormwood, and boil them in vinegar, well, and sprinkle your blankets with it, or savory laid in your chamber will kill them.

Take wormwood well dried, and put it in a bag with holes in it, so place it under your bed ; or fleawort, laid under and about your beds, kills them ; or take wormwoood, nut-leaves, lavender, eye-avernon, and green coriander, put them under the bed or pillow, and the fleas will die. Or,

Take unslacked lime, and strew in your chambers. Penny-royal wrapt up in a cloth, and laid in your bed, drives fleas away : lay fresh once a week.

Or,

Or foup-lees and onions boiled together, and fprinkle in the room, kills them.

Or, marfh-fleabane fpread in your room, or burnt, will drive them away. Elder-leaves gathered, with dew on them, and laid in a chamber, will gather all the fleas thereinto, which you may kill, or throw out of the window.

Or, take an earthren difh or platter, fmear it all round with bulls fat, and it will gather the fleas to it; or fmear it with goat's blood, and they'll come into it ; or the blood of an ox mixed with foot, and rubbed on the infide of the difh, will make them come into it in a day or two.

Or, rub a fmall piece of board over with hog's greafe, and all the fleas will gather to it in the middle of the room.

Or, take the blood of a badger, fmear a trencher over with it, and it will gather all the fleas to it, and kill them : or, coloquintida, oil, and wormwood, boiled in water, and fprinkled about the room, kills them.

Or, take fouthernwood, rue, wormwood, favory, walnut-leaves, lavender fleafed . lay all thofe, or fome of them, under the blankets ; or elfe boil them in vinegar and fea-onions, and with that befprinkle the bed.

To deftroy RATS and MICE.

TAKE ratfbane, powder it, and mix it with frefh butter, or make it into a pafte with barley, or wheat meal and honey, and lay it on trenchers or boards where they come ; they will eat it, and it makes them drink till they burft. It is a ftrong poifon, therefore be very careful in :

N 3.   ufing

uſing it, and waſh your hands after it. Or unſlacked lime and oatmeal mixed, and laid on
boards where they come, kill them.

Or, mix powdered glaſs and oatmeal with
freſh butter, and lay it where they come ; or
filings of iron, mixed with oatmeal, or dough,
of oatmeal flour, will anſwer the ſame purpoſe.

Or, take wheat or barley flour, mix honey or
metheglin with it, and make it into a ſtiff paſte ;
if you mix a little white hellebore powdered with
it, it is better. Hemlock ſeed thrown into their
holes kills them.

To kill Field Rats.

The fields are generally bare in the dog days,
then is your time to find out their holes or neſts,
which are little and round, like an augur hole ;
you muſt put hemlock ſeed therein, or hellebore
mixed with barley : they will eat it greedily,
which kills them.

To preſerve Artichoaks from Rats or Mice.

They are great lovers of artichoaks, and will
come to them in troops ; to prevent this, wrap
wool about their roots, and they will be gone.
Or, hog's dung, or fig-tree aſhes laid about them,
will drive them away.

To deſtroy MOLES.

TAKE a head or two of garlick, onion, or
leek, and put it into their holes, and they
will

will run out as if frighted, and you may with a fpear or dog take them.

Or, pounded hellebore, white or black, with wheat flour, the white of an egg, milk and fweet wine or metheglin, make it into pafte, and put pellets as big as a fmall nut into their holes, they eat it with pleafure, and it will kill them.

In places you would not dig nor break much, the fuming their holes with brimftone, garlick, or other unfavoury things, drive them away ; and if you put a dead mole into a common haunt it will make them abfolutely forfake it.

Or, take a mole fpear or ftaff, and where you fee them caft, go lightly ; but not on the fide betwixt them and the wind, left they perceive you ; and at the firft or fecond putting up of the earth, ftrike them with your mole ftaff down-right, and mark which way the earth falls moft : if fhe cafts toward the left hand, ftrike fomewhat on the right hand, and fo on the contrary to the cafting up of the plain ground, ftrike down, and there let it remain : then take out the tongue in the ftaff, and with the fpattle or flat edge dig round about your grain to the end thereof, to fee if you have killed her ; and if you have miffed her, leave open the hole, and ftep afide a little, and perhaps fhe will come to ftop the hole again, for they love but very little air, and then ftrike again ; but if you mifs her, pour into her hole two gallons of water, and that will make her come out for fear of drowning ; mind them going out of a morning to feed, or coming home when fed, and you may take a great many.

Or, it is faid, that in engendering time, if

you

you lead or draw a bitch mole in a ſtring a-
long the ground, the buck will trace her, and ſo
you may catch them in a pot ſet in the gronnd.

To deſtroy Weaſles.

Take ſal-ammoniac, pound it, and with wheat
flour and honey make it into a paſte, with the
white of an egg, lay it in pellets where they
come, and it will kill them.

To prevent their ſucking hens eggs, lay rue
about the rooſt, and they will not come near
them.

To deſtroy Caterpillars.

Te prevent their numerous increaſe on trees,
gather them off in Winter, taking the prickers
away that cleave to the branches, and burn
them.

Or, anoint the bottom of the tree round a-
bout with tar, then get many piſmires and put
them in a bag; hang them ſo that they may
touch the bottom of the tree; the piſmires not
being able to get down for the tar, will devour
the caterpillars for want of food.

Or, when they are upon cabbage or coleworts,
take ſome ſalt water, and water them with it,
and it will kill them.

Or, ſhake them off the plants betimes in a
morning, for while they are touched with the
cold of the night, they eaſily drop off.

To deſtroy Green Bugs that hurt plants and roſe-trees.

Sprinkle the places where they fix with ſtrong
vinegar

vinegar mixed with the juice of henbane; or, fome water the plants haunted by them with the cold decoction of muftard and laurel feed in water; fome quafh them with their fingers, which is a good way; or fiee-bane boiled in water, and fprinkled, will kill them.

To deftroy Vine-Fretters.

Stick a rod half a foot high in the ground, with mugs or cups turned over the top of it, and you will find that they creep under them for fhelter, fo you may eafily kill them.

Or, put eight or nine crabs in an earthen pot with water, and let them ftand eight days in the open air, then take off this water, and fprinkle your plants in their infancy, repeat this once in eight days, and it will kill moft fort of vermin.

To deftroy Frogs.

Take a fheep, ox, or goat's gaul, and bruife it by the water fide; the frogs will gather to it, and it will kill them.

To prevent their croaking, fet a candle and lanthorn upon the fide of the water or river, that waters your garden.

Toads will not come near your garden, if you plant fage and rue round about it.

To drive Snakes and Adders from the Garden.

Plant wormwood in various parts of it, and they will not come near it.

Or, fmoak the places with hartfhorn, or lily
roots

roots, burnt in a fire-pan, and they will fly from
the place.

Or, old fhoes burnt, or other ftinking ftuff will
drive them away ; or afh-tree boughs, while green
leaves are on them, laid about your ground will
have the fame effect.

Or, take a handful of onions, and ten river
crab fifh, beat them well together, and lay it in
the place where they come, and you may kill
many of them together.

To keep Earwigs and Pifmires from Flowers.

Take glue boiled in linfeed oil, and lay this
round a tub four inches broad, and if they go to
climb up, they will ftick in it : but if any fhould
get up, lay on the top of the flowerfticks, paper
caps, lobfters claws, with fome wool or tow in
them, and in the morning you will find many in
them.

Or, make a box with cards or pafteboard, prick
it full of holes with a bodkin, and put in them
powder of Arfenick and honey mixed together :
having the boxes on the trees, and it will kill
them. You muft be careful the holes are not
made too large, left the bees get in, and be poi-
foned.

. Or, hang a glafs bottle in a tree, with a little
honey in it, or other fweet liquor, and it will
bring the ants into it, which you muft fhop and
wafh, and place there again.

To deftroy Snails.

Set tiles, bricks or boards, hollow againft the
walls, pales. &c. and they will creep under
them

them for shelter. About Michaelmas they get to such places for security the whole Winter, except you prevent it by destroying them in December, which is the easiest, best and surest way to destroy them.

Or, look for them by break of day, or after rain, then they come out of the earth to feed, and are easily killed.

Also observe, not to pluck that fruit they have begun with, but les it alone, for they will end that before they begin another.

To prevent Flies *teazing Cattle.*

Boil bay-berries in oil, and anoint them with it, and they will never sit on cattle ; or, wet the hair of horses with the juice of the leaves of gourd at Midsummer, and they will not molest them. If cattle are anointed with the juice of aresemart, flies will not come near them, tho' it is the heat of Summer.

To destroy Earwigs.

Place hoofs, horns, crabs, or lobsters claws on branches of trees, and they will creep into them ; early in the morning take them gently off and shake them into a tub of water, of on the ground, and tread on them.

To destroy Wasps *and* Hornets *that detriment Bees.*

In Spring or Summer, before they are increased, destroy the old ones, for a few increase to a multitude.

Or,

Or, fcald them, if in the thatch or hollow tree, or fmoak them with any ftinking combuftible matter.

Or, put cyder, verjuice, or four drink, in a fhort necked phial, and you may catch many in it. Alfo lay fweet apples, beafts intrails, or other fifh, or treacle in an earthen difh, and a little water mixed with it, or any thing they love, and they will flock about it, that you may kill many at once.

Or, put pieces of lighted brimftnne-rags into the wafps holes, where the neft lies, and then fill it up with earth.

Swallows are great enemies to bees ; therefore take care to deftroy their nefts wherever you find them.

To deftroy Gnats.

Shut your windows clofe in Summer towards, the evening, and fmoak your rooms with brimftone, and burn ftraw in them, and they will fly into the flame, or be choaked.

Or, the fmoak of burnt fern will drive away gnats, ferpents, and other venemous creatures.

Or, afh-leaves hung up in a room attracts them, that they are lefs troublefome ; alfo, balls made of new horfe-dung, and laid in a room, will do the fame ; by this means you may overwhelm them with a bafon, and keep them there.

To deftroy Worms.

Water, wherein the leaves and feeds of hemp

are

are fodden, fprinkled on earth, will bring them out.

Or, fea water fprinkled on the ground, kills th m. Some fay, foot ftrewed on the ground, kills them. Others commend chalk and lime, ftrewed on the ground.

Take a quantity of green walnut hufks, and rub them on a brick or tile, holding them at the bottom of a pail of water till the water is become bitter, which fprinkled on the ground, will bring the worms out in a quarter of an hour.

Or, water your garden with the brine of falt meat, and it kills them ; or, with a ftrong lixivium made of afhes : or, lay afhes or lime about any plant, and neither fnails nor worms will come near it ; as the moifture weakens, you may renew it. Some fmoak their holes with ox or cow dung ; or the mother of oil fprinkled on their holes kills them.

Or, after rain or fun-fet gather them when they come out of their dens, and kill them.

Or, fet the leaves and feeds of hemp in water, and fprinkle it on the earth, brings forth worms.

Or, take a poker, with two prongs is beft, and ftick it in the ground, and fhake it well, brings out worms ; morning and evening is the beft time.

To deftroy Worms in Apple-trees.

Lay a fea onion about the trees, to preferve them from worms ; if they come naturally, bull's gall, or hogs dung mingled with man's urine, and poured to the roots, deftroys them ; but if they are hard to deftroy, the bark muft be digged into with a brafs pin, or fuch like tool, and

O

tended

tended till the point take upon the worms, and drives them from the place; but where there is a place ulcerated, stop it with ox dung: an apple tree plant, the root being anointed with bull's gaul, they and their fruit will be free from worms.

To prevent Worms eating Chests of Drawers, or Wood.

Rub them with linseed oil ; or rub them with wormwood, rue, or other bitter herbs, preserves them, and all wooden houshold stuff, that is rubbed with the lees of linseed oil, and polished, will look pleasant.

To destroy Polecats.

If you can conveniently have a channel about your pigeon house, it will preserve them and all other fowl, for no beast of prey will take the water.

Or, some make a dead fall to take them, which is made of a square piece of wood, weighing 40 or 50 pounds ; they bore a hole in the middle of the upper side, and set a crooked hook fast in it ; also they set four forked stakes fast in the ground, and they lay too sticks acrofs, on which sticks lay a strong staff to hold the dead fall up to the crook, and under this crook, they put a short stick, and fasten a line to it, and this line must reach down to the bridge below ; and this bridge you must make about five or six inches broad. Then set on both sides of this fall boards or pales, or hedge it with close rods, and make it ten or twelve inches high ; let the passage be no wider than the fall is broad.

To

To *deſtroy* Badgers.

Badgers are pernicious creatures, and deſtroy lambs, pigs, and poultry.

Some take them in a ſteel trap, or a ſpring, as foxes are taken.

Others make a pit-fall five feet deep, and four long, making it long at the top and bottom, and wider in the middle ; then cover it with ſome ſmall ſticks and leaves, ſo that he may fall in when he comes on it. Sometimes a fox is taken thus.

Others hunt the badger to his hole in a moon-light night, and dig him out.

Hedgehogs always make their cave or cabbin contrary to the wind.

To *deſtroy* Foxes.

Take a ſheep's paunch, and tie it to a long ſtick, then rub your ſhoes well upon it, that he may not ſcent your ſweaty feet; draw this paunch af-ter you as a trail, a mile or more, and bring it near ſome thick headed tree ; leave your paunch, and get into the tree with a gun, and as it begins to be dark, you will ſee him come after the ſcent of the trail, where you may ſhoot him : draw the trail if you can to the windward of the tree.

The beſt way is, to ſet a ſteel trap in the plain part of a large field, out of the way of all paths, yet not near a hedge, or any ſhelter : then open the trap, ſet it on the ground, and cut out juſt the form thereof in a turf, and take out ſo much earth as to make room to ſtay it ; then cover it a-

gain

gain very neatly with the turf you cut out ; and
as the joint of the turf will not clofe exactly, get
fome mold of a new caft up mole-hill, and put it
clofe round the turf, fticking fome grafs in it as
if it there grew ; make it curious and neat, that
it might even deceive yourfelf. Ten or twelve
yards from the trap, three feveral ways, fcatter
fome of the mole-hill mold very thin, on a place
fifteen or fixteen inches fquare ; then on thefe
places, and where the trap is placed, lay three or
four fmall bits of cheefe, and then with a fheep's
paunch draw a trail of a mile or two long to each
of the three places, and from thence to the trap,
that the fox may come to one of thefe places firft,
for then he will approach the trap more boldly ;
and thus you will never fail of him. Be fure let
your trap be loofe, that he may draw it to fome
hedge or covert, or he will bite off his leg and be
gone.

To make a Spring Trap.

Tie a ftring to fome pole fet faft in the ground,
and to this ftring make faft a fmall, fhort ftick,
made thin on the upper fide, with a notch at the
lower end of it ; then fet another ftick faft in the
ground, with a nitch under it ; then bend down
the pole, and let both the nicks or notches join as
flight as may be ; then open the noofe of the
ftring, and place it in his path or walk ; and if
you lay pieces of cheefe, flefh, and fuch like, it
will entice him that way.

Or, greafe the foals of your fhoes with hog's
fat a little broiled, and as you come from the
wood, drop in feveral places as you pafs, a piece
of roafted fwine's liver, dipt in honey, drawing
after

after you a dead cat, and he'll follow you, fo that you may fhoot him.

A Hook to take a Fox tied to a tree.

This hook is made of large wire, and turns on a fwivel, like the collar of a greyhound ; it is frequently ufed in catching wolves, but oftener for the fox. They hang it from he ground fo high that he muft leap to catch it ; and bait it with flefh, liver, cheefe, &c, and if you run a trail with a fheep's paunch as before directed, it will draw him the more eafily to the bait.

Methods of taking fmall Birds with Lime-twigs.

Cut down the main branch or bough of any bufhy tree, whofe branch and twigs are long, thick, fmooth and ftraight, without either pricks or knots ; when you have picked off the leaves, make the twigs neat and clean, then take the bird lime, well mixed and wrought together with goofe-greafe, or capon's, which being warmed, lime every twig therewith within four fingers of the bottom.

The body from whence the branches have their rife muft be untouched with lime.

You muft be careful not to daub your twigs with too much lime, for that will give as much diftafte to the birds, as too little will not hold them when they are there.

Having fo done, place your brufh in fome quickfet, or dead hedge, near the town's end, back yard, old houfe, or the like ; for thefe

are

are the reforts of fmall birds in the Spring-time.
In the fummer and harveft in groves, bufhes, or
white thorn trees, quickfet hedges, near corn
fields, fruit trees, flax and hemp lands ; and in
the Winter, about houfes, hovels, barns, ftacks
or other places, where ftand ricks of corn, or
fcattered chaff, &c.

As near as you can to any of thefe haunts,
plant your lime bufh, and plant yourfelf alfo at a
coovenient diftance, undifcovered, imitating with
your mouth feveral notes of birds, which you muft
learn by frequent practice, walking the fields for
that purpofe very often, obferving the variety of
feveral birds founds, efpecially fuch as they call
one another by.

To *scare* Crows, Ravens, Jack-daws, &c.

Make a hole in the ground where they come,
let it be about a foot deep and two feet over, and
ftick the long back feather of a crow, or other
fowl, round the edges thereof, and fome at the
bottom ; then make feveral of thefe holes, if the
ground be large, and it will fright them away.

Dead crows hung up will much affright them ;
but among cherry-trees and other fruit trees,
draw a line from tree to tree, and in various places
fatten a black feather, and this will do.

To *take* Bulfinches, Goldfinches, &c.

The bulfinch is a very pernicious bird, and
in the Spring will make great deftruction among
the

the plum and currant trees. The beſt way to take them, is to lime the twigs.

Goldfinches are as bad for gooſeberry-buds, and muſt be taken the ſame way.

Sparrows are great devourers of corn ; uſe the ſame method for them, and all other ſmall birds.

A Remedy by which a dog bitten by another that is mad, may be cured.

Take three plants of that herb which is called roſe-plantain, and having chopped it ſmall with a proper quantity of butter, let the dog that is bit take it the firſt day; the ſecond day give him five plants ordered as before ; the next day ſeven.

The following are the evident ſigns by which a mad dog may be known, and likewiſe avoided.

A mad dog is ſeemingly rapacious and thirſty, yet eats and drinks nothing ; his eyes are fierce and flaming ; he hangs down his ears and thruſts out his tongue ; froths much at the mouth, and barks at his ſhadow ; oftentimes runs along with a melancholy countenance, without barking at all; frequently pants for breath, as if tired with running ; carries his tail bent inwards ; runs without diſtinction againſt all he meets, with great fury, and bites ; hurying on in a haſty and uncertain courſe. Dogs that are well are afraid, and fly both at the ſight and barking of one that is mad. The firſt mad ſympton in a dog, is an unuſual trembling.

Receipt

Receipt to cure Poultry stung with any venomous Worms, or other poisonous Thing.

This you perceive by their lounging and swelling; in which case anoint them with rue and butter mixt together.

To prevent your Trees from being peeled by Hares, Rabbets, or other Animals.

Take tar, which mix with any kind of grease, and boil it over the fire so as both many incorporate, then with a brush daub over the stem of the trees as high as they can reach; do this in November, and it will secure the trees for the whole year, it being the Winter-time only when they feed on the bark.

To cure the Pip in Poultry.

A pip is a white thin scale growing on the tip of the tongue, and will hinder poultry from feeding. It is easy to be discerned, and proceeds generally from drinking-puddle-water, or for want of water, or eating filthy meat. The cure is, to pull off the scale with your nail, and then rub the tongue with salt.

To cure the Rup.

The rup is ordinarily known by the staring or turning of the feathers backwards. To cure this you must pull away the feathers, and open the sore, thrust out the core, and then wash the place with salt and water, or with brine.

To cure the Flux.

The flux in poultry comes with eating too much moist meat. The cure is, to give them peas and bran, scalded.

To cure a stoppage in the belly.

This is a distemper contrary to the flux, and affects them so that they cannot move. To cure it, you must anoint the vents, and then give them small bits of bread, or corn, steeped in urine.

To cure Lice.

If you poultry be much troubled with lice, as it is common, proceeding from corrupt food, or want of bathing, or fluttering in sand, ashes, or such like, take pepper, small beaten, and mix it with warm water, wash your poultry therein, and it will kill all sorts of vermin.

To cure Sore Eyes in Poultry.

In this case take a leaf or two of ground-ivy, and chewing it well in your mouth, suck out the juice, and spit it into the sore eye, and it will assuredly heal it, as hath been often tried.

THE

THE

Shepherd's Barometer;

Or, certain Rules *to judge of the* WEATHER : *grounded on fifty years experience and observations, by an ancient shepherd on the* South Downs, Suffex.

THE fun. If the fun rifes red and fiery, it certainly betokens more or lefs wind and rain, this obfervation agrees with the old Englifh rule ;

> If red the fun begins his race,
> Be fure that rain will fall apace.

If cloudy at fun-rifing, and it foon decreafes, it is a certain fign of fair weather : agreeable to this an obfervation of Pliny's, in his natural hiftory, which fays—If at fun-rifing the clouds are driven away, and retire as it were to the weft, it denotes fair weather.

There is an old proverb to this purpofe, which alfo deferves our notice :

A red evening, and a grey morning, fet the pilgrim a walking.

Clouds. Little round clouds like a dapple grey, and at the fame time a north-wind blows, denotes fair weather for a few days.

Lord

Lord Bacon fays, he had always obferved, that if clouds appear white, and fly to the north-weft, we had generally feveral days of fine weather. One of our old English minor poet fays, (and it generally holds good)

> If woollen fleeces fpread the heavenly way,
> Be fure, no rain difturbs the Summer day.

And Pilny, to the fame purpofe, fays :
If the fun be furrounded with an iris, or circle of white clouds, and they equally fly away, 'tis a fign of fair weather.
And this old English proverb in often right ;

> In the decay of the moon,
> A cloudy morning bodes a fair afternoon.

Large clouds, like rocks, denote large fhowers : this is an old obfervation, and generally proves true : in one of our old kalendars it is exprefled thus :

> When clouds appear like rocks and towers,
> The earth's refrefh'd by frequent fhowers.

But the quotations from other obfervers do not in the leaft diminifh the credit of our fhepherd, who certainly made his obfervations from nature and experience, and then compared them with what others had wrote before him.
If the weather be hazy, and the wind falls away, and fmalls clouds increafe, depend on much rain, and that foon.

If

If large coulds break away decreafe in bulk, and afcend higher in the atmofphere, it is a certain fign of fair, pleafant weather. The large black clouds in Summer evenings, which feem- ingly threaten much rain over night, are fre- quently refolved into dews, and produce a very mifty morning, and a fine warm day.

Mifts. When they rife in low ground, and foon vanifh, nothing is a furer fign of fair wea- ther; when they are heavy, rife flowly, and keep vifible on the hill-tops, they are foon con- denfed, and fall down in rain, which, however, feldom lafts long.

A mift in the morning, before fun-rifing, and at or about the full of the moon, betides fair weather; but if mifts appear in the new moon, you may depend on more or lefs rain in the old; and when they arife in the old, there is generally rain in the new.

Winds. South weft winds and rain, north- eaft winds and fair weather, generally come together; and in nine years time I have ob- ferved, there is as much fouth-weft as north- eaft wind; confequently, as many wet years as dry ones.

If the wind gets into the north-eaft, and re- mains three days without rain, it generally con- tinues in that quarter for nine or ten days, which will be fair; and then it commonly turns to the fouth, and fome rain follows.

If the wind fhifts from the fouth to the north- eaft, and it rains at the fame time, and continues north-eaft but two days without rain, it com- monly abides chiefly in that quarter for two, and fometimes three months.

If

If the wind has been chiefly north for two month, and then comes to the south, you may expect a few fine days notwithstanding; but if it continues south five or six days, depend on rain: but if it turns to the north again, it is undoubtedly dry.

If the wind shifts from the north to the south in a few days without rain, and turns north again with rain, returns to the south in one or two days, and so on for two or three times keeps shifting, it will afterwards fix south or south-west for two months or more.

A week of fair weather, with a south wind, forebodes a great drought, especially if there has been much rain out of the south before.

When the north wind first clears the air, which generally happens once a week, you may depend on a fair day or two.

Clouds. In Summer, or Autumn, when the wind has been in the south two or three days, and the weather very hot, and the clouds rise one above another, with white tops, like battlements of a tower, and joined together, and black on the hills, depend on thunder and rain very speedily.

You may sometimes see two clouds, one to the left, another to the right, which denotes a sudden shower.

When clouds float in a serene sky, you may expect winds, and if they rise from the south, depend on rain; and if you see them driving at sunset, come from what quarter they will, depend on a tempest approaching. Clouds that have a dusky hue, and move slowly, are laden with hail; if they have a blue cast, with large hail; if yel-

P   low,

low, fmall. Lord Bacon remarked, that the proverbs are the philofophy of the common people,
and as many are founded on experience, and are
undoubtedly true, fuch are worth our notice, and
ought to be remembered.

The fafter it rains, the fooner it will be over,
and fudden rains never laft long. But when the
air grows thick, and the fun, moon and ftars
fhine dim, then it is like to rain fix hours fuccef-
fively.

If it begins raining in the fouth, attended with
a high wind for two or three hours, and afterwards falls, but the rain continues, it will in all
probability laft for ten hours or more, unlefs a
ftrong north wind fhould rife, which generally
clears the air, and carries off the rain ; thefe rains
feldom happen above once a year.

When it rains an hour or two before fun-rifing,
it generally clears before noon, and continues fo
the whole day : but if the rain fets in an hour or
two, after fun-rifing, it generally rains all day,
unlefs the rainbow appears a little before the rain
begins, then it feldom lafts long.

Of Spring and Summer.

If the laft twenty days of February and ten firft
days of March be chiefly rain, then the Spring
and Summer are generally wet.

A rainy Winter betokens a dry Autumn ; a
dry Spring denotes a rainy Winter.

When October and November are warm and
rainy, January and February are frofty and cold :
but if October and November be fnow and froft,
then January and February are open and mild.

As

As the following old proverbs are in some measure true, they ought not to be forgot, and are therefore here inserted.

If the grass grow in Janiveer,
It grows the worse for't all the year.
The Welchman had rather see his dam on the bier,
Than to see a fair Februeer.
March wind, and May sun,
Makes cloaths white, and maids dun.
When April blows his horn,
Its good for both hay and corn.
An April flood,
Carries away the frog and her brood.
A cold May and a windy,
Makes a full barn and a findy.
A May flood
Never did good.
A swarm of bees in May,
Is worth a load of hay ;
But a swarm in July
Is not worth a fly.

To shew the approach of wet and dry weather.

Take a piece of dry whipcord, and tie a plumbet at the end, hang it against a wainscot or dry wall, and draw a line under it, exactly at the bottom, where the plumbet reaches ; do this in moderate weather, that is, when neither very dry nor very wet ; and when it is like to be wet weather, the plumbet will be above the line, and when dry, it will reach below the line ; but what is better, take a pair of scales, in one put a brass pound weight, in the other a pound of dry salt ;

let

let there be a fhelf or board under the fcales to
prevent their finking too low, and when it is inclined to rain, the fcale with the falt will fink the
loweft ; when inclined to dry, the fcale with the
brafs weight will weigh up the falt.

Bat-Fowling, the manner of it.

OBferve where thefe birds rooft in great numbers, as they generally do in fhrubs, hedges,
or trees ; then go in a dark night, and have a
wicker with a handle to hold on high, in which
place pieces of link or great candle, to make a
great light ; fome have a pan to make a fire, and
carry it at their back ; but then one muft put fire
on as faft as it burns out ; then let one go with a
pole, and beat the contrary fide, and two or three
with you, carrying long boughs ; and when they
are unroofted with beating, they will come flying
about the light, fo that they with the bough may
eafily ftrike them down ; if among fhrubs, as in
a wood, let one on each fide beat at a pretty diftance. This muft be done in a pure ftill night.
Depth of Winter is the beft for this fport. Some
ufe nets made like a racket at the end of poles
with which they are eafily knocked down.

A

A Secret to hinder pigeons from quitting a pigeon-house.

TAKE the head and feet of a gelt goat, and boil them together till the flesh separates from the bone ; take this flesh and boil it again in the same liquor, till the whole is consumed ; bruise into this decoction, which is very thick, some potter's earth, out of which you are to take all the stones, vetch, dung, hemp, soot and corn ; the whole must be kneaded together, and reduced to a paste of dough, which form into small loaves about the thickness of two fists, and dry them in the sun or oven, and take care they do not burn ; when they are baked, lay them in several parts of the pigeon house, and as soon as they are set there, the pigeons will amuse themselves with pecking them, and finding some taste therein which pleases them, they will not afterwards leave it but with regret. Others take a handful of salt, which they candy, and afterwards put into the pigeon house. Some take a goat's head, and boil it in water with salt, cummin, hemp and urine ; and then expose it in the pigeon house, with which they amuse the pigeons. Lastly, there are those who fry millet in honey, and add a little water thereto to prevent its burning too ; this preparation is a repast to them, and will cause them to have such an affection for their ordinary habitation, that they will be so far from abandoning it themselves, that they will draw strange pigeons to it.

P 3

☞ As it is very probable that this Book may fall into the Hands of many Perfons in the Country, whofe occafional Bufinefs may call them to London, or whofe Inclinations may lead them to fettle in the Metropolis, I would earneftly recommend to their Perufal the following Book, which is Publifhed with the *moft benevolent intention* of guarding the *honeft* and *unwary* from the Tricks and Artifices of *villainous* and *defigning* Wretches of both Sexes ; and I the rather recommend this Work, as the Perufal of it has *already faved* feveral very worthy Perfons from *ruin :* for though Country People are no Way deficient in point of *Abilites,* yet it is impoffible that they fhould guard againft Snares they have never heard or thought of, and which the Honefty of their Hearts would never allow them to fufpect. Therefore the Perufal of it to thofe who defign going to London, may very truly be allowed worth its Weight in Gold, although,

The Price is only One Shilling.

Adorned with Six curious Copper Plate Cuts, beautifully Engraved from original Defigns, which alone are worth the Price of the Book,

The Cheats of *London* Expofed;
Or, the TRICKS of the TOWN
Laid open to BOTH SEXES.

Being a clear Difcovery of all the various Frauds and villanies that are daily practifed in that great City.

Among many others, are the following, viz. Highwaymen, or Scamps, Sharpers, Gamblers, Kidnappers, Waggon-hunters, Money droppers, Duffers, Setters, pretended Friends, Mock Auctions, Regifter-Office, Quacks, Bullies, Bawds, Whores, Pimps, Jilts, Goffips, and Fortune tellers.

The whole laid down in so plain and easy a manner, as to enable the most innocent Country People to be completely on their Guard to avoid the base Impositions of such vile and abandoned Wretches, who live by robbing and ruining the young and innocent of both sexes.

Together with General Remarks on the present State and Condition of the Town, interspersed with useful Admonitions to Person of all Ages and Conditions.

By the Author of the LONDON SPY.

Herein are shewn the various Feats
Of Whores and Rogues, and other Cheats;
Here Youth are taught those Snares to shun,
By which *too many* are undone.

☞ To prevent Imposition, be careful to ask for *The Cheats of London exposed, adorned with Curious Copper-Plate Cuts,* and to observe that every Book is signed on the Back of the Title Page, by J. COOKE, of Pater-Noster-Row, London, for whom it is Printed; but it may be had also of most Booksellers and news carries in England.

Of whom may be likewise had, the following Books; but the Public are intreated to observe, that, unless the name of J. COOKE is at the bottom of their title pages, they are spurious editions, imposed on them by a set of literary pirates, who live by dafrauding the fair trader.

II.

THE COMPLETE

ENGLISH FARMER;

Or, HUSBANDRY made easy,

In all their various Branches,

Containing a greater Variety of useful Articles than are to be found in any Book of the Kind, though Four Times the Price ; particularly, the Management and Qualities of the different Kind of Grafs, and of making Hay.

Defcription of different Soils, and of manuring and ploughing Land.

The Cultivation and Management of Wheat and Barley, &c. &c.

Together with great Variety of other very ufeful Articles, too numerous to be inferted in this Advertifement.

By GEORGE COOKE, Farmer, at Weft End, in Hertfordfhire, Adorned with a beautiful Frontifpiece, finely engraved, from an original Drawing. Price 1s. 6d.

The Whole freed from the Errors, Obfcurities and Superfluities of former Writers on the Subject.

III.

A handfome Pocket Volume, Price Two Shillings in marble Covers.

The Complete ENGLISH Brewer;

Or the whole Art and Myftery of BREWING, In all its various BRANCHES :

Containing plain and eafy directions for brewing ALL forts of malt liquors in the *greateft* Perfection, from the fmalleft to the largeft quantities.

Alfo inftructions for the choice of *barley and hops*, and all other ingredients and utenfils ufed in brewing. Together with the very beft methods of *cafking, cellaring, fining, bottling, curing* and *recovering faulty or damaged Liquors.*

The whole made eafy to every capacity, and calculated not only for the ufe of Publicans in general, but private Families in particular.

By GEORGE WATKINS.

Who has practifed BREWING in all its BRANCHES upwards of Thirty Years.

IV.

The Servants Book *of* Knowledge,

Containing *Tables* of *Wages*, ready cast up, for any Number of Pounds, or Guineas, they may have to receive for odd Days, Weeks or Months, up to a Year; which will explain to Servants what they may have to receive for odd Days, Weeks, Months, or Years; nicely calculated to the Hundredth Part of a Farthing.——Together with a *Table*, for *Marketing*, from One Penny and upwards per Pound.——Likewise *Tables*, shewing the even Parts of Pounds, Shillings and Pence, from One Penny to a Thousand Pounds. The whole made perfectly easy to every Capacity.

By ANTHONY HEASEL.

To which are added plain and easy Instructions for Servants of both Sexes, to qualify themselves · for places in general, in order to obtain the Favour of their Masters and Mistresses in the Discharge of their several Stations; but more particularly for the *Valet de Chambre*, *Shopman*, *Apprentice*, *Gardener*, *Footman*, *Farmer's Man*, *Groom*, *Housekeeper*, *Lady's Maid*, *House Maid*, *Chamber Maid*, *Cook Maid*, *Dairy Maid*, *Laundry Maid*, *Nursery Maid*, *Scullery Maid*, &c.— Including several curious Articles for the Use of Servants in general, never before published— Price sewed in blue Covers. 1s. 6d.

V.

Price one Shilling, adorned with a curious Frontispiece of all the most favourite singing Birds.

The Complete BIRD-FANCYER;

Or, BIRD-FANCYER's Recreation.

Containing the best instructions for Taking, Breeding, Feeding, and Rearing, all Sorts of

Song-Birds, particularly Canary-Birds, Nightingales, Larks Black-Birds, Starlings, Thrushes, Linnets, Gold-finishes, Bullfinches, &c. Together with an account of all their Distempers, and the best Methods of curing them. Also the surest Means of distinguishing the Cock from the Hen, and learning them to Sing, to the greatest perfection.

By GEORGE WRIGHT, who has made the rearing Birds his diversion near twenty-years. The Lovers of Harmony reading this Book.

   May the Moments of Pleasure prolong,
For here we are taught by the Feather and Lock,
   To judge of the Bird and his Song.

VI.

A Treatise on English Shooting,
Under the following Heads.

Of the Knowledge of a good Fowling-piece. The Ordering and Managing of the Fowling-piece. The Appendages of the Fowling-piece, The choice of Powder, Shot and Flints; or Partridge Shooting, with the Choice and Ordering of Pointers; of Pheasant Shooting, with the Ordering of Spaniels: of Woodcock shooting; of Snipe shooting; of Water and Fen Fowl Shooting, and the Use of proper Dogs. Of Upland Winter Shooting; with necessary Observations for the young Sportsman when out, and returning Home.

By GEORGE EDIE, Gent.
In Demy Octavo, Price 1s. 6d.

VII.

The NEW LONDON SPY;
Or, A Twenty-Four Hours Ramble
through the BILLS of MORTALITY.

Containing a true Picture of Modern high and low Life; from the splendid Mansions in St.

James's, to the subterraneous Habitations of St.
Giles's, &c. Wherein are displayed the various
Scences of Covent-Garden and its Environs, the
Theatres, Jell -Houses, Gaming Houses, Night-
Houses, Coteries, Masquerades, Public Gardens, and other Places of Entertainment, as well
as of civil Reception, public and private. Together with the various Humours of the different Inhabitants of the Metropolis, &c. &c.
The whole exhibiting a striking Portrait of London, as it appears in the present Year; and interspersed with Moral Reflections.
By the Author of the CHEATS of LONDON.

Adorned with a humorous Frontispiece, finely engraved by a capital Artist. Price, sewed in
Marble Covers. 2s.

VIII.

In a handsome pocket volume, (Price 2s. 6d. sewed.
or 3s. neatly bound) adorned with a curious fron-
tispiece, from an original painting, representing the
Four great Dangers.

The Companion for the FIRE-SIDE:
Or Winter Evening's AMUSEMENT.

Being a valuable and curious Collection of amu-
sing and instructive *stories, tales, fables, allegories,*
historical facts, eastern tales, novels, remarkable events,
and singular occurrances.

Selected from the most celebrated writers in
several languages, many of which never appeared
in print before.

To pass the dull evening in pleasure away,
    And laugh at the cares of mankind ;
Accept of a chearful companion to day,
    To mirth and amusement inclin'd.
The contents of our volume will amply repay
    The expence that the purchase has cost ;
And none but a blockhead will seriously say,
    That his time or his money was lost.

Part of Europe to the prefent Times; but alfo a very great Variety of ufeful Difcoveries, which have been communicated to the Authors of this Work, by Gentlemen of diftinguifhed Abilities; whereby every Difficulty attending the Study of the Arts and Sciences is diftinctly cleared, and the whole explained in the moft eafy and intelligent Manner.

The *Anatomical, Chemical,* and *Medical* Parts,
By M. H I N D E, M. D.

The *Mathematical* Parts,
By W. SQUIRE, Author of *The Modern Book-keeper.*

Gardening and *Botany,*
By J. MARSHAL, Gardener, at Knightfbridge.

Criticifm, Grammar, Poetry, Theology, &c.
By the Rev. THOMAS COOKE, A. B.
Author of *The Univerfal Letter Writer* ; or, *New Art of Polite Correfpondence.*

And the other Parts by Gentlemen of Eminence in the feveral Departments they have undertaken to elucidate.

Adorned with upwards of One Hundred large and beautiful Copper-Plates, engraved from real Objects; among which are *twelve* large Plates of the Zodiac, curioufly engraved from original Drawings made by eminent Aftronomers. In Two large Volumes in Folio; Price, neatly bound in Calf and Lettered,   £ 3   3*s*

*** This Work being completed in One Hundred Six-penny Numbers, each containing at leaft One Copper-Plate, may be had in the fame manner as the Hiftory of England, abovementioned.

ᵀII.

By the KING's Royal Licence and Authority.

A New and Univerfal Collection of Authentic and Entertaining

VOYAGES AND TRAVELS;

From the earlieft Accounts to the prefent Time.

Containing

Containing a full Account of whatever is most worthy Notice in *Europe*, *Asia*, *Africa*, and *America*.

Illustrated with a great Number of Maps, and Copper-Plates by GRIGNION, and other celebrated Masters, exhibiting the most remarkable Occurrences of the History.

By EDWARD CAVENDISH DRAKE, Esq;

In a large Volume in Folio. Price, neatly bound in Calf and Lettered, —— —— £ 1 16s

*** Those Gentlemen who prefer taking in the above Weekly to having it complete, may have one or more Numbers at a Time, the whole being comprized in Sixty Six-penny Numbers, every one of which is adorned with One or more Copper-Plates, finely engraved.

IV.

By the KING's Royal Licence and Authority.

A NEW and COMPLETE
HISTORY AND SURVEY
Of the CITIES of
London and Westminster,
The BOROUGH of SOUTHWARK,
And PARTS adjacent;

From the earliest Accounts to the present Time.

By HENRY CHAMBERLAIN, of *Hatton Garden*, Esq;

Enriched with a great Number of elegant Copper-Plates, containing Views of the Public Buildings, Churches, &c. In a large Folio Volume. Price, neatly bound in Calf and Lettered, —— £ 1 16s

†₊† This Work is comprized in Sixty-Numbers, which may be had in the same Manner as the Voyages and Travels above-mentioned, each Number containing One, or more Copper-Plates, elegantly engraved.

A 2 V.

V.

Elegantly printed on an excellent new Letter and fine
Paper, embellished with upwards of Sixty elegant
Copper-Plates, drawn by WALE and other eminent
Artists; and engraved by GRIGNION and other cele-
brated Masters.

THE

Complete Englifh Traveller;

OR,

A New Survey and Defcription of *England* and *Wales.*

Containing a full Account of whatever is curious and
entertaining in the feveral Counties of England and
Wales, the Ifles of Man, Jerfey, Guernfey, and other
Iflands adjoining to, and dependant on, the Crown of
Great Britain.—To which is added, a concife and ac-
curate Defcription of that Part of Great Britain called
Scotland; its ancient and prefent State; Antiquities,
and natural Curiofities. Together with the Manners and
Cuftoms of the Inhabitants, &c.

By NATHANIEL SPENCER, Efq.

In a large elegant Folio Volume. Price, neatly bound
in Calf and Lettered,   ———   £ 1 16s

+++ The above Work being comprized in Sixty Six-
Penny Numbers, any Perfon may be fupplied with one
or more at a Time, as may fuit their own Convenience;
each Number embellifhed with *at leaft* one beautiful
Copper-Plate, curioufly engraved.

VI.

By the KING's Royal Licence and Authority.

England's Bloody Tribunal;

OR,

POPISH CRUELTY DISPLAYED.

Containing a complete Account of the Lives, Religious
Principles, Cruel Perfecutions, Sufferings, Tortures, and
Triumphant

Triumphant Deaths, of the most pious *English* Protestant Martyrs; who have sealed the Faith of our Holy Religion with their Blood.

By the Rev. MATTHEW TAYLOR, D. D.

Embellished with Twenty-Five curious Copper-Plates, reprefenting the various different Tortures inflicted upon the several Martyrs, whose Lives are recorded in the Work.

In a large Volume in Quarto. Price, neatly bound in Calf and Lettered, —— —— 16s

†‡† The above Work is comprized in Twenty-Five Six-Penny Numbers, which may be had by one or more at a Time, as may suit the Readers Convenience; each Number embellished with a beautiful Copper-Plate, curioufly engraved.

VII.

By the KING's Royal Licence and Authority.

A New and Complete HISTORY of

The HOLY BIBLE;

From the Creation of the WORLD to the Incarnation of our blessed Lord and Saviour, JESUS CHRIST; during a Period of above Four Thousand Years.

Together with

A History of THE APOCRYPHA, which is authorized to be read in Protestant Churches.

By the Rev. JOHN FLEETWOOD, D. D.

Adorned with upwards of Forty beautiful Copper-Plates, finely engraved.

In a large Quarto Volume. Price, neatly bound in Calf, and Lettered, —— —— £ 1 4s

†‡† For the Convenience of those who may not chuse to purchafe the above Work complete, it may be had in Forty Six-Penny Numbers, one or more at a Time, each of them containing at least One Copper-Plate.

A 3   VIII.

VIII.

The LIFE of

Our Blessed Lord and Saviour, JESUS CHRIST.

Containing the Genealogy of our Glorious Redeemer; his Nativity, Preservation, Circumcision, Baptism, Fasting, Temptation, Ministry, Doctrine, Calling the Apostles, Miracles, Parables, Travels, Transfiguration, Passion, Institution of the Sacrament, Crucifixion, Burial, Resurrection, Appearance, and Ascension.

Together with the Lives and Sufferings of his Holy Apostles, Evangelists, and other Primitive Martyrs, who have laid down their Lives in the glorous Cause of Christianity, the Foundation on which all our Hopes of Eternal Happiness are fixed.

By the Rev. JOHN FLEETWOOD, D.D.
Author of the History of the Holy Bible,
Published by the KING's Authority.

Enriched with Twenty-Five beautiful Copper-Plates, finely engraved.

In a large Quarto Volume. Price, neatly bound in Calf, ——— ——— ——— 16s

✝✝✝ This Work may be had in Twenty-Five Six-Penny Numbers, in the same Manner as the Bible before-mentioned, each Number being embellished with One beautiful Copper-Plate, finely engraved.

IX.

IX.

THE

CHRISTIAN's PRAYER-BOOK;

Or, Complete Manual of Devotions.

In FOUR PARTS.

By the Rev. J O H N F L E E T W O O D, D.D.
Author of the Life of our bleffed Lord and Saviour, JESUS CHRIST
and of the HISTORY of the HOLY BIBLE, with the APOCRYPHA.
Published by the KING's Authority.

In a handfome Pocket Volume, embellished with a well
adapted Frontifpiece. Price, neatly bound,   —   3s

X.

THE

COMPLETE SPORTSMAN;

OR,

Country Gentleman's Recreation.

Containing the Whole ARTS of Horfemanfhip, Racing,
Cock-fighting, Hunting, Angling, Shooting, &c.
Together with feveral other equally curious Articles, too
numerous to be mentioned in this Catalogue.

By T H O M A S F A I R F A X, Efq;

In a handfome Pocket Volume, adorned with a curious
Frontifpiece. Price, neatly bound,   ——   3s

XI.

A NEW

GEOGRAPHICAL DICTIONARY.

Containing a FULL and ACCURATE Account of the
feveral Parts of the Known World.

By J O H N B A R R O W, Efq;

Adorned with upwards of one Hundred and Forty
beautiful Copper-Plates. In Two large Folio Volumes,
neatly bound in Calf and Lettered. Price £ 3 3s.

XII.

XII.

By the KING's Royal Licence and Authority.

ENGLAND DISPLAYED.

Being a complete and accurate Survey and Defcription of ENGLAND and WALES.

By P. RUSSEL, Efq; and Mr. OWEN PRICE.

In Two beautiful Folio Volumes, neatly bound in Calf and Lettered. Price ——— — £2 12s 6d

XIII.

A COMPANION for the FIRE SIDE;
Or, Winter Evening's Amufement.

Being a valuable and curious Collection of amufing and inftructive Stories, Tales, Fables, Allegories, Hiftorical Facts, Eaftern Tales, Novels, Remarkable Events, and fingular Occurrences; in Profe and Verfe. Selected from the moft celebrated Writers in feveral Languages. Together with many original Stories, which never appeared in Print before.

In a handfome Pocket Volume, adorned with a curious Frontifpiece, from an original Painting reprefenting the Four great Dangers. Price ——— — 3s

XIV.

THE

MODERN BOOK-KEEPER;
OR,
Book-keeping made perfectly Eafy.

Wherein the Theory and Practice of that excellent Art is clearly explained, in the Manner of real Bufinefs, both Foreign and Domeftic, according to the moft approved Method

Method. Calculated for the Use of SCHOOLS IN PARTICULAR, as well as for the Compting-House.
By WILLIAM SQUIRE,
Master of the Academy in Hoxton-Square, and one of the Authors of the New Royal and Universal Dictionary of Arts and Sciences, now publishing in Weekly Numbers, Price Six-Pence each.
In a large Demy Twelves. Price — — 1s 6d

XV.

MODERN EDEN;
OR,
The GARDENER's Universal Guide.

Containing plain and familiar Instructions, for performing every Branch of Gardening, whether relating to Ornament or Utility. In which are laid down the best Methods at large for raising all the Products of the Kitchen and Flower-Garden, and the Training, Pruning, and entire Management of Fruit-Trees. The whole founded on Experience, according to the Methods of the best Gardeners of the present Time. With many useful and curious Experiments, which have been repeatedly practised, and proved, not only by Gardeners, but the Virtuosi in General.

By JOHN RUTTER, Gardener, at *Wandsworth,*
And DANIEL CARTER, Gardener, at *Battersea.*

In a handsome Octavo Volume. Price, neatly bound, —————— 5s

XVI.
An ENTIRE ORIGINAL WORK.
The Universal LETTER-WRITER;
Or, New Art of Polite Correspondence.

Containing a Course of Interesting Original Letters on the most important, instructive, and entertaining Subjects, which may serve as Copies for inditing Letters on every various Occurrence in Life. Particularly on Advice, Affection, Business, Children to Parents, Condolence, Courtship, Diligence, Education, Fidelity, Friendship,
A5 Generosity,

Generofity, Happinefs, Humanity, Induftry, Love, Marriage, Mafters to Servants, Modefty, Morality, Oeconomy, Parents to Children, Paternal Affection, Piety, Prodigality, Prudence, Religion, Retirement, Servants to Mafters, Trade, Virtue, Wit, &c. &c.

To which is added,

The COMPLETE PETITIONER,

Containing great Variety of Petitions on various Subjects, from Perfons in low or middling States of Life, to thofe in higher Stations; fuited to all the different Occafions in Life.—Alfo a new, plain and eafy GRAMMAR, of the Englifh Language; and Directions for addrefling Perfons of all Ranks, either in Writing or Difcourfe.—Likewife Forms of Mortgages, Letters of Licence, Bonds, Indentures, Wills, Wills and Powers, Letters of Attorney, Bills of Sale, Releafes, &c. as they are now executed by Gentlemen of diftinguifhed Abilities in the Law.

By the Rev. THOMAS COOKE, A.B.

One of the Authors of *The New Royal and Univerfal Dictionary of Arts and Sciences.*

N. B. The Public are intreated to obferve that this Work will ferve for indicting Letters, and writing Petitions, on all Occafions; and thofe Perfons who are poffeffed of other Books of a like Kind, will make a valuable Addition thereto by the Purchafe of this New One; it being entirely Original, as not a fingle Letter is copied from any Book whatever.

** Be careful to afk for COOKE's *Univerfal Letter Writer.*

Price, neatly bound in Red, and embellifhed with a beautiful emblematical Frontifpiece, finely engraved from an Original Drawing, ⸻ ⸻ ⸻ ⸻ 2s

XVII.

AN ENTIRE NEW WORK.

The MIDNIGHT RAMBLER;
Or, New Nocturnal Spy.

Containing a Complete Defcription of the modern Tranfactions of London and Weftminfter, from the Hours of Nine in the Evening, till Six in the Morning. Exhibiting great Variety of Midnight Scenes and Adventures in real Life comic and ferious; wherein are difplayed the various Humours and Tranfactions of the different Inhabitants of the Metropolis, from the Duke in high, down to the Cobler in low Life; and from the Dutchefs in St. James's to the Oyfter Woman at Billingfgate, &c. &c.

In a neat Pocket Volume. Price, fewed, adorned with a humorous Frontifpiece drawn from the Life, ⸻ ⸻ 2s

XVIII.

XVIII.

The ADVENTURES of

A KIDNAPPED ORPHAN.

A NOVEL.

In a neat Pocket Volume. Price, bound, — 3s

XIX.

THE

SPOUTER's COMPANION;

OR,

THEATRICAL REMEMBRANCER.

Containing a select Collection of the most esteemed Prologues and Epilogues, which have been spoken by the most celebrated Performers of both Sexes. Together with Variety of curious Originals, written on purpose for this Work. Among which are several Prologues and Epilogues, to be spoken in the Characters of Bloods, Bucks, Choice Spirits, Fribbles, Bravoes, &c.

To which is added,

The SPOUTER's MEDLEY.

Containing select Parts of the most celebrated Comedies and Tragedies, contrasted in such a Manner as to render their Assemblage extremely diverting to the Readers, Speakers and Hearers.

Together with the Spouting Club in an Uproar, or the Battle of Socks and Buskins.

Embellished with an elegant Frontispiece, representing Mr. GARRICK speaking the Prologue to Britannia, a Masque. Price — 1s

XX.

THE COMPLETE ENGLISH BREWER;

OR,

The Whole Art and Mystery of Brewing,

In all its various BRANCHES.

Containing plain and easy Directions for Brewing all Sorts of Malt Liquors in the greatest Perfection, from the smallest to the largest, Quantities.

By GEORGE WATKINS.

In a handsome pocket Volume. Price, neatly Bound, — 2s 6d

A 6   XXI.

XXI.

The YOUTH's POCKET COMPANION;
Or, UNIVERSAL PRECEPTOR.

Containing a Syſtem of uſeful Knowledge, proper for every Young Man, who deſires to thrive in the World; particularly a complete Grammar of the Engliſh Language. The beſt Inſtructions for Writing, making Pens, &c. Familiar Letters in the common Occurrences of Life, on any Subject whatſoever. Arithmetic made plain and eaſy. Forms of Receipts, Bills, Notes of Hand, &c. Rules to be obſerved in the Conduct of Life, to lead to Happineſs and Proſperity. The Pocket Farrier. The Gardener's Directory, &c. Examples of the moſt neceſſary Forms in Law.

By GEORGE WILSON, Teacher at an Academy in London.

Adorned with a moſt beautiful Frontiſpiece, finely engraved. Price ⸺ ⸺ ⸺ ⸺ 1s

XXII.

FRANCIS QUARLE's
Emblems and Hieroglyphics of the Life of Man,
MODERNIZED.

In a handſome Pocket Volume. Price, neatly bound, and embelliſhed with near One Hundred beautiful emblematical Cuts, ⸺ 2s

XXIII.

CURTAIN LECTURES;
O R,
MATRIMONY DISPLAYED.

In a Series of intereſting Dialogues between married Men and their Wives, in every Station and Condition of Life. Inſcribed to the young and unmarried of both Sexes. In a handſome Pocket Volume, adorned with a moſt beautiful Frontiſpiece finely engraved from an original Drawing, taken from the Life. Price, neatly bound, ⸺ 3s

XXIV,

XXIV.

The LADIES POLITE SONGSTER;
Or, Harmony for the Fair-Sex.

Containing a felect Collection of all the neweft and moft admired
SONGS; as they are fung at the Theatres, Public Gardens, &c.
Alfo a great Variety of curious Originals, particularly adapted to the
Ear of the Fair-Sex. Likewife plain Directions for Singing with a
good Grace; by which Perfons with bad Voices may render themfelves agreeable; and fuch as have tolerable ones will fhine to the utmoft Advantage.

Price, neatly bound in Red, adorned with a moft beautiful Frontifpiece, finely engraved from an original Drawing, —— 1s 6d

XXV.

BACCHUS AND VENUS;
OR,
The Harmony of Love and Wine.

Confifting of a droll Collection of SONGS in high Humour,
as they are fung by the Votaries of Bacchus and Venus, as well as
by the Sons of the Chace, and by the Bucks, Bloods, Geniuffes,
Choice Spirits, and other Fellows of High Fun and Good Fellowfhip,
including a much greater Variety of droll Originals, than were ever
publifhed in any Collection before.

To which is added,
A felect Collection of TOASTS and SENTIMENTS.

Price, bound, and adorned with a humorous Frontifpiece, 1s 6d

XXVI.

THE

COMPLETE ENGLISH GARDENER;
OR,
Gardening made perfectly eafy.

Containing Directions for the proper Management of the Flower,
Fruit, and Kitchen Garden, for every Month in the Year. The
whole laid down in fo plain and eafy a Manner, that all who are
defirous of managing a Garden, may do it effectually, without
any

any other Inftruftions whatever. To which is added, The COMPLETE BEE-MASTER; or, Beft Method of of Bees, as well for Profit as Pleafure. Together with the whole Art of Breeding and Rearing Fowls, Ducks, Geefe, Turkies, Pigeons, and Rabbits. Likewife plain Inftruftions for deftroying Vermin, particularly fuch as infeft Houfes, Gardens, Dairies, Barns, Bees, Poultry, &c. Alfo Rules to judge of the Weather, and many other Articles equally ufeful, too numerous to infert in the Title Page.

By SAMUEL COOKE.

Adorned with a beautiful Frontifpiece, elegantly engraved. Price, ————— —— ———— — 1s 6d

XXVII.

THE POLITE TUTORESS;
Or, YOUNG LADY'S INSTRUCTOR.

Being a Series of Dialogues between a fenfible Governefs and feveral of her Pupils of the firft Rank. In which they are made to think, fpeak, and act in a Manner fuitable to their refpective Tempers, Difpofitions, and Capacities. The natural Defects of Infancy are reprefented in the ftrongeft Light, and proper Rules laid down for correcting them; Care being taken to form their Minds to Virtue, as well as to cultivate their Underftandings.

Price, neatly bound in Red, ———— —— 1s 6d

XXVIII.

The BOOK of FATE;
O R,
UNIVERSAL FORTUNE-TELLER.

Containing the Arts of Fortune-Telling, Conjuring, and Juggling, in all their Branches. The Method of throwing Cups and Balls, eating Fire, and other curious Feats of Legerdemain. A true Interpretation of all Kinds of Dreams, digefted into Alphabetical Order. The Art of Palmeftry, or Prognoftication by the Lines of the Hand. To which is added, an entire new and extraordinary Method of telling Fortunes by Cards and Dice; with many Particulars never before publifhed:

By WILLIAM PARTRIDGE, Doctor of Aftrology.

Adorned with a moft beautiful Frontifpiece finely Engraved from an original Drawing, taken from Life; Price ——— — 1s 6d

XXIX.

XXIX.

The Second Edition, with the Addition of great Variety of made Dishes, &c.

THE

COMPLETE ENGLISH COOK;

O R,

PRUDENT HOUSEWIFE.

Being an entire new Collection of the moft genteel, yet leaft expenfive Receipts in every Branch of Cookery and good Houfewifery, viz. Roafting, Boiling, Stewing, Ragouts, Soups, Sauces, Fricafeys, Pies, Tarts, Puddings, Potting, Cheefecakes, Cuftards, Jellies, Candying, Collaring, Pickling, Preferving, Made Wines, &c. Together with the Art of Marketing, and Directions for placing Difhes on Tables, and many other Things equally neceffary. The Whole made eafy to the meaneft Capacity, and far more ufeful to Young Beginners than any Book of the Kind extant.

By CATHARINE BROOKS, of Red-Lion-Street.

To which is added, the Phyfical Doctor. Alfo the whole Art of Clear-Staiching, Ironing, &c.

Adorned with a moft beautiful Frontifpiece, and other ufeful Cuts (being the moft plain and eafy Book of the Kind ever yet publifhed,) Price ——— ——— ——— —— 1s

XXX.

T H E

COMPLETE BIRD FANCYER;

O R,

BIRD FANCYER's RECREATION.

Containing the beft Inftructions for taking, breeding, feeding and rearing all Sorts of Song Birds, &c. Together with an Account of all their Diftempers, and the beft Methods of curing them, and of diftinguifhing the Cock from the Hen, and learning them to fing to the greateft Perfection.

By GEORGE WRIGHT.

Price, adorned with a curious Frontifpiece of all the moft favourite Singing Birds, ——— ——— —— 1s

XXXI,

XXXI.

THE

LOVER's INSTRUCTOR;

OR,

The Whole Art of Courtship.

Containing, among a very great Variety of other curious Articles, equally instructive and entertaining, The most ingenious Letters, written to and from both Sexes, relative to Love and Courtship. Love Epistles in Verse, written in an elegant Stile. The politest personal Conversation between Lovers, &c.

To which is prefixed, a Preface, directing each Sex how to make a prudent Choice in a Partner for Life, and several other curious Particulars. Price ⸺ ⸺ ⸺ 1s

XXXII.

THE

COMPLETE HORSE DOCTOR;

OR,

FARRIERY made perfectly easy.

Explaining the best Methods of curing the several Diseases to which Horses are subject. Together with a succinct Account of the various Symptoms of their approaching Disorders. Also the best Manner of taking proper Care of them, during the Time of their Illness. The whole laid down in the most plain and intelligible Manner, that those who have Horses may manage their own, and cure the Distempers to which they are subject, without the assistance of a Farrier. With an Introduction, containing the most certain Methods of choosing Horses of all Kinds. Also easy Directions for Riding, whereby a Person from small Experience, may become a complete Horseman, as well as a complete Farrier. Likewise the most proper Manner of managing a Horse on a Journey. Being the result of 37 Years Practice and Experience.

By J. THOMPSON, of Clifton, in Yorkshire.

Adorned with a most curious and useful Frontispiece, representing at one View, in near Fifty Figures, all the various Names of every Part of a Horse's Body, (being the completest, cheapest and plainest Book of the Kind ever yet published.) Price ⸺ ⸺ 1s

XXXIII.

XXXIII.

By the KING's Royal Licence and Authority.

The Cheats of LONDON Exposed ;
O R,
The Tricks of the Town laid open to both Sexes.

Being a clear Discovery of all the various Frauds and Villanies that are daily practised in that great City. Among many others, are the following, viz. Highwaymen, or Scamps, Sharpers, Gamblers, Kidnappers, Waggon-Hunters, Money-droppers, Duffers, Setters, Pretended Friends, Mock Auctions, Register Offices, Quacks, Bullies, Bawds, Whores, Pimps, Jilts, Gossips, and Fortune-tellers. The whole laid down in so plain and easy a Manner, as to enable the most innocent Country People to be completely on their Guard how to avoid the base Villainies of such vile and abandoned Wretches, who live by robbing and ruining the young and innocent of both Sexes.

Adorned with Six curious Copper-Plate Cuts, beautifully engraved from original Designs, which alone are worth the Price of the Book. Price ———— ——— —— —— 1s

XXXIV.

T H E

MERRY QUACK DOCTOR;
O R,
The FUN-BOX broke Open.

Containing an entire spick and span new and curious Collection of brilliant Jests, frolicksome Joaks, witty Quibbles, arch Waggeries, humorous Adventures, smart Repartees, queer Puns, funny Stories, Irish Bulls, and entertaining Humbugs. To which is added a choice Collection of Conundrums, Riddles, Rebusses, jovial Songs, sharp Epigrams, droll Epitaphs, amorous Poems, &c. The Whole containing a great Variety of High Fun and Good Fellowship, calculated

to

to promote Mirth in all its entertaining Branches, by laughing Care out of Countenance.

By TOM KILLEGREW, Junior, President of the Wits Club, in Piccadilly, and Great Grandson to the Famous Killegrew, Jester to King Charles the Second, of Merry Memory.

Adorned with a most humourous Frontispiece, finely engraved by a capital Hand, being the completest, cheapest and merriest Book of the Kind ever published. Price ——— —— 1s

XXXV.

The GOOD SAMARITAN;

Or, Complete English Physician.

Containing Observations on the most frequent Diseases of Men and Women, Infants and Children; with Directions for the Management of the Sick; and a Collection of the most approved Receipts for making and preparing cheap, easy, safe and efficacious Medicines, for their Recovery. Likewise Directions concerning Bleeding. By Dr. LOBB, late Member of the Royal College of Physicians in London. To which is added, a Method of restoring to Life such Persons who are thought drowned, or any other Manner suffocated. Price, sewed in Marble Covers, and adorned with a curious Frontispiece, ——— —— ——— —— —— 1s

XXXVI.

The SCHOOL of VIRTUE;

O R,

POLITE NOVELIST.

Consisting of Novels, Tales, Fables, Allegories, &c. &c. Moral and Entertaining; in Prose and Verse.

In a handsome Pocket Volume, neatly bound and gilt, Price 2s

XXXVII.

XXXVII.

THE
COMPLETE DUTY of MAN;

O R,

A System of Doctrinal and Practical Christianity.

To which are added Forms of Prayer and Offices of Devotion, for the various Circumstances of Life.

By H. VENN, A. M. Vicar of Huddersfield, in Yorkshire.

In an Octavo Volume. Price, neatly bound, ——— 5s

XXXVIII.

AGENOR AND ISMENA;

O R,

The War of the Tender Passions.
A NOVEL.

Translated from the FRENCH.

In Two Volumes. Price, neatly bound, ——— 6s

XXXIX.

THE
FORTUNATE BLUE-COAT BOY;

O R,

MEMOIRS

OF THE

Life and Happy Adventures of Mr. Benjamin Templeman, Formerly a Scholar in Christ's Hospital.

By an ORPHANOTROPHIAN.

Price, handsomely bound in Two Volumes, ——— — 6s

XL.

XL.

T H E
NEW LONDON SPY;
OR,

A Twenty-four Hours Ramble through the BILLS of MORTALITY

Containing a true Picture of Modern high and low Life; from the splendid Manfions in St. James's, to the fubterraneous Habitations of St. Giles's, &c. Wherein are difplayed the various Scenes of Covent-Garden and its Environs, the Theatres, Jelly-Houfes, Gaming-Houfes, Night-Houfes, Coteries, Mafquerades, Public-Gardens, and other Places of Entertainment, as well as of *civil* Reception, Public and Private. Together with the various Humours of the different Inhabitants of the Metropolis, &c. &c. The Whole exhibiting a ftriking Portrait of London, as it appears in the prefent Year.

Adorned with a humorous Frontifpiece, finely engraved by a capital Artift. Price, fewed in Marble Covers, ——— — 2s

XLI.

The DEBAUCHEE,
A POEM, in Six Cantos.
With an ELEGY on the Death of a Libertine.
By FRANCIS BACON LEE.

Neatly printed in large Quarto, and enriched with a beautiful Frontifpiece. Price ——— ——— 2s

XLII.

The BOOK of ODDITIES;
OR,

Wonderful STORY-TELLER.

Containing an uncommon Collection of Curious Stories, which may be valued for being queer, ftrange, amazing, whimfical, comic, abfurd, out o' th' way, and unaccountable.

By JACK STRANGE.

Price ——— ——— — 1s 6d

XLIII.

XLIII.

THE
COMPLETE MARKSMAN;
OR,
True ART of SHOOTING FLYING;
A POEM.

In large Demy Octavo. Price   —   —   1s

XLIV.

MEMOIRS of a SCOUNDREL;
By an INJURED FAIR.

In Two handsome Pocket Volumes. Price, neatly bound, — 6s

XLV.

By the KING's Royal Licence and Authority.

THE
TYBURN CHRONICLE;
OR,
Villainy Displayed in all its Branches.

Containing an Authentic Account of the Lives, Adventures, Trials, Execution, and Last Dying Speeches of the most notorious Malefactors, of all Denominations, who have suffered for various Crimes, in England, Scotland, and Ireland, from the Year 1700, to the present Time.

Neatly bound in Four large Octavo Volumes, embellished with Forty beautiful Copper-Plates, finely engraved from original Drawings, made by Wale, and other eminent Artists. Price   —   £ 1 4s

XLVI.

XLVI.

THE
COMPLETE CONFECTIONER,

O R,

The whole Art of Confectionary made plain and easy.

Shewing the various Methods of Preferving and Candying, both dry and liquid, all Kinds of Fruit, &c. &c. Also Directions for making Rock-works and Candies, Bifcuits, rich Cakes, Cuftards, Jellies, Whip Syllabubs and English Wines of all Sorts, Strong Cordials, Simple Waters, Knicknacks and Trifles for Deferts, &c. Likewife the Art of making Artificial Fruit, fo as to refemble the natural Fruit. To which are added, fome Bills of Fare for Deferts for private Families.

By H. GLASSE, Author of the Art of Modern Cookery

In a handfome Octavo Volume. Price, neatly bound, — 5*s*

XLVII.

The CRIES of BLOOD;

O R,

JURYMAN's MONITOR.

Being an Authentic and faithful Narrative of the Lives and melancholy Deaths of feveral unhappy Perfons, who have been Tried, Convicted, and Executed, for Robberies and Murders, of which they were intirely Innocent. Together with a brief Relation of the Means by which the faid Crimes were difcovered, after the Deaths of the feveral unfortunate Perfons therein related.

In a large Octavo Volume. Price ——— 1*s* 6*d*

XLVIII.

TIMOTHY GRIN's Merry Jefter,

O R,

New Ways to Kill Care.

Being an entire new and comical Collection of lively Jefts frolickfome Joaks, witty Repartees, humorous Tales, Ridiculous

Bulls, entertaining Humbugs, &c. To which is added, a beautiful
Collection of new Conundrums, and Rebuffes, Acroftics, Fables,
&c. &c.

Adorned with a beautiful Frontifpiece. Price ·——— — 6d

XLIX.

T O M G A Y's Comical Jefter ;

O R,

The Wits Merry Medley.

Being a new and moft beautiful Collection of brilliant Jefts, Merry
Stories, Irifh Bulls, &c. &c. To which is added, a curious Collection
New Conundrums, Rebuffes, and Riddles, and fharp Epigrams,
amorous Poems, Songs, Fables, &c. &c.

Enriched with a curicus Frontifpiece. Price ——— 6d

L.

J E M M Y B U C K's Merry Jefter ;

O R,

The Merry Mortal's Companion.

Being an entire new and Curious Collection of excellent Jefts,
whimfical Stories, Humorous Tales, Irifh Bulls, and queer Adventures, &c. &c. The Whole being a moft excellent cure for Spleen,
Grief and Dulnefs, and calculated for the Tafte of all who love Mirth,
Fun and good Humour.

Embellifhed with a humorous Frontifpiece. Price ——— 6d

†↓† Be pleafed to obferve that the above three Jeft Books are
entirely different from each other ; and therefore being all printed
in the fame Size, may with great Propriety be bound up together.

LI.

LI.
THE
COMPLETE ENGLISH FARMER;
OR,
Husbandry made perfectly easy, in all its various Branches.

Containing a greater Variety of useful Articles than are to be found in any Book of the Kind, though Four Times the Price, particularly, The Management and Qualities of the different Kinds of Grass, and of making Hay. Description of the different Soils and of manuring and ploughing Land. The Cultivation and Management of Wheat and Barley, &c. &c. Together with great Variety of other very useful Articles, too numerous to be inserted in this Advertisement. By GEORGE COOKE, Farmer, at West-End, in Hertfordshire.

Adorned with a beautiful Frontispiece finely engraved, from an original Drawing. Price ———— ———— 1s 6d

The Whole freed from the Errors, Obscurities, and Superfluities of former Writers on the Subject.

LII.
The YOUNG LADIES MONITOR;
OR,
Polite Instructions for the FAIR-SEX.
Translated from the French of the celebrated MADAM DE MAINTENON, by Mr. ROLLOS.

In a handsome Pocket Volume. Price neatly bound, — 3s

LIII.
NATURE the best PHYSICIAN;
OR,
Every Man his own Doctor.
Containing Rules for the Preservation of Health and long Life; and a Collection of simple, cheap, and palatable Receipts for the Cure of the various Disorders incident to the human Body.

In a Large Demy Octavo, Price — — 1s 6d

www.ingramcontent.com/pod-product-compliance
Lightning Source LLC
Chambersburg PA
CBHW021957050726
47498CB00006BA/1711